OFF TRACK

E.M.HIBLER

OFF TRACK

E.M. HIBLER

To all the girls the world told to be invisible.

Be invincible.

Terms to know:

DNF- Did Not Finish

Staging – When a driver pulls up to the start line on a drag strip, illuminating the starting lights. Engaging in car processes to start the race.

Pro-Mod- A purpose build car based on a factory model.

Win light- A light at the end of the drag strip to show who won the race.

5.9- In regards to race times this in measured in seconds.

Chapter 1

Lola

She could see the finish line. She was going faster than her last winning pass and she knew it by the way the car was singing to her. She looked over and saw the red car next to her, Greyson was in that car about to cross the line behind her. She saw his head turn, the helmet gave it away, he should not have moved his head. The next then she knew his car was turning towards her with nowhere to go, the wall or the car those were her options.

Trying to push the gas more to avoid the accident, she knew she failed when she felt the impact hit the right side of her car pushing her towards the wall. She let out of the gas and held on to the steering wheel, hoping to keep the car straight and out of the wall. Then the front panel hit and that was the end of all control, the car began to raise up and she knew she was about to roll. Feeling weightless for half a second, colliding with the ground, feeling weightless again she knew she was going over a second time. The car jolted to a stop, and she rushed to pull off her safety equipment. The five-point harness and the roll cage were blocking her way. Once she got those off, she tried to open the door but found it was jammed. Leaning to the right despite the shooting pain in her side she positioned herself to kick the door.

She kicked so hard she was able to get the door open, thank

you adrenaline. She climbed out of the car as smoke was surrounding it. The sounds of sirens and people screaming from the stands hit her as she pulled her helmet off. That was a bad idea she decided as she felt the pain in her neck. She ran towards the retaining wall as far away from the car as she could. Passing the other car, she saw Greyson getting out and rushing over to her. Rage filled her, that was no accident and she knew it. He had always been a sore loser. She sat down at the foot of the wall when she got there and the whole world went black.

Lola bolted awake, when would the re-living dreams end. It had been four months since the "accident" and she was still having them more than not. The smallest ray of light came into her room from the crack of the curtains. If the sun was up then she would have slept for a little bit at least, even if she could use more.

Getting out of bed was always the worst she felt all day. She was still sore from the accident and still going to see her trainer to make sure she was ready for the next racing season. She would make a comeback, and no one was expecting anything less from her. Heading into the attached bathroom she turned on the light. It felt like an assault on her eyes, but she rubbed away the little bit of sleep left in them and looked at herself in the mirror. Her long blond hair was a mess, and she reached for the brush to run it through it. Grabbing a hair tie, she pulled it in a low ponytail before looking at her face. The bags that were under her eyes were not that big today, but they would require make-up to hide them.

She should have the day all to herself. It was Saturday, and she had no private training or meetings today. She rubbed her face again and her blue eyes looked brighter than they had in a long time. But the tan of her skin was the cause of that, she had been spending a lot of time outdoors even in the brisk early spring days. Being outside was good for her, it made her feel less pathetic. When she moved here, she was hoping it would help her have an escape and relax and recover after the accident, but it was a bit of a challenge for her.

None of her friends knew where she was, just how she wanted it. Most of those friends were on Greyson's side of things. She was trying to keep a low profile and heal under the radar. The car community was not as crazy as celebrities, but she knew that all it took was one Instagram post to make her followers raise concerns about her health. There had been official press releases made after she was out of the hospital. They gave the impression that she was fine, and she would be back. For the first two months she felt like that was a lie. She had fractured her ribs, tore a muscle in her leg and had a very serious concussion. But training and physical therapy helped her get better and she knew she would be ready for the opening of the season in a month.

She had just received her new car for the season this week and now the real struggles were starting. She had to get down the track and be ready to race again. Thankfully there was a small-town track here and she was hoping to get a private session so no one would know how scared she was to get back in a car with that type of power.

Her phone rang, pulling her out of her own head, glancing over at it on her bedside table. The name Greyson flashed across the screen. She turned back to the bathroom to wash her face. She had not talked to him since the accident but that didn't stop him from calling her three times a week. She never took the call, or any of the messages he left. He was relentless and it made her giddy at one time in her life but no more. She knew he was a sore loser, but to see what he would do to win made her angry. She knew he would not come here as he didn't know where she was, but she still wasn't sure any of their team members wouldn't ruin the secret.

They shared a race team as they were signed to most of the same sponsors, so a lot of their information overlapped. Even though things were supposed to be separate, they merged when they were dating, it was easier on the team for the last four years. Her manager was surprised when she told him that she wanted separate teams this year. Duke was an older man and was not fond of her relationship with Greyson anyway, but she worried that she may have tipped him off as far as motives for the wreck.

Her phone rang again, and she saw Dukes' name flash over it. Grabbing the phone she hit the green answer button.

"Were your ears ringing?" She smiled as she answered the phone.

"Why were you talking about me?" Dukes' deep voice came through the phone.

"I was thinking about how the team is being split and how I need to get track time. Is that why you called?" She abandoned the idea of makeup and headed to her closet.

"Partially, but I was calling just to check in on you." Duke was the closest thing she had to family anymore and he was always there for her.

"I will make sure and get in touch with the track this week." Pulling a black shirt out of a drawer she decided she was going to the

4

car show today in town. She needed to make some kind of contact to figure out who owned it.

"Is the trailer covered? The car is not branded yet, but I don't want it seen." He was concerned.

"Yes, it is. I promise I will protect it with my life. Plus no one here knows who I am thankfully." She pulled the shirt on and grabbed a pair of jeans that had a few rips on them.

"You have for sure done a good job of taking time off. How is therapy going?" His voice calmed down a little.

"It's good, I feel ready to get back in the seat." She pulled on the jeans and went to get socks and sat back on the bed to begin pulling them on.

"I wish you would let me be at the track for the first time." He sounded like a dad to her.

"Duke, I will be fine; I need to be able to go at a slow pace. I promise when I'm ready to make a full pass you will be there. At this point I need to be able to get the car to the staging lanes without breaking down." She slid her socks on and headed towards the door of her room.

"Magnolia Rae, if you tell me that, I am going to make sure I am there. If this is not something, you can do this season I need to know. I don't want you pushing yourself too hard." Dad mode activated; she was in trouble now.

"I am fine, I have been driving daily and that helps. It's just the track that freaks me out. I'm still having flashbacks to the crash, and I just need to mind over matter it and boss up. I will be fine, but I need to do it by myself, so I don't feel pressure to be perfect." She talked to him like an old friend, but she knew it had to happen. Duke was her coach and mentor since she was sixteen and her parents passed away.

"Fine. But you better call me when you need me, or I will come there. I do in fact know where you are miss. Better yet, I will get Tayler to go out there." He was serious, but she knew that he meant well.

"I know, nothing gets past you. But I will call you when I have a track date. I am going to the local cars and coffee this morning to see who knows the track owners." She was not planning to tell him, but she felt she owed him for being so protective of her. Pulling open the door to her room open she headed to the rest of the house.

"Be careful there, what are you driving that no one has noticed you?" She smiled knowing he was not going to like her answer.

"The new Supra, it's all grey. But I don't drive it crazy I drive like a normal person. Thankfully this town is not exactly a poor area, so I blend in for the most part." Knowing he would protest she felt the need to explain the choice of car.

She had ordered this car when it was still brand new. Then the accident happened, and she was not sure she would want to drive it. When it was delivered a month after she was still in love with it, and she knew she still wanted it. It took two more weeks after delivery to even be able to get into it and drive it.

"Send me a picture of it please. I need to make sure you don't end up on social media after the show. You didn't enter, did you?" She could hear the worry in his voice.   She headed down the small hallway towards the kitchen to grab water on her way out.

"No, of course not. I knew if I entered it might be shared. Plus, even at the doctor's office they know me as Magnolia or Rea, no one here has made the connection." She opened the door of the fridge in her kitchen just as the sun was coming through the windows filling the room with soft light.

The entire house was light and bright. She wanted to keep it simple and not overdue it like her other house. When she bought it, her designer wanted to send a crew over, but she decided to do it herself. Her simple white kitchen with natural wood tones leads into her living room that is similar. She found a sectional that was the most comfortable thing she had ever sat on. The room had bookshelves and a tv in it and she spent most of her time here.

"Duke, I have to go though I am going to be late and never find parking at this rate." Looking at the clock on the stove it read 9 am and she knew the show was starting now.

"Ok, be safe and call me if you need me."

"Promise." Smiling, she hung up her phone and slid it into her back pocket.

Her small purse was on a hook by a door on the other side of the kitchen leading to the garage. She only had the two cars here, but she made sure to keep them inside. The Supra did not have any identification on it but her truck did. The trailer was in a covered garage in the back of the property so that no one could see it. She had no idea how she was going to get it to the track without anyone noticing but it was a later issue at this point.

She headed through the door and flipped on the light. The grey supra was sitting there next to her black Dodge Ram. She did have a thing for black cars that was for sure. They had made fun of her saying that girls were supposed to drive something lighter, but she knew what she liked. The grey on the Supra is a darker shade but she loved it, the way it makes the body lines show up better than white but doesn't hide them like black. She had not picked an accent color

7

yet, but she had not been into working on her cars lately either.

She hit the button to open the garage and unlocked the car. Opening the door and sliding into the driver's seat she threw her purse on the passenger side. She put the key in the ignition and took a deep breath. It was just a regular drive, and it would be nice to be around more cars again. She turned the car over and it roared to life.

Chapter 2

Lola

The car show was already full when she got there 30 minutes after it started. She was hoping getting there later she would fly under the radar even more. The town's main road was blocked off and there were cars running down the street on both sides. The median was large, vendors were set up on the grass. She was realizing this was a bigger event than she had thought. But this was the best thing about small towns. These events made weekends great in places like this. As she got to the front of the line the parking attendant waved her forward.

"Exhibit cars closed 30 minutes ago." He informed her.

"Thanks, I am just spectating today though." Smiling at him she explained.

"Sorry I just thought since this is what you brought you would have entered. Next time you should. There is parking on the back row still. Have a great day." He smiled at her with his baby face as he pointed to the back of the lot.

"Thanks, you have a great day as well." She rolled up the window and slowly continued towards where he pointed. She passed a few people as she drove to the back but most of the parking lot was empty of people walking around, everyone was on the street looking at the cars already.

She pulled the car into one of the chalked off spots and turned it off. She pulled the mirror down and looked at herself. With the hat on and her sunglasses on she hoped people wouldn't be able to tell who she was. Grabbing her phone and keys she moved her purse to the floor of the car. Opening the door, she was glad she had a jacket in the car already. She popped the trunk and pulled out her jean jacket and pulled it on.

Heading toward the cars she was excited to see the variety of them here. There were a handful of exotic cars like GTR's, Lamborghini, and Maclaren. There were some imports like Hondas, Toyotas, more on the classic builds like NSX's and plenty of Civics. Then there was the American Muscle, which was the largest group here. They were organized by classic and modern, also by make which she smiled at. There were classic Mustangs and modern ones, as well as Corvettes and Camaros. All organized from oldest to newest; the organizer of this show took time thinking this out. When she got to the Mopar section she took her time to walk around the Chargers and then the Challengers.

When she got to the modern cars, she saw a group standing around a drag pack just like what she started racing in. This was the dark green stock color, and the owner had pulled off some of the decals that came stock on it.

"It is running well; I do want to get more power out of it though." The older man standing next to the car said. He must be the owner because he is leaning on the car slightly. He was taller and looked to be in his mid-50's with some salt and pepper hair. He was clean shaven, but you could see some age on his face.

"Why not put a Whipple on it if you are looking for more power?" She immediately wanted to take it back, asking a question like that was going to get her caught.

"There is only one guy in town who can put them on, and he is backed up months. It's on the list though. Haven't seen you around here before?" He smiled at the group of guys standing around. Each seemed very comfortable with one another and now each was looking at her waiting for an answer. Car guys could be intimidating but she knew how to handle herself.

"I am new to town, only been here about three months. Nice to meet you." She adjusted her glasses as she looked back up from the car.

"Are you the Supra owner?" a deep voice from one of the other guys asked. Turning towards him, his bright blue eyes were gorgeous, and his chiseled face made her want to trace it with her fingers. He had a hard jaw line and hair that was a little long for the area reaching just his shoulders, dark brown with some light areas from the sun.

"I am, how did you guess?" She had to know what gave her away.

"That's the newest non-normie car in town and someone who knows what a Whipple is would not be driving a Prius." He smiled at her as he explained.

Her body grew warm with his smile. She felt comfortable in this conversation but knew she would not be able to hide if she kept talking.

"The dang car always gives me away. Well, I should get going, lots of other cars to see. Nice talking with you." She attempted to end the conversation again.

"Wait, you want to go to lunch? We know a great spot." He was very forward in this request, but most car guys were when they found a girl that they could talk with about cars.

"I have plans today sorry." She tried to turn and walk the other way but there was a crowd of people forcing her only way out to be past the four guys.

"Gideon, you don't have time to be dating anyway, you have cars stacking up at the shop." One of the guys said slapping him on the shoulder, they look identical, she assumed twins but brothers at least, except for their hair this mans was shorter.

"Whatever Emory, you should be there working. That's what you get paid to do." Gideon said swatting the hand away.

"Oh, do you own a shop here in town?" She had to shut up or she was really going to blow her hiding place by noon.

"We own HPS Motorsports here in town." Emory told her with a smile that she was sure got them all the girls in town.

"I have heard of you; you guys are also in control of the track here in town, right?" It was all clicking together now, and she needed to get to be able to get a track day soon.

"That's us." Gideon smiled at her; the kind of smile that says "be impressed with me please so you will go out with me."

"That's awesome. What does HPS stand for?" Curiosity was getting the best of her and she was committed to getting the track time she needed.

"It is a combination of our last names. Gideon and Emory Henderson, Slade Presley, and Tobias Smith." Gideon point to the other two men standing there.

Slade gave a smile when Gideon pointed at him causing his cheeks to rise a little. He was not wearing sunglasses so she could see his hooded dark eyes sparkling a little when he looked at her. With little facial hair on his chin and upper lip he looked older than he would have without. His face was well defined, and she could tell there was some Asian influence in his family. His longer black hair hung in his face just a little.

Tobias nodded to her causing his brown hair to fall on his face just a little, which he swept back quickly. His bright green eyes lighting up when he looked at her. A smile filled his face as he got closer to where they were all standing. The crowd around the car was starting to move down the road.

"That's great, I guess it's good to be in business with your family and friends." She used to enjoy the fact that her life was filled with friends on her team but now she knew things were going to change.

"It is but these two have the twin telepathy going on all the time and we get left out." Slade pointed to Gideon and Emory confirming her twin suspicion.

"Well, it seems to work for you all to be so busy. I do have a question about the track." She held her breath a little as all four of their eyebrows raised.

"We have a monthly race if you're thinking of bringing your cute little car down the track." Tobias had a cocky tone to his voice; it usually pissed her off when guys talked to her like this, but something was different here.

"I actually need to have a private track day if that is possible?" She knew she was about to be screwed if she had to tell them who she was right here.

"It can be arranged. Send me a text to this number and we will get it set up." Gideon took a longer look at her and she shifted a little on her feet. He handed her a card out of his wallet.

"I will do that, thanks. You guys have a great day." She quickly turned and headed back towards the other cars in the row. She did not want to give them another chance to ask her to lunch, she felt like she needed to hit the gym though.

Chapter 3

Lola

Pulling up to the track at 6am gave her a mix of emotions. She had messaged Gideon yesterday after the car show and he said today would work for them all best so here she was bright and early on a Sunday morning.

She knew that she had not been seen leaving town since there were no other cars on the road. But she also knew that Gideon and the others were waiting for her. There was no way to hide the fact that she was a professional driver at this point. The gate to the track was open and she drove the truck through them and headed as close to the starting line as possible.

She saw the four of them standing around an enclosed trailer pulled by a red Dodge. How she had found a group that was into the same make of cars she had she would never know. Maybe that just meant they knew what was good.

As she got closer, she could see Toby elbow Gideon to get his attention from the trailer as he was getting ready to open it up. They were all in HPS gear today. Toby was wearing a hat holding his hair away from his face. Gideon was in a tee shirt with their logo on the front. She felt his eyes boring into her as he made eye contact with her, she could see the realization in his eyes.

Slade and Emory came around the other side of the truck and had the same look on their faces. They both were in the same tee shirt Gideon had on, Slade had a matching hat to the one Toby was wearing with his hair pulled back. Anxiety was rising in her body, and she felt the small shake coming to her hands.

"Its fine Lola, they would have found out eventually." Taking a deep breath, she kept telling herself this as she pulled into the spot next to them. She killed the engine of the truck and took a few more breaths before opening the door.

"You felt the need to hide that you are Magnolia Rae from us for what reason?" It was Gideons deep voice that came to her as soon as the door was open. She met his sharp gaze with his eyebrows raised at her.

"I am supposed to be recovering from my accident last year still. No one knows where I am or what I have been up to." The rest of them were now standing on the same side of the car just looking at her. She had braided her hair back today per her usual racing style and was wearing her team shirt with black leggings since she needed to put her fire suit on anyways.

"I cannot believe the Lola Bunny is racing here on our track!" Emory smiled at her, reaching out a hand to shake hers. His hand was rough with callouses but warm despite the cool morning as she took it in hers.

"Thanks, but I need you not to tell anyone. I will pay extra if that is what it takes to keep this all private." She looked at Gideon hopefully. She had two objectives today, get the car down the track and not to blow her cover being here. They all held the outcome in their hands right now.

"I am not going to take your money and I am not going to tell anyone you are here. We have three hours before anyone shows up." He softened his face as he spoke now, with a look of understanding in his eyes.

"How were you able to arrange that?" She started to move to the back of the truck so she could unload. She would need as much time as possible.

"It helps when you're a co-owner of the track." Slade said to her as they all followed her.

"Wow." She was impressed. He owned a very successful shop and part of the track at his age that was a very successful start.

"My dad owned it and when he passed away, he gave part to me and part to Emory, we co own it." Gideon explained as they got to the back of the trailer.

"I am sorry for your loss." She looked at him to see his face fall as she expressed her condolences.

"Thank you. Let's get you unloaded and on the track ok." Gideon reached for the latch on the trailer just as Slade reached for the one on the other side.

Inside sat her new car, the one she was bound to win in according to Duke and Sam, one of the mechanics and tuners for the team. It had all the newest technology in it and was built just for her and the big return. But the whole thing terrified her. She had made Sam leave it in the trailer for her because she could not even sit in it yet. But today was different, she could take all the time in the world she wanted.

"I can get it out if you need to take your car out as well. Don't let me reduce your time either." She was hoping this would let her get in the car and just breath for a bit, but she didn't think they were going to go anywhere at this point.

"We can help guide you out then get ours." Toby smiled at her, this was happening, and she had to just pull up her big girl panties.

"Ok give me a min to get in." She walked back to the left to get into the side door that would put her right at the driver's side window.

Pulling the latch off the door and opening it she paused for a brief second, but she felt their eyes watching her. Taking a deep breath, she climbed into the trailer and then through the window of the car into the driver's seat. The shaking in her hands was getting worse but she had to do this, there was no other option.

Taking another deep breath, she flipped the switches to engage the car and pressed the ignition button. The sound of the car starting in the trailer was loud and it rumbled through her body. Now the anxiety she had before was mixing with her natural adrenaline of being in a car.

She put the car in reverse and made sure to stay as straight as possible as she backed out of the trailer. As she got into line with the opening, she could see Toby behind her telling her to keep backing out. Gideon was on her side of the car just watching her, his face having a slight look of concern on it. Toby signaled to stop as she was clear of the door to the trailer and so she stopped and pulled the break but left the car on.

"It needs to run for a bit before I can run it." She said getting out of the car through the door this time.

"Are you ok?" Gideon was right there, the closeness of his body making hers feel even more excited. The overwhelming smell of cars filled her senses as he got closer to her. It was a smell that she sought out for comfort, and it was currently attached to a very attractive man.

"I am fine." She felt like she choked on the last word. That was all she had been saying for months now but it felt wrong to be telling it to him right now.

He just looked down at her for a second, like he was going to call her a liar. "Okay" was all he said as he headed toward his car that was now coming out of their trailer with Slade behind the wheel. The white Dodge drag pack was as clean as she had ever seen one, they were not popular cars to be going down the track in a regular race considering their price tag. But it was what her car was based on with more mods and improvements.

She only looked for a second before heading into her trailer. She went to the storage area to grab her suit and helmet. The teal and black suit was brand new but the same as her old one and her new helmet was the same color scheme as well. She slid off her Vans and put her legs into the pants, pulled the suit up, slipping her shoes back on. She wouldn't need her fire shoes right now, she almost felt like putting the car back in the trailer and going back home right now. Taking another deep breath, she pulled the suit over her shoulders and zipped it up. Grabbing the helmet, she headed back out of the trailer towards the car.

"Emory is going to go run the prep on the track both lanes. By the time he is done the cars should be ready to run. Do you need anything?" Gideon was back by her car when she made her way there.

"I should be good. Can I have the lane not next to the wall?" Steadying her breath as she asked hoping to not tip him off that she was terrified.

"Of course, this is your track day. We just hijacked it to get some more test time." He looked at her with the same concern as earlier.

She felt like his eyes knew her struggle but he was not going to ask her to talk more about what he already knew she was feeling.

"Are you okay Gideon?" Hoping to pull the attention off her, maybe there was something he was worried about.

"I am fine it's just early. Is this why you wanted to come before anyone was here?" He gestured to the trailer that represented her.

"Yeah, I told you I am supposed to be keeping a low profile." She tried to brush it off.

"Well, you have certainly been doing that here haven't you." He raised his eyebrow at her.

"I do own my house here Gideon, I have for years. Personal situations just changed where I was." Too much information, stop while you're ahead, she wished she could kick herself.

"Yeah, you broke up with your longtime boyfriend Greyson after your crash, or that's what media is rumoring." He was focused on her now there was no way she was going to avoid this conversation.

"Yes, we did, he has been having some issues with my choices." Struggling to find the right way to say he didn't agree with her version of the accident.

"But you are still planned to be team mates this season?" That hit a nerve, she was hoping to have a plan before the season but there was not one right now.

"That is going to stay the same, but we have some team changes that need to happen. All a work in progress though." She looked up at him to see a change in his face, a trace of relief.

"Hey, the track's ready. Let's smoke some tires." Emory called over to them from the side of the pits as he walked towards them.

"Let's go Lola." Gideon smiled at her as he walked toward her car.

"Let's get you strapped in."

They walked over and she got into the driver's seat. As she pulled the seat forward to get the right distance, she felt his hands moving the straps of the five-point harness over her legs. His warm hands on her thighs drew her attention to his face again. It was softer, like the idea of racing calmed his worries.

"Thanks," She said pulling the buckle towards the middle and clipping them all together. "Can you pull them tight?"

"Of course." He began to pull the straps that tightened her to the seat. "Good to go."

She pulled them more, trying to move forward to test their tightness. Pulling them one more time, he caught her hands, which were shaking again.

"Lola they are as tight as they will go. You're fine." Right, there she knew why he looked concerned, he could see her worries all around her and she couldn't hide them.

"I am fine, just want to make sure they are tight; they're new harnesses, and they like to be sticky." She was trying to find an excuse for her concern, but you can't bullshit a car person like Gideon. She pulled her hands away from his hoping he didn't realize how bad they were shaking now.

"Ok, here. Put the neck harness on and then the helmet." He handed her the foam harness, and she began to pull it around her neck tucking her braid into her suit as she did. When she finished, he handed her the helmet. She pulled it onto her head and could feel the panic coming. She should have just sat in the house with this on before now.

She took some deep breaths and closed her eyes as she looked away from him. But she felt his hand on her thigh again, he was not going anywhere until she could convince him she was ready.

"Let's go. Burning rubber is my favorite smell so let's get to it." She smiled at him as she could see Slade getting into their car.

"Ok, I will pull the parashoot pins and back you up. Just go to the right after I get you on the staging lanes." He stood up taking his hand off her as he did, the warmth stayed for a second and she missed it when it was gone. He shut the door to the car, she watched him go to the back and pull the pins out, giving her the thumbs up.

She began to back up and when he gave her a forward signal, she shifted into first. Turning to the right to head towards the lanes she kept trying to take deep breaths. Into the burnout box she went, and she began to getting the wheels spinning. The car was filling with smoke as she warmed up her tires. Gideon was back in front of her at the start of the lanes right before the light. She could see their car in the lane next to her and then there was the wall.

Turning forward Gideon was signaling her to move up. The first light on the stage came on, just a tad further and the second one came on. She could see Slade staged as well. Gideon gave them both a thumbs up and then took a step back. All she could see now was the light and the track in front of her with the end marked by time lights at the end of the track.

The lights came in yellow, yellow, then the flash of green. Slade took off but she was frozen. Hand on the trans break, car ready to go but she couldn't move. She let out of all staging causing the car to just idle. The panic was taking over, and she had to get out of the car. Her breath was fast, she was trying to rip off the harness again. Flashes of rolling and the wall coming right towards her were taking over her brain. She couldn't get hold of the door handle and as she began to panic and cry the door flew open.

"Lola!" Gideons voice demanded her head move toward him.

"Get me out of here!" She realized then she had been screaming. Her voice was horse.

"I got you, you're ok." He was unhooking and pulling the harness back as fast as he could. Once it was off, he took her hand and pulled her out of the car.

She resisted his attempt to pull her towards him and she took off towards the trailer. Unstrapping the neck harness as she walked, the walk was short so by the time she got there it was off, and she threw it into the side of the trailer as she got there. Not stopping, she turned into the trailer and ripped off the helmet and was about to throw it also when a hand caught it.

"This would be bad to ruin doll." Gideon was there again.

"Don't call me doll." She yelled, not meaning to but she had been called it so much it was the reason Lola Bunny was her alter ego.

"Ok. What's going on? Talk. That's the only way you're going to get down that track in that car." He set the helmet on the floor and was looking at her now. She could tell he was resisting the urge to grab her.

"Why would you care? I do enough talking in therapy which clearly is not working." She yelled as she kicked the spare tires at the front of the trailer. She could hear her car pulling back into the pits and could hear the rest of the voices starting to fill the area as the cars shut down.

"Hey you, ok?" Slade's voice came into the space.

"She's having a panic attack Slade, back off for a second. Lola talk, that's all that's going to help, and maybe some water." Gideon was trying to pull her focus to reality, but it wasn't working, All she was hearing was Greyson yelling that it was an accident repeatedly.

"Here drink this." Toby was putting a cold bottle of water in her hand, and she could see Emory coming into the trailer. The space was getting small with all of them in here.

She twisted off the lid and took a drink, the cold of the water made her throat feel better, but she could still hear the screaming and feel the fear.

"Why don't we go sit outside. We have chairs." Emory turned away to leave without an answer.

"Lola, come sit outside for a minute. We have all the time in the world. I will shut the track down all day if I need to." Gideon was reaching for her hand again. She wanted to take it, to feel his warmth in her hand. It was a slippery slope to take that hand, she shouldn't feel like she needed it from someone she had known for less than 24 hours. But she did, she reached out for it and let the warmth fill her body from a single touch.

He pulled her along a bit as if he knew she wouldn't move willingly even if her brain told her to. The air outside was still crisp and it helped her breath better. They walked towards Emory who had four chairs already out and was setting up another. Gideon stopped her in front of one and pulled another closer. He sat in that one while pulling her to sit in the one she was closest to.

"We were there the day of your accident Lola. That is a huge wreck to try and come back from." Toby was the one to speak first, and she scoffed at the word accident.

"What was that for?" Gideon seemed offended by the involuntary noise she made.

"It wasn't an accident. Greyson couldn't stand to lose so he turned towards me just before the finish." She felt the rage escape, she had not said those words to anyone except Duke who made her stop as soon as she had started. There was a moment of silence.

"No, no way! Why would he do that?" Anger came out with Slade's voice.

"I would have won the season. I should have won the season." The tears were coming down her face and she reached up to wipe them away.

"But they said there was a failure with your car, and you had hit oil causing the accident." Emory was right, that is what they said.

"They also said I had minor injuries and was fine when I left the hospital. They left out the fractured ribs, concussion, abdominal issues, and torn muscle in my leg from kicking the door open." Their faces were serious and sad.

"God, no wonder you're freaking out. Is this your first-time back at a track?" Gideon squeezed her hand.

"Yeah." She nodded as well.

"There is no way you are going to go down in that car. You need to start smaller. Emory, go to the shop and get the track hawk." Gideon through the truck keys towards him.

"Got it." Emory caught the keys and headed towards the truck.

"I will go with so we can bring the truck back." Toby got up also having been silent for the last few minutes.

"I don't think a bigger car is going to help Gideon." She tried to get up and his hand pulled her back down.

"No but a non-track car might. The jeep is a regular car, but it sounds more like a racecar than most. But there is no shifting, you just hit the gas, like at a stop light. I have seen you in the Supra Lola, you do not take stop lights like a normie." He smiled at her and she realized he had been watching her for a while.

"I should have brought that. It still took me a month to drive that when I was first cleared to drive again." She was starting to calm down, but she still felt terrified to try and go down the track.

"What about the truck? Let's unhook it and just drive it down the track a few times. We can go 15 miles per hour if that's what you want." Slade suggested looking at Gideon.

"Lola, what do you think? I could even drive it if that helps just be the passenger princess." He smiled at her with the last suggestion.

"I am not a passenger princess, but I might let you try just to see if it would work." She felt like it might work. She had to be able to send Duke a video today of her driving something down the track or he was going to come here, and she did not need that.

"Ok let's drop this trailer and get going." Slade jumped out of his chair and walked toward the truck and trailer.

"Why are you helping? You don't even know me." She looked at Gideon as he stood up.

"Because I have had a wreck like you, and I know the feeling of missing something you love and being terrified of it all at the same time." He reached out his hand to pull her up. "Plus, if I never see you in this outfit again, I might die, because your hot."

She felt the blood rush to her cheeks as he pulled her into him. He smelled like race fuel, oil and she never wanted to leave it. She felt him place a small kiss on the top of her head, she was not short but compared to how tall he was her head fell right below his chin.

"We should go help Slade, the lock on the latch can be tricky." She took one more deep breath before pulling away.

"I bet he can figure it out." Gideon smiled at her putting a little bit of pressure on her to stay but not forcing it.

"Let's go. Time will pass quickly and I need to get the trailer hidden again before people see me out here. The press would have a hay day if they saw any pictures of me going down the track in my truck." She pulled away dropping her hands to her side and starting to walk away so he couldn't pull her back. She didn't know what was going on here, but she couldn't let herself fall for this man, she had other things she needed to focus on.

"This thing is a bitch! Why do you have this latch on here?" Slade yelled as he was about to kick the junction between the trailer and the truck.

"You have to pull it up." She rushed over as fast as she could before he kicked it.

Chapter 4

Gideon

Gideon watched Lola rush towards Slade to stop him from kicking her truck and he let out a laugh. This girl was incredible, and he was going to make sure she knew it. After hearing the real story about her crash, he wanted to kill her ex-boyfriend. If he had anything to do about it, she would not be around him ever again. This girl was all he had been able to think about since seeing her yesterday. Heck she was all any of them could think about. He thought he recognized her at the car show, but he was not sure until today.

"Is Duke still your team manager?" He was curious if they were staying together as a team at this point.

"He is planning on it. But we are not sure on the entire team split at the moment. How do you know Duke?" She had a curious look in her eyes.

"He knew my dad. He used to race here." Hiding that he knew Duke very well would be good for him for now. He did not want Lola to think he was going to blow her secret of fearing the track.

"Oh, well I guess I should have known it was something like that when I told him what track I was coming it." She turned and pulled up on the latch Slade was trying to get off and it released as soon as she applied the right pressure to it.

"Is that right?" He was curious now what Duke had said, the old man could have called and warned him.

"Yeah, I told him your name and said you were able to get me a private track day and he instantly calmed the heck down. That man forgets that he can trust me sometimes." She was walking towards the driver's side of the truck now to pull it forward.

"How about we try the passenger idea for the first time?" Slade suggested before Gideon could, his best friend watching Lola just as closely as he was. It was hard not to when she was in her fire suit still.

"Ok who's driving then." She dangled the keys as if to challenge them both.

"I will." Reaching out and taking the keys while shooting Slade a look that said, 'sit in the back.' Slade huffed but did not argue at this point, they all wanted her but right now he wanted to be selfish. She was an addiction he was not willing to kick.

She smiled at them and walked the long way around the front to get to the passenger side. She opened the door and hopped in. Her truck was cleaner than he had expected, but that was not fair to her. Being a car girl usually meant their cars were well kept and not a hot mess like most.

"We will go in the right lane, away from the wall and take it slow, ok." He wanted to make sure she knew what was going to happen. He knew she needed the help and could tell she had hidden how bad it was from Duke because there was no way he would have let her come today by herself if he knew everything.

"Sounds good." She was taking deep breaths as he started the

29

truck and began towards the lanes.

"Why didn't Duke come today?" He knew she would probably avoid this question, but he needed to know.

"I told him he should stay home. I needed to try and do this for myself. Clearly, I was stupid to think I could do it alone. But he turns dad mode on when things happen, and I don't need him freaking out while I am. Plus I think if he saw me this bad, he would try and kill Greyson. I am pretty sure he is the only one who knows what I saw and believes me." She let out a sigh.

"How do you know he did it on purpose? Not saying I don't believe you but how did you know it?" Slade asked the question on both their minds.

"I saw his head turn towards me. The front windows are not tinted on the cars, so I glanced over right at the finish and saw his head turning back and then the car coming right for me. His explanation is he thought I was losing control and had looked and seen smoke coming from the car. But I know there was not any smoke until he hit me first." She stared forward down the track as they pulled into the lane. He avoided the burnout box because they would not be going that fast.

"Did you confront him about it?" Slade again asked. This was good, he was pulling her focus from the track and into a conversation, Slade was the talker of the group.

"Yeah. He kept just yelling at me saying it was the car, and it was an accident. He told me I was crazy, and I couldn't know what happened because I had blacked out. But I didn't do that until I made it to the fence." She was still staring forward and taking deep breaths.

"How do you know that?" Gideon asked as he began to go down

the track, slower at first and controlling the launch so it was smooth.

"I have flashbacked every night I think I know when it was when I blacked out Gideon." The pain in her voice was there, she didn't sleep, and he could see it on her face.

"Well, he is an ass." Slade cut the tension causing her to laugh. Her face lit up as they got closer to the end of the track. He had gotten to 45 mph, and she was still doing all right. This was working, he knew it. She needed baby steps and to trust those round her.

"That's it. Lola welcome back to the track." He said as they passed the bars at the end of the track a ridiculous time showed up.

"A great first run back." She laughed again. Gideon could listen to that every day for the rest of his life. Slade's face lit up in the rear-view mirror and he could tell his friend was on the same wavelength.

"You ready to try it now?" He asked her just as he saw his brother driving into the parking lot in the red track hawk and Toby in the truck behind him.

"Maybe in this, not that." She was looking at them as well.

"Don't worry doll, we can take this as slow as you want. The first race of the season is not for two months." She shot him a glare at the nickname.

"Don't call me doll." The spice was there, he knew her to be fierce in the car world. She was a force to be reckoned with. She was the youngest girl to ever to be signed to a major team in drag racing at the age of 16 and she held the world record for her class on two tracks. When people asked her how she felt she faired against the boys she always said anything they can do I can do better, and she proved it over and over again. She should have won last season and would have without the crash.

"There she is." Gideon smiled at her as they drove back to the pits.

"So how are you liking living here?" Slade broke through his thoughts as they pulled back into the pits.

"I love it, I am so used to being in the bigger areas of the world that it's nice to be somewhere small and simple." She smiled as she talked about their town.

He loved living here; you could make greatness out of something small here and that's why he chose to stay here after school. He wanted to own his own shop for as long as he could remember. Emory was the same way, though he had gone away for school to handle the business side of their shop.

"I mean it's not like you have a lot of down time. You run in what? Two different seasons a year?" Slade knew that answer and it made him roll his eyes. They had stopped in the spot next to her car as Toby and Emory were getting out of the other cars.

"Yes, usually the worlds. But I did not race last year. I also am not planning on it this year, but we will see how the season goes. Duke swears this is the car that is going to make me need to get a new tattoo so we will see." They both raised their eyebrows at her as they got out of the car.

"You have tattoos?" Gideon could not imagine them as he had never seen her in anything other than long sleeves and pants.

She began to unzip the fire suit and pulled out her left arm. When she went to lift the hem of her shirt, he caught his breath. Right under her bra strap on her left rib cage there were roman numerals. A set of three were in a line going down her side.

"They are my personal bests. The first one is the fastest I ran at 16 and the other two are from my records at the tracks. I thought

I would have been adding one last year and Duke says that it should have been that way." She pulled her shirt back down and began to pull the suit back on.

"What did we miss?" Toby's eyes were watching them as they walked towards them as Lola finished zipping up the suit.

"Lola was showing us her tattoos, and she made it down the track in the truck. She was just about to go down driving herself this time." Slade winked at her as a form of encouragement.

"I think you need to put the helmet on this time though." Gideon looked at her and saw the flash of panic on her face. He knew every little thing about this process was going to be a lot for, but he wanted to be there with her. He wanted to walk beside her as she overcame this pain and struggle.

"I should have been wearing that dammed thing in the living room watching tv." She had a harsh tone to her voice as she headed toward her trailer.

"I still cannot believe she is here at our track. What are the odds?" Emory slapped his hand on his shoulder as he watched her pick up the helmet.

"Possibly higher than we know considering her manager is Duke." Gideon raised an eyebrow at his brother as Lola walked back towards her truck. He could see her taking deep breaths as she pulled the helmet on her head and went for the door of the truck.

"Meet us at the line, I think she should try with the lights this time." He began to head towards the truck as well, he still had the keys.

"Ok." Emory said as they all headed towards the start line.

Gideon opened the door of the truck as she was climbing up in it as well. "I think you need these." He said, holding the keys out.

"Thanks." She almost whispered, he could see her breathing quickening up.

"You can go as slow as you want. It's just like at a stop light Lola." He wanted to reach out and take her hand in his, but that felt to forward at this point. He was beginning to feel protective of her and seeing her in this state made him want to do whatever it took to fix it.

"Ok." She whispered again, he patted her leg and shut the door.

"Should we wait for a second car to go with her?" Toby asked, watching Lola drive towards the track.

"I think that would be best." They walked to the track and realized Slade had snuck into the truck with her.

"Hey, what's on your mind man?" Toby pulled his focus away from the truck.

"I don't know. I just know that I have never felt this strong about helping anyone get over their issues. I want that girl to run down all the high scores." He confessed to his best friend.

"Yeah, me too man, but you know she is in too fragile of a state for us to try to be with her." Toby gave him the look he only remembers seeing one other time and none of them talked about that situation anymore.

"I know." He said as they got to the fence line.

Emory was lining her up and he could see Slade had moved into the front seat. The lights lit up and Emory backed up to the box with the controls. The yellow lights came down fast and on the green the truck launched quickly. Lola did not lift till the end of the track, and Gideon knew that he was smiling just as big as his brother and friend. They were doomed, he was hooked already to this feeling for this girl.

Chapter 5

Lola

By the end of the track day, she was able to make it down the track in the jeep and set down a good time. Duke had not said anything about the car not being hers when she sent him the video.

"Hey Lola." Toby walked over to her as she finished checking the trailer to head home for the day.

"What's up?" She looked up at him and his smile really felt like it was going to knock her over at this point. All day the four of them had been so nice to her and she was just waiting for the shoe to drop.

"We are having a bonfire tonight you, should come." Toby leaned against the trailer. She could not help looking at his toned arms in his tight t-shirt.

"Come on. I am sure you all are sick of me at this point." She was sure their night would be better off without her there.

"If I told you we enjoyed our time with you today, would you believe me?" Toby raised an eyebrow at her.

"I might. But it's different depending on the setting." She glanced over at the others and could see them watching their conversation.

"Just come and hang out. Promise we won't hold you hostage if you want to leave, you should celebrate your accomplishment today." Toby smiled at her again and it melted the wall she was trying to build here.

"Fine, send me the address and time. Should I bring anything?" She hated going to parties without bringing anything.

"Just you." Toby laughed a little and the sound made her blush a little. There had been little comments from all of them all day and she was now worried she was going to cause issues within their group.

"Alright, thank you guys for today." She called out to them as Toby climbed into the Jeep with Slade already inside.

She did not wait for a reply and climbed into the truck and heard her phone go off. She had gotten all their numbers earlier in the day and Toby had just sent her an address in a group chat with the other three.

She headed out of the track when her phone rang, and she saw Duke's name come up on the screen in the truck.

"Hi." She answered as the call connected.

"What are you doing now? How are you feeling?" Duke had his worried dad's voice on again and it made her roll her eyes.

"I am heading home. I feel good." She was not lying, but she knew it was not fully the truth, pulling the car back into the trailer was difficult still but going down the track was not hard.

"Do I want to know how you got your hands on a track hawk?" She could hear his eyebrow raised through the phone.

"The owner of the track had one at his shop and he brought it so I could drive it." She was honest since Duke would know if she was lying.

"Did they figure out who you were?" He did not sound mad, but he was not quite happy either.

"The moment I pulled up Duke, it's not hard to put two and

two together with the car and trailer." She answered as she saw another call coming in.

"Who all was at the track?" She ignored Greyson's call before answering Duke.

"The owners and their friends. The four of them have a shop in town. HPS Motorsports have you heard of it?" She knew he lived in this area even if he moved away to be closer to their team home.

"Yeah, I have heard some good things about them." He said after a long pause.

"They seem nice, and the jeep drove well, so if that indicates anything it explains why they are busy in this town." She turned down the back road of the town that led to her house.

"That's good, let me know when you go back again ok. If you want me there call, Lola." She smiled as he went back to dad mode.

"I will let you know. Bye Duke." She hung up and let the music fill the truck as she drove the rest of the way home.

She would need to shower and get ready but did not know what time to show up at the house. She finished parking the trailer, leaving the truck hooked up, and headed into the house. Pulling her phone out as she entered the back door.

What time? She sent in the chat Toby had started.

6pm A reply from Emory was almost instant after her message said read.

Ok see you then. She glanced at the clock and realized it was almost 1pm now and she had plenty of time to get her work out in and shower.

She headed into her bedroom to change before going to the spare room she had set up as a gym. She needed to stay up on her work outs to maintain her physical fitness to race. As she set her music up, she started her stretching and mentally prepared herself to do leg day.

By the time Lola ate and showered she was almost too exhausted to go to the bonfire, but she felt obligated to show up now. The address was only ten minutes from her house and as she pulled in, she did not see that many cars out front. It was what only could be called a shop house, the front looked like a simple one-story house but as she followed the driveway around the side of the house the four garage doors were open. Inside were more cars than she could see at the moment, but she saw the track hawk she had driven earlier and the truck, the drag pack still on the trailer off the side of the house. There were a few cars with covers on them and she was interested in seeing what was under them. Surprisingly there were four bikes inside as well.

There were several people she could see all around the bon fire in the middle of the driveway and she could make out Gideon among them as he stood up and walked towards her. She rolled down the passenger window as he got close to the car.

"You can pull to the end of the driveway there's a spot open for you." He pointed to the corner closest to her next to a white mustang was next to a beat up S15, and a light blue corvette.

As she pulled up, the people in the seats looked in her direction, she could make out the others and see the guests. There were two other guys and four girls. She felt a little bit of her excitement drop, of course their girlfriends would be here, now just to see which one was connected to who.

She grabbed her phone and went to grab the door but found it opening before she got ahold of the handle. Gideon was there pulling the door open with a smile that made his blue eyes crinkle a little. He was in a long-sleeved shirt hiding his tattoos.

"I am glad you came, find the place ok?" Gideon was holding the door open for her stepped out of the car.

"Yeah, gps works well here." She put her phone and keys in her pants pockets.

"Good, come meet everyone." Gideon held his hand out in the direction of rest of the people were ushering her towards them. His other hand landed on her lower back as she walked with him. She could feel the heat rising to her face as his hand contacted her back.

"Holly shit, its Lola Bunny!" One of the guys said as they walked up and she got into the light of the fire more.

"Her name is Magnolia. Brighton don't be an ass." Gideon said before she could react, the girl on the guy's lap just laughed at him.

"Ignore him Magnolia he's crass, I am Penelope, but you can call me Penny." The girl reached out a hand and her red hair fell over her shoulder with the movement.

"Lola is good, Gideon didn't have to scold him. I am used to it, it's one of those lean into it situations." She laughed as she shook Penny's hand.

"Sorry Lola. Brighton." The guy reached out his hand as well and she smiled as she shook his hand.

"You made it." Slade walked out of the garage and right up to her.

"I said I would come." She said before he gave her a quick hug, the smell of cars filled her nose as she breathed in. She was a little stiff still not knowing if one of these girls was his girlfriend.

"Did you get introduced to everyone?" Slade asked as he stepped back from her.

"I was just getting to it." Gideon answered with a gruffness to his voice as if he was annoyed.

"Yeah, Brighton sort of jumped his pants when he realized who Lola was." One of the other girls laughed leaning forward picking up a beer off the ledge on the fire pit.

"That is Aurora, her boyfriend is Granger he was just over here but must be on the phone now." Gideon looked around as Aurora reached out her hand.

"It's a pleasure to meet you Lola, you are an amazing racer." She noticed how the girls' green eyes lit up in the firelight as she shook her hand.

"Thank you." She smiled back at her as another guy walked up.

"Sorry, Cody's piece of shit broke again he needs me to go get him. Aurora, you want to come or stay here?" He was tall and had sandy blond hair but smiled at her as he joined the group.

"I will stay if you have to take him home there won't be room for me." Aurora answered.

"You could take the truck." Gideon offered but Cody shook his head.

"He was able to get it to the shop but needs a ride here. Nice to meet you, Lola." Granger headed towards the corvette after kissing Aurora.

"Cody has the typical yellow Camaro, and the damn thing is always broken. Alaska." One of the other girls got up and held her hand out, she had dark hair but, in this light, she could not tell if it was

40

black or brown.

"Nice to meet you." She shook Alaska's hand, and she saw Toby and Emory coming out of the house into the garage smiling at her as they walked over.

"Like you're one to talk, at least his car is all one color." Emory laughed as he also came over and gave her a quick hug before taking one of the empty chairs.

"Oh, is the S15 yours?" She asked Alaska.

"Yeah, they make fun of me for being the only import, but I guess they can't pick on me anymore now that you're here." Alaska laughed but Emory glared at her.

"If anyone makes fun of Lola, I will beat them up." Toby pulled her into a hug, and she was just as stiff hugging him as the others. Was it possible they were all unattached.

"Toby you wouldn't hurt a girl." Alaska lounged back in her chair and the last girl just raised her eyebrow.

"No, but still." Toby took a seat after letting her go from their hug.

"I would kick your ass if you put a hand on my girl." The blond who had not introduced herself says.

"Noelle is Alaska's girlfriend, and a volunteer fireman who could absolutely demolish Toby in a fight. You want a drink?" Gideon asked her before leaving her side, moving in the direction of the house.

"Just a water would be nice," she said as Noelle held her hand out to her.

"Nice to meet you, Lola. As everyone said you are an amazing racer, glad to see you are recovering from that wreck." Noelle got up from her seat and pulled Alaska to standing before taking her seat and pulling her down on her lap.

"Thanks, it has been a journey," she said just as Gideon returned holding a bottle of water out to her.

"Grab any seat. We have food on the grill to eat when the others get back." Gideon motioned to the three empty seats, one next to Noelle and Alaska, one next to Slade and Penny and the last one on the other side of Emory.

She sat in the one next to Emory as it was the closest to her. The involuntary wince escaping her as she took the very low seat.

"Are you ok?" Emory asked her with a worried face.

"Yeah, it was leg day today." She laughed opening the water bottle.

"Leg day sucks but it's so worth it." Alaska laughed as Noelle tapped her butt.

"Yeah, I just went heavier also so it will be a day or two of soreness." She leaned back but could still see some concern in the guys' faces.

"You work out a lot?" Brighton asked, taking a sip of his beer.

"Yeah, training for the season is important. Part of going fast is being in shape, need to keep weight on track so we keep the car working properly. It also helps to have strength when you're driving at the speeds we can get up to." She stopped before saying she was pretty sure it was the reason she was alive too.

"I can see that. Gideon you use to work out a lot too when you were racing right?" Brighton asked and she saw Gideon's face shift a little at the thought.

"Yeah, but now just working in the shop is enough." Gideon took a drink of his drink and winked at her. She felt her cheeks warm and was thankful for the darkness of the night.

"If you're hungry now there are some snacks in the house Lola, I was going to grab something if you want to come with me." Aurora got up and asked her.

"I could use a snack I guess." She got up, she noticed the guys were watching her as she did so she tried to keep her pain level from showing on her face.

She followed Aurora into the garage and she could see that it was a fully equipped. They had a lift and everything, she also could see a few more cars tucked away and covered. There was a loft which Aurora went up to with tables of food and drinks on it. There were two doors up here as well once she looked around.

"The bathroom is through the black door and the house is through the brown one. I would not recommend going in there though the guys are super private about their space." Aurora was putting chips and vegetables on her plate.

"I get that, privacy is important, and no one should feel like theirs is being exposed." Lola said as she reached for some of the vegetables and a fruit salad.

"Some people think it's weird that they live together but they are all so close they never thought any differently when they moved back home." Aurora leaned against the railing of the loft before taking a bite of her food.

"Where did they live before?" She couldn't help but ask, she wanted to know more about them.

"Well, when Gideon raced, they all lived on the road. They would stay at their parents when they stopped in, but it wasn't until after his wreck that they all moved back and pushed to be part of the shop and the track." As Aurora explained, she looked out towards the bonfire.

She couldn't help but watch Gideon as he talked to the others. He had trauma in this sport just like she did, but he was so much more adjusted than she was, could she really get back to that point? As if he knew she was watching him he looked up at her and his blue eyes wrinkled as he smiled at her. She felt her body react to this and she turned away quickly.

"So, what they all just live here with their girlfriends, and they are cool with that?" She asked, needing to know if she was stepping into something she should be running from.

"Oh, they have not had girlfriends in a while. It's hard to find a car girl you know. It's even harder to find one that is willing to live with your best friends and honestly come second to their passion." Aurora chuckled as Lola grabbed a brownie on the table.

"So, they just what don't date at all?" She took a bite of the treat and moaned. "Holly shit this is amazing."

"Thanks." Aurora said with a amile.

"You made these; I swear they taste just like the ones from the bakery in town." She went there most days after therapy because she needed a treat after that shit show.

"They should, I own it." Aurora laughed again.

"Oh my god. I love your shop! I go weekly." She said taking another bite.

"I know, I have seen you in there." Aurora gave her that face that told her she understood way more about her than she had told anyone.

"But you know who I am?" She was not use to people not ratting her out.

"I do but when you gave Rae as your name the first day, I got the feeling you just needed your space." Aurora smiled at her as she took the last bite of brownie into her mouth.

"Also, no they don't usually date. They don't want to date a girl that's not into cars because of the drama when they want to race, and the car girls around here piss them off honestly." Aurora laughed just as she heard steps on the stairs.

"You four are the exception to that." Slade's deep voice made her turn around.

"Well, we also have been friends since what elementary school so you can just deal with it." Aurora took a drink of her beer as Slade came towards her and grabbed a plate.

"Don't let her scare you off Angel." Slade bumped into her as he spoke.

"I am not trying to scare her off god you're the worst sometimes. I was just explaining a question she had." Aurora ratted her out, but it did not bother her.

"Oh, and what question was that?" Slade looked at her and she turned her face to meet his eyes.

"I was curious if I was going to have to deal with a crazy chick pissed off that you all invited a new girl to the group. I don't do girlfriend drama, especially crazy car girlfriend drama. There is plenty of that at the tracks." She was honest about it; she had enough drama to deal with.

"No crazy chicks here, unless you count Alaska, but she drives about as straight as she is." Slade's comment made Aurora laugh and then headed down the stairs back to the group.

"Good to know." She almost whispered as she reached for

45

another bottle of water.

"You could have a drink Lola, one of us would drive you home if you wanted to unwind a little." Slade just watched her as he put a cookie into his mouth.

"I don't drink when training. It is a strictly off-season thing." She was blunt, she honestly drank very little.

"Got it. So how are you feeling after today?" Slade motioned towards the stairs.

"Good, I need to get the car down the track though, so I need another track day as soon as possible." She was sure they were busy and couldn't just open the track to her all the time though.

"I will check the schedule at the shop tomorrow and let you know when we can make it over there again." Slade smiled at her as they walked through the garage.

"Oh, if you are all busy, I can manage on my own honesty." She did not want to be an inconvenience to them over this.

"Lola, if you are going to be going down that track, a minimum two of us are going to be there with you. Do you understand me?" Slade stopped her movement and turning her to face him as he asked her.

"Slade, it's not that big of a deal honestly. I need to get over this issue quick." She had two months to get race ready and it would fly by.

"We understand that, but you need people. You don't have to do things by yourself to silence whatever that voice inside your head is telling you. If you wanted to spend the whole week at the track, we would make it work, do you hear me?" Slade's tone and look made her feel safe and cared about even though she barely knew him.

"Yes. But I won't take up that much of your time I promise."
She turned away from him, moving towards the group.

"You can have all of it for I care." Slade said behind her, but she didn't stop, she had to slow down with the feelings she was having for these guys before she crashed again. Because she knew this time recovery would not be easy.

Chapter 6

Emory

Watching Lola enjoy herself tonight was exactly what Emory needed to see, and he would never let this girl leave. She fit right in with the others, she made Slade smile and not run off to work on cars like he usually does around this time. When Granger showed back up with Cody she made fun of him just like the others. This girl was perfect, and he could tell why his brother was trying to keep her to himself all night.

But he was not about to let Gideon keep her for himself, despite how it ended the last time they shared a girl. But that had been years ago that they had tried to fulfill what they all needed with one person. They had shared one-night stands from time to time since then, but nothing permanent. But he was ready to have someone there every day with them, hell he needed it at this point.

None of them wanted to be with each other, no they just wanted to enjoy being with a girl together. To watch her come apart at their hands and be ready for more. It was a little harder for him since he was not like the others as far as enjoyment. Emory wanted to worship a girl, make her beg for release, and wanted to kiss her all over after he made her reach that peak and fall. But that was not usually what you got with a girl that was not even going to stay the night.

But looking at Lola he wanted to do all that and more to her. Emory wanted to watch Gideon control her and Slade be rough with her. He wanted Toby to get enjoyment with Lola and then be left with the puddle of need that she would be for him. He wanted to pull her close to him and wake up next to her the next morning.

The problem was finding a girl who was interested in them all. All of them wanted her, he could see it by how none of them kept their hands off her all night. So, no one was allowed to keep her to themselves, no that would tear them apart and that was not going to happen. They had to show her they were all interested in her and how ok that was. There was a social stigma to what they wanted in a relationship, and they all knew to tread lightly.

"Hey Lola, you want to go for a ride?" He called out to her as he walked over. Gideon gave him a small glair but did not say anything.

"In what?" Lola raised her eyebrow as a challenge, he could see that despite her fears on the track that's where they stayed.

"Not in, on. Want to go for a bike ride?" The others laughed at his wording, but no one said anything.

"Which one is yours?" Lola smiled and he felt his dick getting hard.

"The all black one is mine." He walked over to her and took her hand, making her move away from Gideon.

He walked her over to the bike and grabbed Slade's helmet off his bike as he walked past handing it to her.

"Take this." He grabbed up his helmet before turning the bike on.

"Who's helmet is this?" She asked with her head cocked to the side.

"Mine Angel, and you better put it on if you are getting on the back of Emory's bike." Slade came up behind her and he could see her body's reaction to them, both being this close to her. She flushed a little before moving her hair back to pull the helmet on.

Slade turned her around and fastened the buckle before lifting the visor.

"Have fun out there. Bring her back in one piece." Slade looked right at him in warning. Yeah, he was hooked on her just as bad as he was.

"We will be fine." He said tapping her perfect ass to get her onto the bike.

As she climbed on, he could see Gideon and Toby watching her. Emory was happy to see she was smiling and her breathing was calm and normal.

He got on the bike and pulled his helmet on. He pushed the Bluetooth button that would connect hers to his and waited a second.

"Can you hear me?" He asked.

"Yeah." Her voice distorted a little from the connection.

"Good, if you want to stop or come back let me know ok." He told her as he began backing the bike out of the garage.

"Don't try and take me down the track on this thing and I guarantee you are fine." She laughed and it made him smile.

He was sure someone eventually would tell her how bad of a thrill seeker he was. He was set to race on the next race day on his racing bike, but he thought she might freak out about that.

"No track tonight, just the road and wind." He headed down the driveway and loved how her arms came around him to hold on as he drove.

She didn't say anything as they rode, he would love to have

her comfortable to talk but he knew she was going through a lot. He turned down the best road in town, it was where they used to street race as kids. It was the best paved road in town since the foreman for the city was a street racer and kept it nice.

As he straightened out, he pushed the bike as fast as it would go. It was nothing compared to his track bike, but it did the trick. Lola's laugh came through the helmet, and he could feel her holding him tight to her body.

"Holly shit." Her voice was hushed but he still heard her.

"Yeah, you want to drive it?" He asked as he slowed down at the end of the road.

"Seriously?" She sounded so surprised and when he stopped the bike, he could tell she was not expecting him to actually let her drive.

"Yes, I am not even going to be the ass and ask if you know how to drive it because I assume you can." He flipped up their visors so he could see her eyes and he could see he was right.

"I can but you're going to ride bitch on your own bike?" She was fire and he loved seeing this side of her.

"Not for most girls, but for you. Lola I would ride bitch forever if that's what you wanted." He could see his words sinking in and he patted the seat to tell her to move up.

She slipped down the bike slowly and now he was thinking this was not a good idea. He was not going to be able to hide how much his body wanted her. But he climbed up anyway, getting behind her pulling their bodies close.

She clicked the clutch and began to pull away from the side of the road slowly gaining speed. She was going to run out of time to stop if she did not go faster now.

"Go now so you don't run out of shut down time." He said to her, and she accelerated quickly.

He could feel her breathing slow down and could feel her body shift as she maneuvered the bike. He tapped her leg to tell her to let up and she backed off.

"Think you can get us back?" He asked her as she slowed down to take the turn back to the main roads.

"Yeah, you sure? You can drive back. That was amazing though." He could hear the smile on her face and did not care about the ridicule he was going to get back at the house.

"Its fine Lola. Just take us back." She laughed as she accelerated on the road. She drove beautifully and he was impressed with her bike handling.

"How long have you been riding?" He asked as they turned down the road for the house.

"Off and on since I was 16. But my parents died in a bike accident, so I don't own one. I haven't even been on one for close to 3 years at this point." Her voice changed a little as she spoke, he could hear the sadness in her voice.

"I am sorry for your loss." He knew what it felt like to be left without parents.

"I am sorry for yours, you lost your dad recently, right?" She slowed down as they got to the driveway.

"Yeah, but we knew he was sick, just like mom. They are just watching us now." He was not angry or still mad about his parents dying. He would rather them not be suffering.

"That's the way I look at it. I hope they are watching me proud of what I do." She put the bike back in the garage and he noticed everyone was in the loft when they got back.

"I think they are." He said before she pulled the helmet off.

"Riding bitch on your own bike?" Cody asked as Emory pulled his helmet off.

"Behind Lola Bunny is not a bad place to be." She elbowed him as he made the comment but everyone else laughed.

"You have fun Angel?" Slade was there taking his helmet from her.

"Absolutely, it's always fun to see how fast you can go." She smiled a smile that could melt the fucking ice caps.

"Good. You want some more food?" Slade asked but she shook her head.

"I should probably get going I have an appointment tomorrow I need to make." She said is and he could see Slade's face fall.

"Want one of us to take you?" Slade was not ready for her to leave.

"No, I am fine. But I will message you after to see about track times ok." She patted his arm before waving to the others saying goodbye. He let her walk out like it was the most normal thing, like a regular friend leaving but he wanted her to be staying.

"You let me know when she wants to go back to the track ok?" He said to Slade as they walked up to the loft.

"Everyone already wants to be there the whole time I wouldn't count you out of that." Slade's face told him they were all hooked.

"You guys ready to work a lot this week?" He asked the others as he got to the top.

"Heck yeah, you have to let us show you we can run the shop for when Toby makes it into the season." Brighton laughed but they all knew this was important.

Toby would be racing for them in the prequalifying event in a few weeks to get on the same season as Lola. They would not be in the same bracket but they would all be at the same tracks and together for a while.

"You guys are going to be fine when we make it." Toby smiled at the others. They all knew he would make it in. Now with Lola involved he knew his friend would not drop the ball on this opportunity.

"Glad you think so. We are heading home, early start in the morning." Granger pulled Aurora closer to him as he pushed off the railing of the loft.

"We're going too." Alaska and Noelle waved as they headed out.

"You need a ride or are you crashing here?" Brighton asked Cody who got up from the couch.

"I have to get started on fixing that crap so if you could take me great." They laughed; he would be working on that car till he died.

"We will see you guys tomorrow." They waved and the others headed into the house as he watched them leave. He shut the garage doors before heading in.

"So, who's going to say it first?" Slade was in his seat at the island when he got into their great room. The space was dark with the lights out and only the light over the island on.

"I don't want her to ever leave." He said it.

"I think we all feel that way. But the problem is how do we show her we all want her, and we all are ok with the fact that she wants us also?" Toby spoke the truth and it hurt to think about her leaving.

"We just show her how much we want to be around her. Then

see where it goes. She came here without even really knowing us. If we are at the track with her more, she is going to get more comfortable. We let it go from there, let it build naturally." Gideon was the wisest for a reason.

"That works I guess, but damn if you put her on your bike again with my helmet, I am going to take her." Slade was serious, he was very possessive of his things and if he saw her as his, they were all going to be walking on thin ice for a little while.

"I knew it would fit her." He shrugged as he grabbed water from the fridge.

"Still, now the image of her on your bike is going to haunt my dreams." Slade shook his head and headed towards the dark hallway that led to his room.

"You and me both. Night guys." He left the kitchen and went to his room as well. He needed a shower and to try and get his dick to calm down about that girl handling his bike like a pro.

Chapter 7

Lola

The next morning, Lola felt like she was floating on air and her therapist noticed it as soon as she sat down. It was enough of a change for her to say that she did not want to see her anymore unless she wanted more sessions. She sent Duke that update before she was out the door, mental health checks were a worry for the season. She had to be physically and mentally cleared after an accident that big.

She was now sitting in the bakery Aurora owned having a coffee and a brownie, trying to get the nerve to send the text to the guys about more track time this week.

"Just send it Rae." Aurora pulled Lola the thoughts as she sat in the chair across from her.

"Hey, when did you get here?" She had situated herself against the back wall so she could see who was coming in, but she was clearly distracted. Aurora had her hair pulled into a high pony tail today which made it easier for Lola to see just how pretty she was.

"I got in a few minutes ago but I came in the back. Just send them the message, I know for a fact the track is already prepped and waiting for you. Granger said the guys have been out all morning working on it." Aurora smiled at her, and Lola hit send on the message.

My appointment is done, and I was wondering when the

best time would be this week to go to the track again? She had sent it in the group message.

You can head over now if you want. Toby messaged back before she could even put her phone back on the table.

"Told you. Let me make you a sandwich and you can head over there." Aurora stood up.

"Why are you helping me?" She did not feel strange about it, but it was not normal.

"Because it has been a long time since I have seen them as happy as they were last night. Plus, I like you and want to be your friend, we need more girls around to balance things out." Aurora laughed as she headed into the kitchen.

I have to go get the car and I will meet you there. She typed back while taking a sip of her coffee.

Good, we are grabbing lunch, do you want something? Emory's message popped up and it made her feel gushy inside. Somone caring about feeding her made her feel welcome.

Aurora is making me a sandwich as we speak so I am good. She hated to turn him down, but she did not need that much food.

Oh ask her to make us some and you can bring lunch. Toby's message was followed by a laughing smiley face by Slade.

"Aurora, think you could make me four more? I will pay you for them." She called into the kitchen, but Aurora was already coming out with a bag.

"I already got you. They would throw a fit if you showed up with one and nothing for them. Tell them they owe me." Aurora laughed as she handed her the bag.

"I will. Thanks." She took the bag and grabbed her coffee.

She headed out of the bakery and to her car. She felt good, like today was the day she could drive her own car down the track.

It took around an hour to get to the track and she was starving. She had gone home and changed into a crop top and shorts since she was going to put her driving suit on and had managed her hair. But she waited to eat with them since she had brought them food also.

As she pulled in next to their stall, she saw the white drag pack fly down the track. She couldn't help herself waiting for the time to show up and when the 8.90 lit up the board she smiled. She had put her suit in the back seat this time and began to pull it on, at least on the bottom, before the guys came over.

Just as she was coming around the passenger side to get the food out, they all came back with the car.

"I have died and somehow made it to heaven because you are an Angel." Slade made her laugh as she handed him the bag of food, taking her sandwich out first.

"You owe Aurora, she already had them made before I even asked." She took a seat on one of the chairs they had set out as the others filled in theirs as well.

"We always owe Aurora; she bakes us breakfast most mornings and Granger brings them into the shop." Gideon shook his head as he took a bite of his food.

"That's great, I mean I eat at her shop almost every day at this point." She loved how the downtown of this town was so easy to walk.

"You work it into the diet then?" Gideon smiled at her in a

mocking way, making her laugh.

"It's worth the extra run time for sure." She took a bite, and her body thanked her. She was hungrier than she realized.

"How are you feeling about today?" Emory looked at her with a little worry in his eyes and she could see it was genuine.

"I feel great actually. I got released from therapy today, and the thought of getting in the car doesn't make me want to burn the trailer down." She leaned into the comfort she felt around them, letting them in a little more.

"That's great. You want to take ours down first? It's just the class under you so it might be a little less intimidating." Toby offered and she nodded.

"If you're ok with that." She looked at Gideon knowing he was like the team owner here.

"I think it's a great idea, you were in one when you first started racing right?" She nodded at Gideon as he asked.

"Yeah, we only shifted to the pro mod last season." She was more comfortable in their car probably than her own.

"Well, if you're done eating let's get you in the car then." Gideon smiled at her as he got out of his chair.

She got up and headed back to her truck. She put her helmet in there as well as her neck harness. They headed over to their car and Gideon opened the door for her.

"The far lane is all set up and remember to take it at your pace. We have all day." Gideon's smile made her feel understood.

Getting into the car she went through the startup sequence and began getting the safety stuff set up. After they both checked the straps, she was ready. Gideon shut the door and she headed to the lanes.

This time as she did her burnout and got lined up, she felt excited. She let her mind drift to the enjoyment of just watching this car go down the track and when the lights began to head to green, she couldn't help it.

Muscle memory hit her, and she launched the car hard. Holding it straight she shifted into the next gear and then the next. Not lifting until the end of the track. Looking in the mirror of the car quickly she caught the board light up with an 8.75 and a laugh came from her.

This feeling, the weightlessness of going faster than the last person. The adrenaline high she road all the way to the pits. The way the guys were clapping for her, and the way Toby just shook his head.

"Had to go blow my time out of the water didn't you sweet girl." Toby helped her get out of the harness while the others opened up the car to cool down.

"Just had to show you what this baby can do." She smiled at him and his hand lingered on her thigh.

"Oh, I intend on beating that time. I was doing a warmup lap. You watch next one I will do better." Toby's eyes twinkled with the challenge of going faster and she loved it.

"Oh, I'll watch, from my rearview mirror." She laughed and he squeezed her leg.

"You need a challenge, Lola?" Toby asked, letting her go and helped her out of the car.

"Always, I live for challenges." She was serious, she hated to lose.

"Good. Let's get your car ready." Toby let his fingers trail her arm as he let go of her.

"Ok, but maybe I should run it on my own for a run. No other car in the lane." She was hoping it would help keep the flashbacks from coming back.

"I think that's a good idea." Gideon was there just smiling at them. She blushed at the closeness of Toby and having Gideon see it.

"Ok let me get it out." She headed towards the trailer without waiting for their response.

She opened the back door of the trailer and then headed to the side door to get in the car. As she started it up, she did not feel the same way she had the last time, the anxiety was still there but she was not shaking, and she was excited.

She backed the car up with Slade and Emory's guidance and then climbed back out for it to warm up. Toby brought her helmet over and she pulled it on and got back in the car. Strapping up she did her checks on everything and when Emory came into the door of the car she let out a deep breath.

"I have a treat for after you get down the track no matter what the time is." His smile made her feel comfortable and at ease.

"Oh, what's that?" She was curious.

"Get to the end of the track and you will find out." Emory checked her harness straps again and patted her thigh before shutting the door.

Gideon was in front of her holding a thumbs up and she mimicked this to let him know she was good to go. He backed her up before pointing her towards the track. She headed towards the lanes and again just took deep breaths, just make it to the end nothing else matters. Seat time is seat time.

She drove through the burnout box and did not do one, she

did not want the pressure. Just drive it down the track Lola. Slade looked at her with his head cocked to the side and she just gave him a thumbs up as she lined up. The staging lights came on and Slade hit the button to start the lights falling.

At green she left just like she would a stop light and let her body tell her when it was ok. She let the car tell her when to shift and she let tears fall when she hit the end of the track. Not looking back at the time because it did not matter. She made it down the track and she was going to be ok; she was going to be able to do what she loved again.

Chapter 8

Toby

He held her time slip in his hands; he could tell by the way she left that she was just trying to make it to the end. Emory and his damn promise of a teat probably did it for her. But he could not help but look at her reaction time. It was perfect, even though she was just letting herself have the moment her mind and body lived for racing.

"Look at her reaction time." He handed the slip to Gideon.

"Damn, I have not seen one that good in a while." Gideon passed it to Emory as they all walked back to the pits, they could hear her coming from the turnaround spot.

"This is why her time was better than yours. Her reaction times are off the charts." Slade said taking the slip from Emory who went to their truck to get the brownies he brought with them. Leave it to him to know her favorite treat already.

Lola stopped the car in her area, and he could see she was already out of her safety gear as she stopped.

"I did it!" She jumped up and down with her helmet still on with pure joy in her voice and the smile on his face started to hurt. He wanted to see her happy like this forever, and he had only known her for a few days.

"Damn right you did. Look at this reaction time. You make Toby's look like he is making a whole dinner on the line." Slade took her the slip and she took her helmet off before looking at it.

"Come on that's not nice, I literally have an app and a handheld toy that I practice daily." Lola smiled at him as she realized how good her time was.

"Maybe you need to share your insider training with me then sweet girl." He walked over to her as she set her helmet into the car and began to unzip the top of her suit. Her body was amazing, and he wanted to see everything she had on, he suspected she was in something short since she was suited up when they got back to the pits earlier.

"I can show you the app, but the toy is not going anywhere. I think the app glitches so the toy has more accuracy." She was smiling but serious, she really did east, sleep and breath this sport and damn if that did not make her hotter.

"I would appreciate that." He smiled at her as Emory came up next to them.

"Your treat as promised." Emory held out the brownies and she smirked at him before taking one.

She let out a little moan as she took a bite, and it went right to his dick. He wanted more of those noises and one look at Slade told him his best friend wanted them too.

"Aurora's?" She asked Emory who laughed.

"Of course." Emory responded.

"My favorite." She said before putting the rest of the brownie in her mouth.

"I know." Emory said as he walked off back towards their truck.

"How did he know?" She looked at him with a questioning gaze.

"I told him, and Emory being himself, he had to make sure we had some today." Slade was popping up the hood of her car so it could cool down before their next run.

"Well, that was really nice of you guys." She was sweet. Lola's reaction gave Emory a boost and he could see it. The way she looked so happy Emory thought of her showed not many others did that. Toby hated to think that no one in her life did little things like this for her, but he knew Emory would gladly take up that job.

"It's no big deal, we always try to have snacks on track days," he told her as they headed to the chairs. Gideon was holding water out for them when they got there.

Lola took a seat and accepted the water from Gideon. They all sat around just waiting for the chance to go run again.

"This is the worst part of test time." Lola broke their silence.

"Yeah, waiting for cars to cool down when nothing else is going on sucks." Slade was always moving so this down time was like hell to him. Even now he was bouncing his leg.

"It's better when it's a race day and there are other races to go watch." Lola settled into her chair more, she looked relaxed.

"You should come to the races this weekend." Emory smiled at Lola as he invited her.

"Oh, what's on the schedule?" Lola perked up quick at the mention of racing and he loved how she smiled.

"We have a few different brackets going. Its Friday night, you should come we will leave you a pit pass at the gate." Gideon urged her.

"That sounds like fun but if it's going to be busy, I don't think I should come." Her voice betrayed her as she tried to make an excuse not to go, she was disappointed in making the excuse.

"Why not?" Slade was upset now, his leg stopped bouncing as he leaned forward watching Lola closely.

"I took a risk last weekend by going to the car show, I would really be pushing the limits of being recognized at a track event." She was right of course; it would be easy for others to recognize her.

"Lola, I don't think anyone in town would tell anyone you are here. We are such a small town that most people don't care. The most you would get would be asked for a picture and an autograph." Gideon was trying to calm her down, but Toby could see it was not working.

"I will think about it, but it might not work out. Pictures show up on social media and then people would know where I was." She stood up and walked over to her car, ending the conversation.

He got up and followed her because he was not ok with her, clearly being so upset over something as simple as photos. She was checking the temp on the car when he got over to her.

"Hey, want to talk about it?" He asked knowing she probably would shut it down, but he had to try.

"Not particularly, but the car's cool so we can go do another run if you want." He would let her push it off for now, but he wanted to see her enjoy a track day. Heck, he wanted to see her watch him run in the event.

"Ok, but know any of us are willing to listen if you want to talk, and if it's something that you need let us know because we want to help." Toby ran his hand over her lower back and felt her tense up but then relax into his touch.

"Thanks Toby, it's just not what I want to focus on right now. I need to get back in the saddle completely." She was focused on the car; he could see her force her focus on her task.

"Ok I will go let the others know we are going to run again. You going to go all out for me sweet girl?" He smirked at her as he asked.

"I think I can give you a run for your money." She smiled right at him, and he could feel her mood shift back to the joy she had after the last run.

"Good, lets head out." He pulled his hand away from her and went to tell the others to get ready for a run.

He and Emory got their car ready while Gideon and Slade made sure Lola was set. As Gideon backed her up after pulling the pins out of the parashoot, Slade went to make sure the track was ready. He headed over as Emory followed Slade.

As he got to the stagging lanes Lola was doing her burn out and Gideon was guiding her forward. He did his burnout and then Emory got him staged. He looked over at her from his lane as Slade gave her the thumbs up, as she gave him one, he smiled. She was ready for this, and he was honored to be beside her. He gave Slade a thumbs up before he headed back to the box.

The lights came down and on the green he launched the car, but Lola was already in front of him. He pushed his car as fast as he could, but she would win because she was pushing also. She crossed the line pulling her shoots and a second later he crossed after her.

Looking in the mirror to see the board, Lola's 6.9 and his 8.7 lit up the board. He was faster on this run, and he was sure it was because he was chasing her down. It is always easier to fight when chasing a car down. But all he thought about was her and how she felt about that.

Her car was fast and that was a great pass for only her second in the car. He knew it was not as fast as that car could do with the work that was put into it. He could see now why Duke was convinced she would be adding to her tattoos this year.

As he pulled back into the pits, he could see her happily getting out of her car waiting for Slade to bring her the time slip.

"You happy Lola?" He called over to her as he got out of his car.

"It felt fast, but I did not catch the board before I turned around." She lifted the hood of her car as the others joined them.

"Well, you beat Toby," Slade's smart ass said holding the slip.

"I knew that when I couldn't see him, what was the time?" Lola almost ran to Slade to try and get the slip.

"How badly do you want to know?" Slade taunted her.

"What is this? What would you do for a klondike bar, show me the slip Slade." Oh, her sass was going to get her in trouble with him when they all decided to keep her.

"8.7 for Toby, 6.9 for you and you beat his reaction time again." Slade's words made her smile, and it caught Slade up where she was able to grab the slip from him.

Emory and Gideon laughed as she ran away from Slade to her trailer with the slip. Slade just let out a growl and followed her. He caught the look on all of their faces, and he could see it, they all wanted to be with her and see her this happy again.

Chapter 9

Lola

The track was packed, and she could see why the guys insisted on getting her a pit pass to be in the lanes with them, even though it made her wonder about the actual meaning of it all. They had not talked about what was going on between them all.

It was comfortable today at the track, the weather was perfect for the event. With her hat on and sunglasses she hoped no one would recognize her. She was not ready to have her location spoiled before the season started. Hopefully being in the pits would help with that, as she walked up to the large tent set up, she could see all of them working on the cars they planned to race today.

Gideon and Toby were working on the drag pack while Emory and Slade worked on the track hawk. There seemed to be a few different types of racing going on here today to start off their season.

"Lola!" Slade called to her as he climbed out of the driver's seat of the car.

"Hey Slade." She let him pull her into a hug as if it was the most natural thing for them both.

"You came." Slade looked at her with a smile as he let go of their embrace. He clearly still worried she wouldn't come to things when she said she would.

"I told you I would come." She rolled her eyes a little, none of them had let her forget about today all week. They had worn her down Wednesday after their last track day.

The track day had been perfect Wednesday, she as able to pull data for Duke who was now planning on coming this week for a session. There were some adjustments to her car that needed to be made and that required him to be here. It would also be a great time to talk about team changes in person.

"Yeah, but he worried it would be too public for you." Gideon came around the car to also give her a hug, it felt just as comfortable as the one with Slade, despite him standing right there.

"I mean it is very public, that is for sure. I am surprised there are so many people here." She looked around a bit after Gideon let go of the hug.

"Well, it is opening day for the track, there are three different events as well as prequalifying to get into the same season you are starting in a few weeks just in the lower brackets." As Gideon said it, she realized that this might be a mistake now.

"What do you mean prequalifying?" She now felt her anxiety rise.

"Those who do not have big teams pre-qualify for the season throughout the off season. We host one for this area of the country." Gideon just looked at her like she was crazy as she began to take deeper breaths.

"Hey Lola, what's wrong?" Emory was now beside Gideon watching her.

"Nothing, um maybe I should go home." She hated to leave them while they were going to race but this could end badly for her.

"You just got here." Slade protested with a look that told her he might be pushed to force her to stay somehow.

"People don't know I am here Slade. It's part of my time off, I even pre-post things on my social media to make it look like I am anywhere but here. I am willing to bet this race is being live streamed if it is for the season?" She asked and could see the recognition on Gideon's face as she said it, she clenched her hand to stop the shaking that was creeping in.

"Shit Lola I didn't think about that. I am so sorry. What can we do to keep you here though, chances are your car is blocked in already with how parking is here." Gideon looked at her as Toby joined them.

"Just make her look like she is part of the team. Give her a team shirt and hat, keep the glasses on and no one will guess it." Toby smiled at her before coming to hug her despite the tension around them.

"That might work, you good with it, Lola?" Gideon asked her, taking in her concern, her anxiety spiking but his look made her feel safe.

"Fuck, this is going to be bad but what the heck." She threw her arms up and they all laughed while rushing her into their trailer. This one was bigger than the one they used for their track day, and she was instantly in love. It was more of a toy hauler with a living space in the front.

There was a couch and a table, a small fridge with a sink and she could see bunk beds further back.

"Do you want a tee-shirt as well as a button-down team shirt?" Toby smiled at her as he pulled open a cabinet on the wall.

"Just the button down please." She smiled back but before Toby could hand her the shirt in his hand a warm shirt dropped into her waiting hand.

71

She turned around to find Gideon without a shirt and realized why the one in her hand was warm. She could not help her gaze over his body and how his chest filled with tattoos made him look incredible. His body filled with muscles, each breath he took pulling her focus to his body more.

"Get me a new shirt Toby." Gideon staired right at her as he spoke to his best friend.

"Change your shirt, Lola." Slade's voice was thick with desire as she broke her stare with Gideon to look at him. His eyes were hooded and as he licked his lips, she felt her desire to have him lick anywhere on her body grow.

She turned her attention to Emory who pulled the door shut, she was now trapped in a small space with all four of them. All of whom she had little moments with the past week, all staring at her hungry for more of her.

"I don't think that is a good idea." She choked out trying to take deep breaths, her anxiety shifting to unease in this situation.

"Lola, change your shirt or you are going to make us late to the race." Gideon drew her attention back up to his face, his blue eyes sparkling with need.

Her desire was winning as they watched her, and she let it take control. Grabbing the hem of her shirt she pulled it over her head, as they all saw the red bra underneath a chorus of groans and growls filled the space. Before she could put Gideon's shirt on though there was a pair of lips on her shoulder right by the strap of her bra.

"This is going to be my good luck charm today, the image of you standing here with this lacy red bra. Please tell me your panties match sweet girl." Toby's breath was hot on her neck as he moved her hair.

"They do." She whispered unable to focus anymore as he kissed her neck.

"Fuck, you are too perfect." Toby put another kiss on her neck and backed away. She took the moment to pull the shirt over her head. It was very long so she unbuttoned the last few buttons and tied it at her waist. Toby handed Gideon a new shirt and she did not realize the groan she made as he pulled it on.

"Make noises like that Doll and we are going to have to keep you." Gideon took her chin in his fingers and tipped her head up to look at him. The roughness of his fingers mixed with the desire in his eyes was enough to make her beg for more attention.

"You think you can keep me Gideon? You would have to catch me first." She smirked at him seeing the challenge flash across his face.

"Oh, Doll you have no idea what we will do to you when we catch you." Gideon did not give her a chance to respond before he pulled her lips to meet his. The realization of the others held her stiff for a minute, but as he pushed his tongue past her lips, she felt the resolve melt away.

"I think she likes the idea of being ours, brother." Emory's voice made her pull away from Gideon, feeling her face grow hot as he looked at her with a need that matched his brothers.

"Let's see." Gideon turned her to face Emory and let his brother take her face in his hands. Emory pulled her closer and closed the distance to her lips. She melted into him as he moved his hands to her waist trailing the small space of skin in the gap between the shirt and her pants. She let out a moan as he swiped his tongue along her lips before she let him in.

She was struggling to focus on anything other than Emory's

hands roaming her ass now, but an announcement on the track speakers pulled her back to reality.

"Time to line up." Toby lightly slapped her ass as he walked out of the space.

"Thanks for the good luck kiss, Lola." Emory kissed her forehead and followed Toby out.

"You, ok?" Gideon looked at her and she could see Slade still watching them, his legs swinging off the table he was sitting on.

"Confused a little." She was honest because they had all just watched her make out with most of their team.

"We can talk about it later ok." Gideon kissed her cheek and left her and Slade alone.

"Come here let's get your hat on." Slade motioned her over and she did so without question stepping between his open legs. He took the hat off his head, ran his hands through his black hair to get rid of the hat hair and she felt her heart rate go up because she wanted her fingers running through his hair.

"Slade, how is this ok?" She asked as he fit the hat to her head.

"We have been a team for a long time Lola, we have shared a girl before, we have shared the heartbreak when she left. If you are willing to talk to us all about it later like Gideon said we will, ok. Just enjoy yourself today, you're a track girl for the day just let yourself be that, ok." He tipped her head to his lips before kissing her as well. It was not as needy as the others, but it was soft and loving, leaving her wanting him to worship her body with his mouth.

"Ok." She said as she pulled away, he handed her the sunglasses she did not realize had come off when she took her shirt off. Slade slid off the table putting them close together again, he smelled like car

74

which was comforting to her.

"Good, now come be our good luck charm because I already feel lucky today." Slade took her hand in his and threaded his fingers with hers.

They headed out to meet up with the others and they all smiled at her. Slade led her to the Track Hawk and opened the passenger seat for her. She climbed in as she heard the drag pack start up. They drove to the staging lanes with the other cars before the event started there was the national anthem and then announcements. The entire time they were standing there, Slade was running his fingers up her arms and sides making it hard to focus.

"Lola." Gideon was right beside her saying her name as if he had said it before.

"Sorry, what's up?" She turned to look at him and could see Emory and Toby laughing a little.

"Do you want to line us up in the lanes or wait in the stands?" Gideon repeated his question.

"Um, maybe the stands? Is there a not too public part?" She was not sure how this one was set up.

"Take her to the control room. There won't be to many people there. Plus, as part of the team they won't second guess it." Slade suggested to the nods of the others.

"Alright, you get ready I will take her in there for the first time." Gideon reached for her hand, and they walked into the small room right next to the burnout box.

Inside there were three people watching out the big window with a desk in front of it.

"Gideon, what can we do for you?" The older man turned and asked.

"My girl is going to watch our runs from here ok. Treat her nice Frank." The old man waved Gideon off at the comment.

"You know my old lady would run me over and drag me down this track if I did anything. Come take a seat." Frank pulled out an extra chair before turning back to the track.

"You don't have to tell him your name but know that Frank has been around for a long time and will probably figure you out. But he won't say anything, ok. The other two are Luke and Nate, they are good guys also and won't say anything for fear of being fired." Gideon whispered in her ear before walking her over to the open chair.

"Ok, good luck," she said as she took her seat, pulling her phone out of her pocket before she sat.

"I have you that's all the luck I need." Gideon kissed her head before he turned her chair around and pushed her in.

"Tell Toby to watch the left lane, if he thinks it's too slippery, he needs to tell us." Frank told Gideon as he walked out with no acknowledgement of the comment.

"What's up with the left lane?" She could not help asking after the door to the room shut behind Gideon.

"Somone blew a head gasket during practice; the oil should be gone, but Toby is the best at finding the bad spots. Luke, by the way." He had short blond hair, and he reached a handout to her across the long table.

"Magnolia Rae," she shook his hand and saw the realization from all three.

"No shit, Gideon snagged Magnolia Rae. Man is he one lucky man. Nate, nice to meet you." The last guy held his hand out and she dropped Luke's to shake his.

"Thanks, not sure about snagged, maybe a few car lengths behind at this point. I would be grateful if you did not tell anyone I was here though." She let go of his hand and they all nodded.

"We understand Magnolia, you deserve some privacy and none of us is going to take that from you. Just enjoy the races." Frank turned a softer look on her, she could see he understood.

"Thanks." She turned her focus to the lanes where she could see Toby lining up after his burn out.

"All right who's ready to kick off pre-qualifying? We have our local team HPS Motorsports in the left lane in their drag pack and another drag pack in the right lane piloted by a newcomer Casey." Nate said into a microphone, and she realized he was announcing the race.

She watched as the two cars lined up and the staging lights came on. She was entranced as she watched them take off from the line and she couldn't help standing up as she watched Toby take the car over the line first.

"Toby takes the win." Nate announced and she could see the crowd outside clapping. Inside the box behind the staging lanes, she could see Emory pointing at her and giving her a thumbs up. She felt all of the good luck charm they had dubbed her.

Chapter 10

Lola

The races were taking a break for dinner, and Lola was on her way back from the concessions stand when her phone went off in her pocket.

"Shit, I can't grab it." She muttered to herself as she made it back to the pits. She put her food down on the table the guys had brought outside and grabbed her phone out of her pocket.

Enjoying the races, Magnolia? It was a message from Greyson, and she dropped her soda as she read it, he saw her somehow. Was he here, she turned around to scan the crowd but could not see him.

"Lola what's going on?" Slade is in front of her, and she realizes she is shaking.

"I need to go. Sorry I need to leave right now." She did not bother grabbing her food before turning from the guys and running towards the parking lot. She could hear them calling her, but she didn't stop.

Her car was thankfully not blocked in, and she quickly got in and headed to her house. The panic attack was already threatening to take over and she was thankful she held it together to get to the house, very thankful for the short drive.

Inside the house she shut all the doors and checked the locks.

She was not sure Greyson would show up but seeing as how she was ignoring him all this time; she couldn't chance it.

She put her phone on her bed before going into the bathroom. She caught a glimpse of herself without her sunglasses on and realized how she was found. There must have been a camera in the crowd at the half time break. She had taken her glasses off when it got dark, even with Slade's hat, she was still very noticeable.

She pulled the hat off and put it on the counter before brushing her hair. She could hear her phone going off, but she ignored it, she needed a break, she needed to get out of her head. She pulled the shirt off and tossed it onto her bed, then went and grabbed a sports bra and big tee shirt. As she changed into workout clothes she grabbed her headphones, put her phone on do not disturb, and headed into her spare room.

She began with a walk on the treadmill before bumping it up to a run. Her music letting her just focus on calming her mind, running made her focus on her breathing and soon she could feel the aftereffects of the panic attack coming.

Coming down from a panic attack was rough and she quickly took off the now sweaty clothes and collapsed onto her bed not bothering to put anything on.

There was loud knocking and a ringing that woke her up. As she opened her eyes, she saw the clock on her bedside table reading 11pm and she cursed. The anxiety coming back hard as she realized there was someone at her door and, after Greyson's message, her mind went right to him.

She grabbed Gideon's shirt from on her bed and pulled it back on, not tying it up this time so it hung almost to her knees. Not grabbing her phone though she knew there would be messages waiting for her, she headed into the living room.

"Open up Magnolia." The voice was deep but not Greyson's.

She looked through the peep hole before unlocking and opening the door.

"Angel come here." Slade was the one knocking and, as she opened the door, he pulled her into him. As he held her, she felt the effects of her anxiety crashing into her again and the sob that came out of her was involuntarily. The comfort his arms offered her felt right and like he was meant for her.

Slade walked them to her couch, and she heard the door shut but did not look to see who else was here. As Slade sat down, he pulled her onto his lap, and she let herself just be consumed by him as she straddled him.

"It's ok, we got you, ok. Nothing is going to happen to you with us here." Slade said into her neck as he cuddled into her.

"It's not ok, he found where I am. I am going to have to leave." She sobbed as she spoke, the pressure and sadness of the realization hitting her as Slade held her.

"You're not leaving Lola." Gideon's voice was beside her and she turned from Slade's neck to look at him.

"I can't stay. If I do, he will come and try and make me talk to him." She had not told them how demanding Greyson was about them continuing their relationship.

"Do you want to stay?" Gideon's blue eyes bore into her as he asked the question. It was not just about staying in town, but staying with them, she could see it in his eyes. How could they all make her feel so safe so soon?

"Yes." She admitted and she could see the relief wash over his face.

"Then we will be here for you." Gideon pressed his lips to her forehead and smoothed out her hair.

"I can't handle him Gideon." She breathed out.

"We will handle him, Lola." Emory's voice was on the other side of Slade, and it made her sit up.

"We are all here sweet girl." She felt Toby's hand on her back as she looked at Emory.

"He won't be ok with me moving on." She looked at Emory as she said it knowing it was true. She hated that Greyson still called and messaged as if she was the problem. He wouldn't listen to her when she said they were over after she was released from the hospital, so why should she keep trying.

"Hey, don't worry about it." Emory pulled her face to his and kissed her deeply and she felt her body relax into him and Slade.

"Why don't you pack some things and come stay with us for a few days?" Toby's voice was calm and his fingers tracking lines on her back were distracting.

"I couldn't put you guys out like that Toby." She tried to turn to face him, but Slade was not letting go of her.

"Angel you will not be putting us out, you have not seen the whole house yet, ok. Let's go pack you a bag and anything else you will need." Slade kissed her forehead before standing up with her in his arms, she tried to put her feet on the ground, but he held onto her ass making her wrap her legs around his hips.

She was now very aware of the fact that she only had underwear underneath the shirt as a cool breeze came across her back side.

"I can walk." She wiggled but Slade held on tighter.

"And miss my opportunity to hold your ass in my hands, no way. Plus, I think Gideon likes this view." His comment made her turn to look at Gideon on the couch and she could see the outline of his dick through his pants.

There was a feeling now in the room that made her suddenly very aware of Slade's calloused hands on the bare skin of her thighs. No one said a word, but she could see it in their eyes as he carried her to the bedroom.

"Slade, I am not sure about this being a good idea." She was conflicted with how she felt attracted to all four of them. It was not normal for someone to want to be with four men, how could they be comfortable with her being with them all.

"Lola, pack some clothes and whatever else you need. We have a full gym also so you should bring workout clothes." Slade had set her on the floor now and was moving to the chair she had in the corner.

"Do you need anything else from the rest of the house sweet girl?" Toby walked into her room, and she felt her breath quicken by having two of them this close to her with the growing need she was feeling for them.

"Um, I think I need to bring the car with me. I can't leave it here if I am not going to be here. Plus, if Greyson comes here and sees the trailer, he will know this is my house." She was sure it would give her away.

"We have room, do I need to go hook it up or move it?" Toby stepped closer to her pulling her to his body by her hips. His hands on her made it hard to think. Why was his touch so distracting and addictive?

"No, I left it hooked up the other day. Keys are on the hook by the back door in the kitchen." She was willing her body to focus on tasks and not be distracted by his hands on her.

"Ok, one of us will take it unless you want to drive it." Toby was gently moving his fingers over her as he talked, and the desire she felt for this man and the others in her house building and pulling her focus to be on them.

"Um, sure I don't care whatever is easier." She was losing the battle of focus now.

"You ok, sweet girl?" Toby just smiled down at her as he kept moving his fingers over her hips. Her focus shifting to his lips thinking about the way they felt earlier today, wanting his lips where his fingers were.

"Yeah, fine just trying to think about what I need." She tried to push the thoughts of his lips touching her away, but Toby smirked at her, and she knew she was not able to hid her desire from him right now.

"Anything you need and forget, we will get for you ok. I will go get the truck ready and make sure the car is good for the drive." Toby shifted a hand to her jaw and pulled her face to his.

The moment his lips touched her the resolve to stay away was gone, she melted into his touch. Toby pulled her closer with the hand on her hip and pushed his tongue into her mouth. The first pass of it over hers the moan slipped out and she knew she would need more of him.

"Angel, you are intoxicating." Slade's voice behind her made her pull away and she could feel the blush on her face now. She had forgotten he was in her with them.

"Don't be embarrassed Lola." Toby stepped away and headed out of the room. She was really going to need to have that talk with them like Gideon suggested. Her mind was swimming with emotions, and she felt like she could fall asleep again for hours at this point.

"Start packing before I start grabbing things Angel." Slade pulled her out of her confusion again and she moved to her closet. She grabbed her weekend bag off the shelf and began pulling comfortable clothes out, putting them into her bag. She was conflicted to be going to their house, but she also felt comfortable going with them. She would make them sit down and talk after she got some sleep when her head was clear of the desire, she felt for them all.

Chapter 11

Gideon

Last night had been a whirl wind of a night. First, they all won their races and pre-qualified for the same races Lola would leave for in a few weeks. It would be interesting to be racing with her even if they were in different brackets. The idea of being close to her if she needed them made him calm down a little after yesterday. Her stress about Greyson worried him and he needed to be able to make sure she was safe.

They had set Lola up in their guest room even though they all knew she wanted to be with at least one of them last night. The tension in the car as he drove them here last night almost pushed him to beg her to stay in his bed. The thought of waking up to her next to him naked, her hair spilled over the pillows with complete comfort on her face made him hard just thinking about.

"You're going to scare her away with that thing first thing in the morning." Emory's voice made his thoughts slip away.

"Shut up, like you were not thinking about her all night either. I am willing to bet that's why you're awake so early." Gideon said to his brother who was getting a cup of coffee out of the pot. It was 9am and considering they had a late night that made it early; no one was up before 11am usually after a race night.

"You know it is, but I also know that she is feeling guilty for wanting all of us, and we need to try letting her realize how ok we are with it." Emory was right, Toby told them how she had blushed when he kissed her in front of Slade, and they all agreed to sit and talk with her today if she was willing to.

He just nodded to his brother as he sat next to him at the kitchen island. Their house was not what you would think four bachelors to live in. Everyone thought they were crazy when they first built the split level home with the garage the entire length of their main living space.

The design was simple and clean which complemented the open layout. The middle part of the house was the central location for them all with the kitchen, living room and diffing room there. The door to the garage was between the dinning room and kitchen at the back of the house with the living room right off the entryway. To the left of the dinning room were Gideon and Emory's rooms, while to the right were Slade and Toby's with the guest room.

Lola was in the guest room on Slade and Toby's side of the house, and he had almost slept in the living room to just be closer to her last night. She was in awe when they showed her around last night, and honestly who would expect this type of house on the second floor of the garage downstairs. With each room having its own bathroom there was no chance of bumping into her in the middle of the night. He couldn't remember a time he felt so anxious to be around a girl, but Lola was different.

"You think she is a late sleeper?" Emory asked him taking a sip of his coffee.

"I would not be surprised if she sleeps later considering the anxiety attack, she clearly had last night before we got there." Gideon remembered how scared she looked when Slade picked her up after she finally opened the door.

They had been so worried when she left but they could not leave till the races were over. Thankfully there were no accidents, and they ended right on time. They did not even clean up their pit, leaving it to one of their track crew to put away for them. Emory did not even race the bike last night at the end of the event, which surprised him.

"You upset you didn't race last night?" Gideon asked, trying to think of something other than Lola sleeping in a room just down the hall.

"Not one bit, I will miss every race for the rest of my life to get to that girl if she needs or wants me." Emory surprised him, and he could feel the truth in them from his brother. They were all falling fast for her, the desire to be close and have her happy controlling their thoughts.

"I would never want you to miss a race for me." The sweet voice of Lola made them both turn around. She was coming out of the hallway and was still in his shirt from yesterday, but he could see the smallest bit of black on her legs meaning she had shorts on underneath it.

"I am serious Lola; I would give up ever getting on a bike again for you." Emory got up from his seat and closed the distance between them.

"Wait you race bikes? Damn you're crazy." The look on her face as Emory pulled her to his chest was so damned cute, her worry about his brother making his heart warm even more for her.

"The thrill of racing a bike as fast as a car feeds a dark part of me. But make no mistake love I will give it up for you, no questions

87

asked." Emory looked down at her and Gideon could see both realize how serious this conversation had turned. He could see Lola blush a little and when Emory moved a little, he knew what caused her reaction. His brother was not going to let this amazing girl think they didn't want her all the time.

"Do you drink coffee Doll?" He asked giving them an out of their situation.

"Of course." Her face flashed a little frustration at him calling her doll, but she did not yell at him like she did others.

"How do you drink it?" He got up and went to grab her a cup as Emory moved back to his chair.

"A little milk and sugar if you have it." Lola sat in the cushioned bar stool Slade usually took and he wondered if he would make her move. Slade was not a morning person and usually not coherent till he had at least a cup and a half of coffee.

"Of course, we also can go grab some more food for you if you need anything specific. We eat healthy, but I know how strict training for a race season can be so let me know what you need." He did not want to imply that she had a diet plan, but he knew from the years of being on one himself.

"Thanks, I will look around if that's ok and then I could just order groceries here if that's ok." She smiled at him as he put the cup of coffee in front of her.

"Either way Doll." He took his seat next to Emory and he just watched as she took that first sip of coffee.

"So, do you guys have a busy day today? Don't let me interfere with it please." Lola sounded like she was trying to get out of an obligation to be around them and it made him frustrated.

"We have some work to do over at the track later as far as making sure clean up went ok. But you're welcome to come to that if you want." He tried not to make it sound like she would be going with him because he knew none of them would leave her here alone today.

"I just don't want to inconvenience you guys; I am grateful to be able to stay for the night. I was thinking about calling Duke and having him come get the car. I can go to his house for a while and keep working on getting ready for the season. He won't let Greyson near me so I wouldn't be putting you guys out any longer." As she talked about leaving, he found himself getting out of his chair and walking over to her. He took her face in his hands and looked down at her.

"Magnolia Rae you are going to stay here until you want to leave, and you are going to stop acting like we don't want you here. Do you hear me?" He could tell she was turned on by how he was talking to her, and he was not going to be able to hide his reaction much longer.

"Are you sure?" She was still unsure; Gideon took a step closer to her to let her feel his desire to claim her on her leg.

"Do you think I would lie to you?" He asked, looking into her eyes.

"No." She whispered so quietly he was not sure she had answered for a second.

"Good so stop talking about leaving." He leaned down to put a kiss on her lips and he felt her resolve slipping away again.

"Good morning to all my favorite people." Toby's voice made her pull away and blush and he was damn sure to fix this response today. Toby only had a loose pair of sweatpants on as he came into the kitchen.

"Good morning." Lola tried to turn away from him, but Gideon

89

caught her and kissed her again. She did not resist him and when he let her turn and look at Toby, he could see a flash of desire on her face.

"Looks like someone is tired of you being shy around us Lola. Watch out with Gideon, he is soft and sweet on the outside, but he has decided you are going to be ours which will bring out his territorial side sweet girl." Toby grabbed some coffee and moved to the seat next to Lola.

Gideon could see her processing the concept as Toby kissed her forehead. Before she could respond, he heard Slade's door slam shut and he was now worried about what their morning was going to consist of.

"Slade is not a morning person love, just ignore him till he has a cup of coffee, and you will be fine." Emory put his hand on Lola's thigh as Slade came into the kitchen.

"Morning." Lola's low voice said to Slade as he grabbed his coffee cup and poured a cup.

Slade ignored her as he does everyone but when he turned around and saw her sitting in his seat his lip curled up into a smile. He took a sip of coffee and walked around the counter before walking behind her and leaning forward to put his coffee on the counter and trap her between his arms.

"Angel, you are in my spot." Slade said into her neck as he kissed her, Gideon could see her face still as if she was truly worried she was in trouble, but them it shifted.

"I am so sorry, no one told me. Was your name on it?" Lola had a little sass about her as Slade stepped even closer to her and when his hips touched her, Gideon could see her try to move forward.

"Not a chance missy. You made the problem you're going to

be expected to fix the problem." Slade's arms came around her waist quickly as he pulled her off the chair backwards. Slade quickly took his seat and sat Lola right on his lap. As they made contact, Gideon could see her eyes dart over to him and he just knew she wanted them as badly as they wanted her.

"How's your seat Doll?" He asked her with a smirk on his face.

"It's a little hard actually." Lola said and then ground into Slade who let out a growl and went back to kissing her neck.

"Do that again I dare you." Gideon heard Slade growl into her neck before Lola ground into him again.

"Owe! You bit me." Lola laughed before turning to face Slade.

"You did it to yourself Angel." Slade picked up his coffee and took a sip as Lola glared at him.

"Alright before Slade takes you to his room and kidnaps you, we need to talk. Can you have this conversation right now?" Gideon meant the question to be for Slade, but Lola nodded nervously.

"If this is what I get to wake up to for the rest of my life I think I can kick coffee." Slade answered knowing he was who the question was intended for. The others laughed knowing he would never kick coffee.

"Alright. Lola, as you realize, we all like you a lot. We can see you like each of us and judging by how your face lights up red each time we show affection, I can tell you are not comfortable with that feeling." He started simple to just get her talking.

"I don't understand how you are all ok with it. Slade mentioned something yesterday that would suggest you have all shared a partner before," he could almost kill Slade for telling her even a little bit about their past but knew it had probably let her come around to the idea a little.

"We have. There was a girl we knew from high school; we were all close and decided to have a relationship with her. It ended because she decided she did not want to live this lifestyle anymore. She said she thought it would be easy to be with all of us but because we all need different things in our intimate relationships, it was too much." Gideon was honest with her; he was not going to possibly lose her to not being open from the get-go.

"Can you explain a little more about that?" Lola asked after a long pause and another sip of coffee.

"I am going to be honest with you and will tell you my side of things, but I will leave it to the others to explain theirs if they want. I like to be dominant, nothing extreme like I am sure your mind just jumped to, but I like to be in control in the bedroom. I don't like to be called sir or anything like that, but I like when my partner listens and I like to punish lightly when they don't listen and act fast enough." He could see her processing and not look terrified.

"I will share because I also think honesty is the best policy. I get great enjoyment out of watching others pleasure the one I am with. I get extremely turned-on watching Gideon instruct a woman towards pleasure for not just herself but ours. Coming in here to see him scolding you made me want to claim you right then and there sweet girl." She turned to look at Toby and judging by his face she was truly taking in what they were saying.

"You all interact intimately together?" Her question was towards Toby, but Gideon would answer it for them all.

"We do, we all get enjoyment from the act of sharing a woman. There are other parts to it that we can talk about later if you don't want to go that deep right now." He explained as she turned around towards him again.

"What are you thinking Lola because I can feel your body's response to Gideon's explanation." Slade said to her, and he could see she was struggling to sit still now.

"I am thinking I'm crazy to already want you all to show me how to make you happy. The idea of being shared by you all together should not make my heart race this fast." Gideon could see her taking deep breaths as she spoke.

"Lola, there is nothing wrong with wanting to be with multiple partners. I promise, and can give you some safe research locations to learn about it if you want." He explained and saw her nod. This was not something society would understand and, having been in the situation before, he knew how important it was to guide her towards safe places to look for more information.

"I am very needy in bed love. I want to consume everything there is about a woman with touch and I want to worship her when I am with her. I want her to fall asleep in my bed while I hold her and make sure she is eating well and taken care of." Emory explained to her, not letting her think too much about her guilt right now.

"And I am the opposite of Emory, I like hard fucking. I want to hear you screaming my name as I bring you to pleasure. I do want to take care of you after, like Emory, but I need attention the same as I give. I like to be bitten throughout the day or teased or punished in a bratty way. I don't discipline like Gideon, but I enjoy watching it be delt out." Slade confessed and Lola shifted again making him groan.

"Thank you for explaining." Lola tried to get off Slade's lap and he held her tight to him.

"No, no running." Slade held on as she tried to pry his arms off her.

"I am not, I have to pee and sorry, but if you are into that I am out right the fuck now." Her comment made them all laugh, and Slade dropped his arms.

"No worry about that here Angel." Slade patted her butt as she walked away and down the hall toward the room she stayed in.

"You think she is going to want to stay now?" Emory asked with some worry.

"She wants what was just laid out to her, whether her mind and body realize it. That's a different story." Slade took a long drink of his coffee.

"I think she wants to stay and be with us, but I think the stigma is going to be hard for her. She's probably thinking about her life, she is a public figure in our world, what will people think? We need to show her it's ok to get what you want." Gideon looked down the hallway hoping she was already coming back, but it was just dark, and he wanted to make her tell him what she was thinking. But he knew it would only hurt their chances, she had to come to them.

Chapter 12

Lola

She went back into the room they set her up in last night and grabbed her phone that she left when she left earlier. There were messages from Greyson that she was ignoring because she could not let him know he got to her, and a missed call from Duke. She hit the call back option and waited for him to pick up.

"Magnolia, I swear I was about to get in my car if you didn't call me back by noon." Duke's voice made her feel safe like it always did. Though she knew he would drive here, it would take him two days to drive.

"Sorry I left my phone in the other room," she explained as she walked into the bathroom. The room was simple with the white tile floors that extended into the standing shower. The vanity was long and with the lights in the mirror Lola assumed a woman was taken into account when this was build. The cabinets were a light grey which helped contrast the white but kept it bright inside.

"Ok but are you ok? Greyson has been throwing a fit that none of us told him you were there. I covered saying you were checking out the prequalifying races hoping to deter him from going there." Duke filled her in, thankful for the cover for her appearance yesterday.

"I am ok, um Gideon offered to let me stay at his house for

a while. I even brought the car, so the trailer was not sitting at the house, it's hidden here." She tried to smooth out her hair with her hands and realized she was going to fail without her brush.

"That is unexpected but also the best option right now. I did hear his tier changer talk about him leaving today to go somewhere so they have the week off. Magnolia, I think he is going there so you need to stay with Gideon or his friends please." Duke's concern was what she was used to, since her parents died, he had become her parent and she realized how much she missed him right now.

"I will, but I don't want to inconvenience them. I am not their problem." She grabbed her brush from the bag on the counter and put Duke on speaker while she brushed her hair.

"You are not inconveniencing them honey, if they did not want to offer it to you they wouldn't." He said it like he knew them.

"How would you know?" She was curious now.

"I was hoping to tell you under different circumstances, but I knew Gideon and Emory's dad years ago. I used to live there and work at the track and garage with him. But when I got picked up with a race team, we didn't stay in contact much. He made it on a team, and we raced against each other till Gideon was born, then he retired and moved home. We stayed in touch for years and I was there for the boys when he died a few years ago. It is one of the reasons I recommended you look at a house there and pushed you to go there after your wreck." Duke's words sank into her. He knew she needed to be around people who would keep her safe, so he sent her to these guys. The guys that wanted to be with her and care for her.

"You sent me somewhere I would be cared for. But why not tell me before?" She was still confused.

"You needed to heal not only physically but mentally. You had a terrifying accident Magnolia, the fact that you are saying you are coming back is beyond what I think some could do. I needed you to be around people who would let you melt down and heal. You had to rebuild the bond you have with that car, and you had to do it while having people in your corner supporting you because they wanted to." Duke sounded like he was getting choked up. She knew he was not able to be there 100% of the time with his job, he was partial owner of the team. The requirements of his position were going to outweigh his place as her pseudo parent at some point.

"Thank you. I will call you later ok, but I am ok and thanks for the warning. You are still planning on coming out this week to work on the car, right?" She wiped the little tear that was in the corner of her eye.

"I am here for you Magnolia, always will be no matter what ok. Yes, I planned for mid-week if that works for you guys but call me later to talk about it ok." The words sank a little lower, would he be there if she was sleeping with the four men he sent her to?

"Ok. Love you, old man." She laughed as Duke laughed as well.

"Love you too honey." He said before the line went dead.

She stood there looking in the mirror, could she really let herself explore being with more than one man? Was she ready to open her heart back up? She already felt more for them than she felt she should. Who meets guys and feels like they just fit after only meeting a week ago? People were going to call her crazy, heck the team might not even be ok with it. Could this affect her job?

She shook her head, don't think about that yet. Plus, what does it matter what her personal life is like if she is winning races. She

97

took a deep breath and decided to just jump into this. She used the bathroom and headed back into the room.

It was at this moment she was thankful she loved buying pretty underwear and matching sets. She had grabbed her black lace bralette set last night wanting to have something comfortable but now she was thinking it would be a good thing to just let herself jump into this situation.

She took Gideon's shirt off and hid it under her pillow, he was not going to be able to sneak it out of her. Puling the top on before taking the shorts off with her other panties off. She took one more deep breath before pulling the new ones on and tossed her head behind her.

"You are allowed to go after the things you want Magnolia, take control of the situation and get what you want." She hyped herself up before turning the handle of the door opening it to the empty hallway. The respect for her privacy was a green flag for her right now.

She could hear them all talking as she headed back towards the large middle space of the house, and she was happy to see they had shifted into the living room. But she was caught when she realized there were only three heads on the other side of the couch.

"Fuck me please." It was Slade in the kitchen and his comment made them all turn around to see her standing there in her matching set.

"I am nervous as all hell but there has never been a challenge that I have not won. I like you all, none of what you want makes me want to run the other way. I would like to see how this could work." She had a second after the words registered in them all before Slade was picking her up over his shoulder.

"Slade bring her back; you can't steal her." She heard Emory call as Slade carried her towards his room.

"I thought you shared." She slapped his ass through his pajama pants as he opened his door.

"Oh, I am not being selfish I will share but I get you first now." Slade slapped her ass, and she felt a rush of warmth go to her center.

"I like your room." She said, looking around. It was a simple design with warm wood tones, she honestly would love to curl up with a book in here for how comfortable it was.

"Thanks, now stay there." Slade dropped her into the middle of his bed and pointed at her before turning to the dresser on the other side of the room. The door opened again and now all the others were there, just as some soft music filled the room.

"Don't blush anymore Doll, you asked for this the moment you left your room in this delicious outfit. You better hope Slade does not rip it off." Gideon stalked to the bed pulling his shirt over his head as he got closer. She shivered from her desire.

"Don't worry I have plenty more where this one came from. You are going to have to tell me your favorite colors, I bet I have one for each of you." She taunted as Gideon got on the bed and pulled her face to his.

"Your sassy mouth is going to be the death of me, and you are going to be the one to reaps the rewards. Now tell me simple limits Doll." Gideon held her face to him as she felt someone behind her kissing and running fingers over her.

"I am not inexperienced, I like it rough, I have not dabbled into much kink stuff, but I am willing to try given the right cautions." She tried to focus on the task, but Slade was distracting her, and she knew it was him now because Toby and Emory were behind

99

Gideon watching them.

"I need more Magnolia. Do you like dick in your mouth?" Gideon looked down at her.

"Yes." She almost moaned when Slade sucked her neck a little.

"Do you like all your holes filled?" The question made her blush because she had only ever experimented on her own, Greyson was usually only concerned about his release and not hers for the past few years.

"I am not sure." She struggled to say with the intensity of her desire from Slade's teasing.

"Slade, stop." Gideon's words halted the assault on her focus.

"Are you distracted Angel?" Slade asked, making her shiver. She was already overly stimulated.

"Gods yes. I have never had a full experience with anal, but I am not untouched." She tried to make it sound like she was willing.

"Good to know, it takes working to get there Doll. Now I think we have enough for today. Would you like to suck a dick and show us your other skills with that mouth?" Gideon's words made her almost blush again and she nodded unable to find the words when Slade began his discovery of her body with his mouth.

"Fuck, sweet girl you are perfect you know that." Toby said to her as she reached for Gideon's pants pulling his very hard dick out.

"Thanks, I try." She winked at Toby before stroking Gideon. He was long enough for both her hands to be on top of each other with the tip not covered while she was just able to wrap her whole hand around him.

"Shit." Gideon groaned as she licked the tip before sliding her mouth down his length as far as she could go.

"I am going to cum just watching you suck Gideon off Lola."
Toby moved around to her side and ran his finger over her chin as she
sucked the tip before going back down Gideon's length.

"I want to taste you Angel, up on your hands and knees." Slade
instructed and she shifted her position while Gideon moved to laying
down.

Toby got off the bed and went behind her where Slade was
pulling her underwear off. Emory came over to her now and palmed
one of her boobs making her moan around Gideon.

"You do that again and I will blow in your mouth Lola." Gideon
warned and she just sucked harder and when a tongue met her
dripping core she moaned again.

"So perfect." Toby said from behind her as Slade licked her.
Emory kisses on her shoulder moving her hair out of the way. She
moaned again as Slade began sucking on her clit combined with full
length licks.

"Doll! Stop now or I will blow." Gideon warned again but she
just put more of him into her mouth and when she felt him beginning
to pulse in her mouth, she knew what was coming. She pumped the
base a little before she tasted the come on her tongue. He let out a
groan and unrecognizable words as he filled her mouth.

"Shit show me his cum in your mouth Lola." Toby was back in
front of her, and she pulled off Gideon trying to not swallow or lose
any of his cum.

She sat up slightly and opened her mouth as Toby stroked
himself, his eyes hungry with desire. Gideon shifted to his knees quickly
so he could see it as well and he held her chin while looking at her.

"Swallow it doll." Gideon's instructions made her get a rush of warmth again and she realized Slade's fingers were slipping into her now.

She swallowed with a moan as Slade pushed a second finger into her core. Gideon held onto her chin as Slade fucked her with his fingers.

"Slade is going to give you an orgasm for being such a good girl then he is going to fuck you hard while you suck on Emory. Are you on birth control Doll?" Gideon asked and she could hardly focus on what he was asking as Slade pumped his fingers in her faster now.

"Fuck yes Slade, god. No worry about a baby and I am clean." She was able to answer without wanting to go into details right at this moment.

"We are clean as well. Now kiss Toby while you enjoy how good we can make you feel." Gideon let go of her face, but Toby was right there taking it in the middle of his hands.

"You are going to be my newest addiction sweet girl, with the noises you make, and the pleasure painted over your body." Toby lowered his lips to hers and she felt consumed by the pleasure they were giving her.

Toby seemed to be matching Slade's fingers with his tongue in her mouth and the combined sensation pushed her closer to the weightlessness of her orgasm.

"Give it to me Angel, I need to feel your wetness cover my hands so I can feel it on my dick." Slade's voice was on her shoulder as he kissed her. He increased his movements and as he kissed her, she felt the rush coming.

"Fuck!" She cried out as her orgasm rushed over her making her pull away from Toby as she tried to breath.

"So perfect." Toby kissed her forehead and stroked her cheek as she caught her breath. She was given no break as Slade pulled her back towards him hard and away from Toby.

She had to brace herself on her hands as he pulled her into his hard body. He pushed the tip of his dick at her entrance and Emory quickly put his dick in her view. He was very close to Gideon's size if not a little thicker. She took the tip into her mouth and used one hand to hold his base.

"Do not make him cum in your mouth Doll." Gideon's voice sounded like a threat, but she felt like it was a challenge, and as she pulled Emory into her mouth Slade filled her pussy.

"Oh, fuck she is tight." Slade groaned and she could hear him trying to breath.

"Shit your mouth is magic." Emory said in a rush as she took him completely into her mouth, this angle was easier for her to take more in.

Slade began to move faster and harder and she tried to match the same pace with her mouth but the force of him made her need both hands to hold onto the bed for support. Emory moved and fucked her mouth but in a slow tormenting pace and she felt the difference of the two men consume her.

"There you go giving them both what they need at the same time Doll, such a good girl." Gideon's words making them all groan.

Slade began relentlessly pounding into her and Emory pulled out of her mouth but got to her level on the bed and held her face in his hands.

"Such a good girl for him love, look at her taking him so well Toby." Emory kissed her lightly as the pressure building made her feel like she was going to black out.

"Shit, oh fuck." She could barely get the words out as she felt the air being fucked out of her.

"Angel, take me to heaven." Slade gripped her hips and was now pulling her into him as he fucked into her harder. She was out of breath and lost focus and could not hear what Emory was whispering to her as he put soft kisses along her face and neck.

"Slade." She cried out as she lost the fight to stay up as her second orgasm hit her body with so much force she was shaking.

"Lola, shit you're perfect." Slade gave three more hard pumps into her before she felt him fill her up and the warmth of his cum was a release, she had never felt combined with her own.

Slade pulled out of her, and she dropped her hips and just laid on her stomach trying to catch her breath. Her skin was tingly, and she felt a chill coming over her.

"You broke her Slade." Emory sounded like a little kid whose toy was ruined.

"No, he did not, it's just been a while. Give me a minuet." She rolled over with Emory still at her head she reached up and ran her finger from the base of his dick to the tip and played with the pre cum bead there.

"Shit, my turn." Toby was now palming her boobs before putting his mouth on her nipple. She moaned and arched into his hold.

She felt a warm cloth on her center and glanced over Toby to see Slade there smirking at her.

"He wants to taste Angel, just cleaning you up for him." She shivered as the cloth made another wipe. She was sad to think that Slade was washing himself from her already.

"Hey none of that, he's staying right here Lola." Gideon's voice pulled her focus to the end of the bed here he was leaning over it watching her.

"Next time we will all fill you up and leave it there if that's what you want." Slade's words made her pussy twitch and she arched into Toby again.

"I think she likes that idea guys." Emory was still watching her as she lazily stroked his dick while Toby began to move down her body kissing her as he went.

When Toby got to her center, he kissed her there before licking her. He pushed his tongue inside her and she felt relief from the fucking she just took. She pulled Emory down to her wanting to taste him some more. She had never complained about sucking dick but until this moment she had never begged for it.

"Shit love I want to feel your pussy so go easy on me." Emory breathed out as she took him into her mouth again.

"God, you taste so good." Toby's words made her squirm as he licked her again one more time before lining up with her.

"Be nice to her show her we are not all animals." Emory said as Toby pushed into her slow and she realized why he said it. Toby was bigger than Slade and the stretch would have been painful if she was not as slick.

"Oh fuck, sweet girl you are going to choak my dick with this pussy." Toby rubbed her clit as he pushed into her slowly, the combination of the stretch and his fingers made the incoming orgasm fast. The slow pace of it letting her body relax and ramp up all at ones.

"Oh. My. God." She panted as she pulled off Emory. Toby pushed into her slowly but hard and she felt the orgasm gripping her. She tightened around him, and his slow movements made her orgasm drag out and she felt her legs shaking as he did not let up as it happened.

"Perfection." Toby picked up his pace a little and she could tell he was close. He was still more gentle than Slade and her body opened up for him after the orgasm. He leaned onto her taking her nipple into his mouth as he ground into her. She felt the twitch of his dick inside her before the warmth of him.

"I think I have to agree with Toby watching you is addictive." Slade's words came with a kiss on her neck as Toby pulled out of her.

"You already had your turn." She mumbled feeling exhausted, this would take some getting used to.

"Are you tired love?" Emory looked down at her and she knew she could tell him yes and he would be fine with it.

"No come here, show me what you need. Because so far, I think I need you all more than I realize." Emory moved to the bottom of the bed, and she was already ready to feel him take her into oblivion.

Chapter 13

Emory

She was getting tired but still wanted him to take her and Emory was not going to tell this perfect creature no. As he lined himself up with her, he pulled her face to his and swallowed the moan she made as he pushed into her tight body.

Her noises were intoxicating, and Emory wanted to have them all. He wanted to kiss every inch of her and tell her how much he wanted her all over his body. He wanted to wake up with this naked body plastered to his and make love to her every morning and night.

"Emory, please." She was begging for more movement, and he smiled at her.

"Just enjoy this Lola, feel how each pass stretches you out with sweet pleasure. Feel how warm and thick I am. Let my body hit just the right spot to make your pussy clench around me trying to suck me in deeper." He angled his hips to hit her G-spot as he spoke to her, taking long thrusts as she arched into each one. Her body already pushing her towards another orgasm, and he was going to give it to her.

Slade and Toby were kissing her body in the soft way Emory wanted to even while fucking her and it made her arch into them all. She moaned again and called out their names and he could see the other two react to her just as he did inside her.

"You are perfect love; I am never going to get enough of this, so you better be ready to stay with us forever." He said it and he did not care if it was to early or if it would scare her away. He meant every word as he pushed into her a little faster and moved to rub her clit as she got closer to the pleasure she was chasing.

"That's fine, Emory please." She was begging for more, but he could tell her body was wound up tight despite the release she had already had, and he wanted to give her a bigger one. The slow denial of her orgasm was going to make her fall even harder for the next one.

"Oh, sweet girl you can beg all you want with him, but he will not let you find that release till it's the perfect time and believe me you are going to drown in the pleasure." Toby said into her neck as she moaned and tried to push into him harder.

"It's too much please Emory, I need it please." She was right there, and he could tell she needed just a little more. He pushed in harder but not faster while rubbing her faster as he did, and he could feel her body react.

She screamed out his name as she tightened around him choking him, as if her body was trying to pull him in closer than he was.

"Shit, Lola." He panted as he spilled into her as she came around him at the same time. He was looking down at her and as her eyes opened, he could see her pleasure in her gaze.

"Holy fuck." She panted, pulling his face down to hers kissing him while he was still inside her.

"I could almost go again watching that sweet girl." Toby's voice made her laugh a little as she broke their kiss.

"You had your turn; I think Gideon is next." Lola looked over to his brother who was sitting on the edge of the bed at her head.

"You need more Doll?" Gideon taunted her and he saw the spark in her eyes at the name.

"I mean if you're not up for the challenge that's fine." Lola taunted back and Emory pulled out of her quickly recognizing the look in his brothers' eyes. This girl was going to challenge him in ways he had never seen before.

"Watch it love." He warned as Gideon reached down to her and pulled her chin up to him. Lola arched into Gideons hold and let him control her movements.

"Your smart ass is going to get spanked if your mouth doesn't learn." Gideon pulled her arm towards him with his other hand, and she rolled into the movement. But she continued the movement and ended up crawling onto Gideon's lap before he moved.

"I am just not sure about that threat Gideon." She taunted and kissed his nose as they all gasped at her.

Gideon grabbed both her wrists and turned her to where her chest was on the bed with her ass up towards him. He shifted his grip on her wrists to one hand and gave her a quick sharp slap on her ass before she could say anything.

"No threat Doll, I warned you." Gideon slapped her ass again quickly on both cheeks. Emory watched her face for signs of wanting to run and was surprised. Her moan in response to the pain making Slade growl a little next to him.

"Oh, sweet girl you are going to be Gideon and Slade's favorite toy with that reaction to spankings." Toby made the comment, but Emory was thinking the same thing. Slade pushed past him to see her face up close as Gideon spanked her again and another moan slipped from her mouth.

"Maybe Angel is not the best name for you." Slade lifted her face to his and kissed her as Gideon gave her one more spank.

"You definitely have a punishment kink Doll." Gideon shifted her back to straddling him as he pushed into her, and her moan was louder.

"Yes, please." Lola sounded just as needy as when he was fucking her, and he loved that she wanted what they all were giving her.

"Oh, you think you deserve this?" Gideon asked but Lola did not respond and so he stopped fucking her.

"Shit, no I probably don't. I don't think being a smart ass would get the reward of release." Lola stumbled to find the right words and Gideon just smiled. She was picking it up much faster than any of them could imagine.

"Good girl, and for knowing that I am going to fuck you to that release because I think you deserve it. But know that it's only because I think you will learn quickly. There will be times when I don't let you have this though." Gideon began to pound into her relentlessly, but Emory could see he was not happy with her position.

Gideon stood up wrapped around her and put her on the edge of the bed before spreading her legs wide. Slade took one leg, and Emory grabbed the other to hold them open for him. Toby came up to her head and kissed her neck and looked at Gideon in approval. While they all had their own things, they would never overstep in the moment. When Gideon did not stop him, Toby continued to kiss Lola.

"Shit, Gideon." Lola cried out as he was fast and hard on her.

"Yes?" Gideon stopped moving and Lola groaned but they all chuckled knowing this was one of Gideon's favorite things.

"Please don't stop please, I need more of you please." Lola begged and sounded like she was close to actually crying.

"Oh, you like this?" Gideon gave her a few more hard and quick passes and stopped again.

"Yes." She whimpered and that was all Gideon needed before pushing into her harder again.

This time he did not stop till Lola was shaking with need and he took her legs from Emory and Slade. Toby backed off as Gideon laid over her almost completely hiding her from their view.

"Your body was made for this Lola; I swear I want to give you this pleasure every day for the rest of your life." Gideon said to her, and Emory could see Lola fall into her pleasure and pull his brother down with her.

Toby left to get the washcloth warm again, but Gideon and Lola lay there catching their breath until he came back. Toby handed him the cloth knowing he would need to be there for her after all they just did. Gideon moved off her and he moved towards her stepping in between her legs before she closed them.

"No more, sorry I definitely need practice with all four of you." Lola mumbled with her eyes closed.

"No more right now love, let me clean you up and you can relax a little." Emory said to her running the cloth over her to clean up a little.

He stepped away and Lola curled into Gideon who kissed her forehead and pulled her close to him. The peace on both their faces made him smile as he brought the cloth back to the bathroom.

When he came back out, he could see Lola was drifting off to sleep beside Gideon.

"You need a nap, Doll?" Gideon asked into her hair as he kissed her again.

"Yes." Lola mumbled into Gideon's side before snuggling closer to him.

"Can I take you to your room? Not saying you can't stay here love, but your sheets are clean." Emory said to her as he walked over.

"Don't care." She mumbled again and he could tell she was done thinking.

"I don't think she's thinking straight. Take her to her room but stay with her." Gideon told him and he moved his arms under her to lift her up.

"Enjoy your nap, Angel." Slade kissed her head and she curled into him.

"We will be here when you wake up sweet girl." Toby said to her following Slade's actions as he walked out of the room with him.

Emory walked across the hall to her room, and he already could feel himself shifting knowing this was where she belonged. He never wanted her to leave and would do whatever needed to be done to keep her here with them.

As he got them situated in the bed, he could barely hear her talk, but he could make out her saying she never wanted to leave and the desire to keep her grew bigger than before.

Chapter 14

Lola

The bed was empty when she woke up again, but she was not upset about it. Laying there she listened to the sounds of the house and could hear other people around. So, they had stayed like they promised. Deciding she needed a shower before she went to join them, she got up and walked into the connected bathroom.

She felt the ache between her legs as she got into the warm water, it was perfect, and she still wanted more. How was this ok, to be this attached to people after a week? They made her feel safe yes, but was this her version of rebounding after Greyson? Was she trying to fling herself into the closest thing she could to comfort after what had happened.

She was sure if she brought it up to her therapist even though she was released from weekly visits, she would have some ideas. How do you even bring that up? Oh, so since the last time we talked I think I have fallen in love with the four hot guys helping me get over my track anxiety. I also slept with all four of them at the same time and they were cool with it.

Who would take her seriously after that. She had to talk to someone and as she finished up in the shower, she knew exactly who would not judge her. She owed Tayler a call anyways, so as she wrapped herself up in her towel, she hit call on the contact.

"Bunny you are in trouble." Her best friend's voice came through the phone, and she couldn't help but smile.

"Taz, I have been busy." She and Tayler had been friends since high school and when she started racing, he came along. He became her other half when her parents died, and Duke always included him in their journeys.

"No excuse to leave Duke to update me on things, that man is going to make me crazy." Tayler said as she laughs. Duke over fathers Tayler, despite him having a mom who makes him crazy also.

"Sorry, I am calling now is that ok?" She knew he would forgive her, but it was always hard to feel like she let him down.

"Forgiven, how are you doing?" His voice shifted to worried, and she knew he was aware of Greyson's movements from Duke.

"Fine." She tried to sound confident but when the call turned to a video one, she knew he didn't believe her.

She hit accept and his tan clean-shaven face filled the screen. His honey blonde hair was styled, and his eyes were closer to green today than the hazel they usually were due to his green shirt.

"Liar. Where are you?" He noticed this was not her bathroom of course.

"At the house of the guys helping me get over the car anxiety." She knew she couldn't try lying to him so why try.

"Why the heck are you there?" His southern accent hitting her hard.

"Because they came to my house last night after I ran away and told me they would all keep me safe." His eyebrows raised as she recanted last night.

"All four of them Bunny?" His face was not judgmental but concerned.

"Yes Taz, all four of them." She felt the flush on her face before she saw it.

"You little sneaky Doll. You slept with them didn't you?" He called her out quickly.

"Yes, and they told me they wanted to keep me. Tayler what am I doing? Is this a knee jerk reaction after what has happened?" She sat on the counter as she talked.

"How do they make you feel?" He was in best friend mode now.

"Safe, protected, cared for. I feel like they want to be with me, not just to have sex with. They have been so caring and kind with the car stuff." She let herself feel the care they had been giving her this last week.

"Ok, so I don't think it's just knee jerk but maybe a little. How do you feel after having your fun with them?" He smirked.

"Like I want to do it again forever. God I am a slut." She rushed out, covering her face in some shams.

"You are not a slut Lola; you are someone who has never pushed for what they wanted in a relationship." She rolled her eyes as she lowered her hand, but he continued before she could respond.

"Greyson treated you like shit Lola, do not try and argue with me. You are allowed to enjoy being with whoever you want, you have told me that how many times? This is no different than me being with who I want to be with." Tayler was right of course he always was, damn gay intuition.

"You're right." She huffed out getting off the counter.

"Good, glad to hear it. Now go enjoy your Sunday and when

115

Duke decides he is coming there I am going to come with ok. We have team stuff to talk about." She could see the spark in his eyes, there was a knock on the bathroom door.

"Ok, got to go see you soon." She said to him, and he told her he loved her before she hung up. She hoped whoever was on the other side of the door had not heard it but when she opened it to find Gideon holding a cup of coffee, she could tell he had.

"Enjoy your shower, Doll?" He asked, handing her the cup and looking at the fact she was still only in a towel.

"Yes, this shower is great." She took a sip ignoring the rage building in his eyes.

"Have a little fun without us?" He tipped his head at her phone.

"Oh yeah, I am sure Tayler enjoyed being on the other end of my mental break down." She was not ok with jealousy simply because Greyson had issues with Tayler as well, and she would not have a relationship like that again.

"Why the break down?" Gideon let the issue drop, it would seem, for the time being.

"Just trying to wrap my brain around everything. It's been a week Gideon; how can I feel so comfortable after a week?" She hated that she had this feeling.

"Sometimes when things just fit, they happen fast. I won't say I am not sappy Lola, because heck, my parents were high school sweethearts, and I saw the love. I believe that there are soul mates and that when you find the person who fits it time doesn't matter." Gideon's words made her smile, she felt this too.

"My parents were also." She admitted as he smiled at her.

"Ok so you can see how when you know you know. For me the way I see you caring about my brother and best friends makes me want you more. That's how I know this is right, it's how I know that it's worth being this honest with you after only a week. Plus, we have spent most of the week together for hours on end." He smiled at her as he stepped closer to her now.

"We have, I do feel like I know you guys pretty well." She took a sip of coffee.

"Good, now we need to head to the track. Are you coming with, or do you want to hang out here and relax?" He ran a finger over her bear arm as he asked.

"I wouldn't mind going with." She couldn't help wanting to just spend time with them.

"Ok, then get dressed because we will not be able to get anything done with you like this." He kissed her forehead and turned to leave.

"I will be right out." She said as he headed out of the bedroom.

She drank the coffee as she pulled her clothes on. She had a pair of jeans and a tank top on, but she grabbed a jacket in case it was cold. Braiding her hair since it was still wet before she put a little make up on. She grabbed Slade's team hat out of her bag and her sunglasses before leaving the room.

"Hot damn, you are a wet dream walking sweet girl." Toby's voice in the hallway startled her a little as he came towards her from his room.

"Me, have you seen all of you?" She smiled at him, just leaning into the feeling she was having and letting it ride out.

"Oh, are we distracting?" Toby pulled her into him now as

117

they walked down the hallway towards the main area of the house.

"Extremely, especially when you don't have shirts on." She looked at Slade and Emory who were in only jeans in the kitchen.

"I couldn't wear my towel, but you can be shirtless?" She mocked them as she walked over.

"Who said you couldn't wear a towel, Angel? I will kill them now." Slade pulled her to him, and he smelt clean and fresh.

"Gideon, but in his defense, I don't think he wanted me at the track like that." She looked up at Slade having to tip her head back farther due to the hat.

"I will agree with that though." Slade pulled his hat off her head and kissed her before rushing away.

"Hey, I was wearing that." She complained as Slade grabbed a shirt off the couch and pulled it on.

"Be happy he let you wear it yesterday, Love. Slade is picky about his hats." Emory said kissing her as he passed by as well.

"Fine but I know where you sleep, I will just go find more." She mocked but Slade's expression told her it was a challenge to him.

"I dare you, penalty for getting caught red handed is steep." Slade adjusted his hat as he watched her.

"Might be worth it." The others just laughed as Gideon came around her from behind.

"Are you a brat, Doll?" The question made her get goosebumps.

"I like to call it feisty." She tried to turn to face him, but he kissed her neck and slapped her ass before walking towards the door.

"Let's go before Lola earns a punishment and makes us late, which would earn her another punishment and get us stuck in a loop." Gideon winked at her as he held the door open.

118

Everyone walked out and headed towards the truck.

"Shotgun." Emory called as they got close.

"Looks like you're in the back with us Angel." Slade tapped her butt as he opened the door for her.

She slid into the middle as Toby took the other side. Gideon turned the car on and as they headed towards the track. The two in the back with her could not keep their hands off her. If this was what her life with them was going to be she was sure she would be ok with it.

Chapter 15

Lola

The last few days had been a dream. She ran the car more and, with the guidance of Duke, they all made adjustments to it. Gideon was a genius when it came to tuning the car and she could feel the car wanting to do more. Today Duke and Tayler would be coming in to go over the car and the team set up. They also had to talk about getting the car back to the main shop for the wrap and to get ready for the press week in two weeks.

She was just finishing up getting dressed when she heard the doorbell ring. It had to be them, and she rushed out of her room almost running over Slade in her rush.

"In a hurry Angel?" He asked, holding her tight as she squirmed to get him to let her go.

"Yes, let me go." She slapped his arms. He kissed her and laughed as he let her go. She ran into the main room and right into Tayler as Gideon let them into the house.

"Bunny, give a guy a chance." Tayler laughed after he dropped his bag to catch her.

"Nonsense Taz, you should always be ready to catch me." She hugged him tight, something about hugging your best friend when stressed that made you always feel better.

There was a throat cleared, and she knew it was from Gideon.

"Calm down big guy Tayler here would be more of a threat to me than you." She rolled her eyes as Tayler put her down.

"Flaming gay guys promise." Tayler held up his hands as she let Duke pull her into a hug.

"Want to tell me what's going on?" That signature dad look on his weathered face could make you want to crawl back to your room.

"Come on old man we can all talk over brunch." She passed off the look and question and led the way to the table. Though they all usually ate on the island there was a table big enough for the seven of them.

Aurora had brought over a variety of options since she knew Lola was excited and could hardly cook. As they took their seats she sat next to Tayler and Duke despite the looks on all the guys' faces.

"You cook all this Lola?" Duke asked and Tayler almost choaked on his water.

"No, shut up Taz. The guy's friend Aurora owns a bakery in town, and she brought it over." She slapped Tayler as he was still choaking.

"Good, means we all have a chance to live another day." Tayler mocked her as the guys just watched them interact.

"You give a guy food poisoning one time, and it haunts you forever." She huffs as she grabbed a scone off the plate in front of her. Everyone else started grabbing for food as well and they all slowly started talking casually.

"Ok so I am glad you all seem to be getting along it makes this next part easier." Duke set his coffee cup down and she knew the serious conversation was beginning.

"I have decided to take a step back this year and focus on the overall team growth rather than be a crew chief. With that said I asked Tayler if he would run your team Lola, I did not think you would have issues with that, and it make the transition easier since he was already by our side last year. As far as the rest of the team I gave the others a chance to choose their team and you are going to retain most of your old crew." Duke explained.

"Explain most? Who am I replacing?" She asked, already knowing who.

"Logan and Ripley stayed with Greyson." It did not surprise her since they were his best friends.

"Kip, Marvin, Wyatt and Sam stayed. So along with Tayler joining I think you are set." Duke continued and she could see the guys nodding.

"We will be there too if she needs more, we made it into the season." Gideon said and Duke nodded.

"Oh, I am aware, and that brings me to my next point. I want to sign you boys on to the team. HPS would be the main sponsor, but we would be the parents and top umbrella for you all. Parts, supplies, tires, travel accommodations, everything would be covered by us." She could see appreciation go across Gideons face as Duke explained.

"That's amazing." She said and Gideon smiled at her.

"It is and I absolutely want to accept it. Do you have a contact with you we can look over?" Gideon took control but she could see the others were sure about his decision and no one looked to have issues.

"I do in my bag. With the acceptance of this though it means you all need to fly out with Lola in two weeks to do press stuff. We will announce it this week and I was hoping to bribe Lola into taking some photos for us at the track today." Duke looked at her with his soft eyes and she just smirked at him.

"You can just ask no bribery needed but if we are talking about flying, I would argue about just driving." She hated flying, but she was not ready to talk about it right now.

"You don't have time to drive with the car. It has to come home by the end of the week, and you don't need to be there that early. So, there is no reason for you to drive Bunny." Tayler was the one to break the option apart.

"Damn you. Then promise me this, during press week keep Greyson away from me. I don't want to do any sort of group shots, there is enough money spent on PR that they can photoshop us together if they want." She was firm about this.

"You have a deal, Magnolia; I will not make you be around Greyson where I can control it." Duke held his hand out to her, and she shook it.

"We will get you guys the schedules emailed as well. I know you're probably going to team together at some point, but Tayler is the best at managing the schedules so if you want him to keep you all together with it let him know." Duke suggested and she could see Gideon not quite happy about the idea.

"If he schedules us together, the more time we spend together." She tossed at him, and his eyes narrowed in on her.

"Fine, but only for that reason." Gideon agreed.

"Alright now is your turn for some explanations." Duke said to her, and she took a deep breath and looked at the guys. They each nodded to her in a silent go ahead and so she took a sip of water before talking.

"We are all together. I know it is not something you are used to and do not ask me how I am going to handle the press when it gets out because, hell, it can't be hidden. But I know that they all make me feel safe and comfortable and loved." She rushed to get the words out before Duke could interject but he just sat there smiling at her.

"Magnolia do you not think I have already gotten used to the concept that love is love after Tayler?" Duke asked her and she let out a breath of relief.

"I know, but this is different." She argued but Duke held up a hand to stop her.

"No, it is not, don't go mauling each other in the pits while the camera is there and there won't be an issue. You know that. When it comes out just tell them to mind their own business, you know we won't drop you from the team because we don't care. Be happy Magnolia because you have had enough sadness, it's time to be happy." Duke's words made her get up and hug him tight in his chair and he rose to meet her as well.

"Alright now that everything is figured out, who's ready to run some cars?" Tayler's enthusiasm made her pull away and laugh. The guys all got up and as she walked with Slade and Emory, she caught Gideon and Duke hugging and talking a little before coming through the garage door towards them all.

"You two, ok?" She asked Gideon as he pulled her into a hug.

"Perfect Doll, you, ok? You going to be able to deal with us all season long, right with you?" He held her tight as he kissed her forehead.

"I think I can handle it." She smirked at him, and he kissed her lips hard before letting her go.

"Alright we will see you at the track." Gideon pushed her towards her truck where Tayler and Duke were waiting for her, and she couldn't help but smile the whole time.

"It's good to see you happy Lola." Duke said as she got into the truck.

"It's good to be happy." She smiled as they headed after the guys towards the track. She was extremely excited about the future. Not only for herself, but she was glad things were working out and her team was filled with those who chose to be with her.

Chapter 16

Slade

The last week had been crazy since Duke had been there. The track day was perfect, and Lola was consistent with her times, though they all knew she had more in that car and could get to a faster time. She was currently getting the car packed up and off to the shop to be wrapped. Her crew came to get it and he couldn't help smiling seeing her interact with them when he dropped her off earlier at the track.

She had looney tunes nicknames for all of them and it just fit, well except for Kip but his name was cool enough she said. Marvin was Marv the Martian, and she called him Martian all the time. Wyatt was Wile E. Coyote and Sam was Yosemite Sam. She was so happy to get to hang out with them for a while.

Slade was currently looking over the schedule for the week after next and trying to think about packing everything. Gideon and Toby were going to fly with Lola, but he and Emory would drive the truck, trailer, and car out. He and Emory had to leave earlier than Gideon, Toby and Lola to get there in time and he was not looking forward to missing out on his girl for any time.

There was a comfortable balance between them all now. She had been spending the night in one of their beds all week and it just felt right. Even the guys at the shop noticed their change in moods as well. Though Gideon was a nervous wreck about the car being perfect. He was down in the shop right now making sure all the things they needed were packed. Even though the team was supplying them with stuff everyone had their own favorite things when working.

His phone notification pulled him away from the paper in his hand.

Greyson is here, please hurry. The message from Lola made his heart drop to his stomach.

Where are you? He typed out quickly, heading out of the door fast into the garage.

The track still, he saw the trailer. Slade hurry please. Although it was a text he could tell she was freaking out.

We are coming. Hold on Angel. He sent it out as he rushed down the stairs of the garage from their office.

"Shit Slade what's wrong?" Emory saw him and rushed over.

"Greyson is at the track with Lola right now we have to fucking go now." He yelled to the shop and tools dropped. He looked down to see if Lola had responded and there was nothing.

Everyone rushed to their cars except Emory who was already gone on his bike. He started up his bike and followed Emory with Gideon and Toby right behind him. But Brighton, Granger, and Cody were behind them. They did not bother stopping at the stop signs on the back roads to the track and he was now very thankful the shop was not far from the track.

As they came around the corner to the entrance of the track he could see her. Backed all the way up against the bed of Kip's truck with a guy boxing her in. There was a black Audi in the spot behind the truck and trailer and his rage took over. He barely stopped next to the guy's car as they all pulled up. Emory getting to her before anyone else could.

"Who the hell do you think you are?" The guy shouted at Emory as he pulled Lola to him. He was as tall as they were with brown hair cut short, brown eyes and he knew it was Greyson because he had seen him at the races.

"Your worst fucking nightmare if I ever catch you threatening my girl again." Slade said closing the distance.

"Your girl, you slut, are you cheating on me?" Greyson shouted at Lola.

"Cheating would imply I was still with you. We were over the moment you crashed me into a wall Greyson." She shouted at him, but Slade could see her trembling, it was taking all her strength to stand up to this piece of shit.

"You are going to stop fucking saying that right now." Greyson was moving towards her again and Emory tucked her behind him.

"I suggest you get in that German piece of crap you drove onto our property and leave before we make you." Emory said to Greyson who was right in front of him.

"I see how it is, you went and became a slut for track time from the owners. God you're worse than I though." Greyson barely got the words out before Gideon grabbed him by the back collar of his jacket and pulled him backwards to the ground.

"Call her a slut one more time and we will see how well you race with a broken leg." Gideon was scary when he was in this fight mode, they all formed a shield between Lola and Greyson on the ground.

"What is she sleeping with all of you? Damn she's not even

128

that good too mouthy and gets in the way of things." Greyson was trying to get up off the ground, but Slade punched him back down.

"Shit!" Greyson shouted grabbing the side of his face.

"Get out of here before we press trespassing charges. You also should be on the lookout for a restraining order from Lola." Toby said to Greyson pulling him away.

"One week Lola, you can't avoid me past that. Your protectors won't be around forever." Greyson got up now and got into his car but had to wait for the others to move since they all blocked him in.

Slade grabbed Lola as they watched the car drive off and she trembled into his hold as she sobbed.

"Angel, we got you, you're ok your safe." He said to her as he held her close, kissing her hair and just wanting to take this pain away. Gideon should have beat the shit out of that guy.

He watched as Greyson drove off and off the property before he pulled back to look at Lola.

"Did he touch you before we got here? Did he hurt you, Angel?" He was trying to look at her face and arms to see any bruising.

"He grabbed my arms after I texted you, shit my phone is probably broke." She pulled back to look at the ground and Cody held a phone out to her.

"Found it on the other side of the truck, you are going to need a new one." Cody said handing it to her. As she took it, she started laughing. That laughing crying things you do when you're so overwhelmed by the shit of the day you don't know what to do.

"Great this is what I need for sure. A new phone, a pissed off teammate that I have to go do press week with who knows about us and is going to try to slut shame me despite the team owners not caring." She was ranting and pacing back and forth beside the truck and trailer. Her crew watching her but letting them handle it. Slade was grateful they were here but also frustrated at himself. He should have stayed with her instead of dropping her off.

"Lola I am sure Duke will get it handled, Gideon can call and let him know your phone's broken and why." Emory was trying to calm her down, but he could see she just needed to be mad right now.

"Emory, Greyson doesn't give a shit what Duke says to him. Hell, he could kick him off the team and he would still somehow be the favorite with the media." She was on fire now and Slade loved seeing her fight, but he could see the pain beneath it.

"Maybe we should press trespassing charges then. Public charges can't be faked, and we have cameras all over the track." Gideon was just watching her, no move to make her calm down just letting her be.

"He would get out of them, god what are you guys not understanding." She threw the already broken phone on the ground and that was all it took for Gideon to step in now. The guys from her crew watching the interaction but again not interfering.

"Magnolia enough. We are going to take care of this, do you hear me. You are our girl, and no one gets away with treating her like this. Now you are going to get in Slade's car and go home. But you are going to go find a way to relax while I handle this do you hear me?" Gideon was holding her chin to his face. Slade could see the fight in her eyes still there but softened by Gideon's command.

She nodded a little and Gideon kissed her before letting her chin go, he turned her to Toby who kissed her as well and Emory came in and pulled her close while kissing her. She came over to him and he

130

just held her close as he walked her to the his car. Kissing her before opening the door for her to get in.

"Thank you." She whispered as she turned to get in.

"Angel, you do not have to thank me for caring for you and protecting you. You are ours and this is what we do ok," he said before she dropped into the passenger seat.

The drive to the house was quiet and he couldn't help but put his hand on her leg to hold her as he drove. She let him help her out of the car but as soon as they got into the house she started crying and he could see how hard this was for her.

"Do you want to go for a run?" They had noticed she ran when she was frustrated since she was staying with them.

"A run is not going to make me forget everything he has done to me Slade." She was not loud as she wiped her tears.

"Angel you're not ever going to be able to escape him, but I will always be there to make sure he can not cause any new tears." He rubbed her arms as she looked up at him. He could see the frustration in her eyes.

"Slade will you help me forget him? Will you take me to your room and make me forget he ever touched me?" Her question made his mind run wild with ideas.

"Angel I will do my best to wash away any touch on your body. What do you need?" He needed her to tell him how far he could take this.

"I don't want to be able to think about anything other than you." She stepped into him and buried her face into his chest.

"I have an idea, but you have to be ok with it the whole time ok." He pulled back to look at her face and he could see the desire

131

burning in her eyes.

"Anything Slade, please." Her begging was going to break him down.

"Ok Angel, but at any time you want me to stop you say 'red' ok. Because stop is not going to be enough to make me stop today." He waited for her nod of acknowledgement before grabbing her and tossing her over his shoulder, she made a squeak when he did, and it lit the fire in him more.

Slade walked into his room and put her down at the foot of his bed and just starred at her. She was in just a tee-shirt and jeans today, no makeup and her hair down with a soft wave to it. There was nothing forces about how beautiful she was, and she was all his for right now.

"Take your clothes off Angel and wait in the middle of the bed." He instructed as he walked to the closet where he kept his ropes.

He grabbed the box quickly and was thankful he kept everything in one place. As he walked out, she raised her eyebrow at the sight of the box.

"I think you need some sensory deprivation today. I have a blindfold, and I want to tie you up if that is ok." He needed to be sure.

"I am ok with that." She looked eager to take this step with him.

"Alright I am going to blindfold you first ok, remember say 'red' if you want me to stop." He took the black fabric out of the box and moved onto the bed.

As he put it on, her body got a little stiff, most people do this as a regular reaction. He kissed her neck and chest before kissing her mouth and getting off the bed. She was trying not to move as she sat on the bed waiting for his next move. As he pulled the ropes out, he watched her. She shifted a little not knowing what to do with her hands or body.

"Stop moving Angel, just sit there. Let me control the senses around you ok." He spoke softly as he ran a finger over her body before deciding what exactly to do.

"Arms above your head Angel." She followed his directions quickly and he smiled as he began to tie up her boobs with the rope. Wrapping the soft rope around her body, tying simple knots and adjusting the tension on them as he went along.

He did not talk to her as he pushed her onto the bed and pulled her arms to the top of the bed before tying them to the headboard. Watching her breathing as he traced down her body with a finger, she was focusing on every touch he was giving her. Pulling his hand away and waiting a moment before touching her again told him she was already desperate for more of his attention.

Chapter 17

Lola

Slade had taken her request and done exactly what she needed. He had tied her to the bed where she couldn't move. She didn't know how it worked but she was only able to focus on him and his hands. She was on her back with rope around her chest, arms tied to the top of the bed and her legs tied bent and pulled to each side holding her open to him. The rope was tight to her body but soft, the slight discomfort helped her feel grounded.

"Angel you are a work of art." Slade said into her chest as he sucked her nipple into his mouth.

"Thank you." She moaned as the sensation of his mouth on her took over her mind.

Slade continued to kiss and suck on various parts of her body making his way to her core. When he licked her, she shuttered a little pulling against the ropes.

"You taste like heaven." He licked her again and this time sucked on her sensitive nub, she arched into him as much as she could begging for more.

"Please Slade." She moaned out as he continued his assault of her body with his mouth.

In response he picked up his pace pushing her to the release her body needed. As she moaned and arched into his mouth, she wished she could push his head down farther.

"Just let me show you the pleasure you deserve." He said pulling away from her.

He ran a finger up her inner thighs before spreading her wide and diving back in with his mouth. This time, after a few passes of his tongue, he pushed two fingers inside her and her body gripped him tightly, needing more. He worked her in unison with his mouth and tongue and soon she was panting and moaning.

"Give it to me Angel." He said to her sliding a third finger inside her. She was so full and as he hit the spot with his fingers she fell apart.

"Slade, oh my god! Fuck!" She couldn't help the scream that came from her as she found the high of her orgasm.

"That's it, Angel, scream my name so the others hear what I am doing to you." At his words she felt her body trying to hold him tighter while also getting wetter at the thought of the others coming in to join them.

"Oh, you like that idea, maybe you're a little like Toby." Slade pulled away from her kissing her as he stopped touching her completely now.

She whimpered at the lack of touch, and Slade laughed a little before moving back to her. He was closer to her head now, his body heat hovering over hers and he was kissing her neck and chest. The aftereffects of her orgasm left her tingly and needing more.

"Slade please I need more." She begged, hoping he would listen to her. Her body arching into his touches as he kissed his way back down her body.

"You want this, Angel?" He asked rubbing the tip of his dick over her clit making her moan.

"Please." She begged louder, not caring how desperate she sounded.

"Well since you asked so nicely." He said before pushing into her hard and completely. She let out a loud curse as he did this, he did it faster and she could not help crying out.

"Slade fuck, please don't stop." She cried.

"Look at the good Angel using her words, whose are you?"

"Yours." She answered in a cry.

"All mine, well I think that's an interesting concept Angel. Maybe we need consultation on that." Slade drove into her harder but then she felt a mouth on her nipple.

Being blindfolded she couldn't see if it was Slade, but the mouth felt different than his and his hands were holding her legs as he pounded relentlessly into her. When a hand began to palm her other boob, she knew someone else had slipped in and her body arched into him. There was a slight noise, and it gave him away.

"Emory, fuck that feels good." She heard a deep laugh as she called Emory out.

"If you're all mine Angel then maybe he needs to leave." Slade taunted slowing his pace making her lose the push to another orgasm.

"Shit, I meant all of yours. I am all yours." She corrected herself and Slade picked up his pace again while Emory pulled off her boob.

"I like that answer much better." Emory said into her ear before kissing her neck around the ropes holding her still.

The stimulation of the two of them threatened to pull her under the deep need for another orgasm. She needed it, she needed to feel free of the weight on her shoulder about today.

"Please Slade I need more." She begged, hoping he would help her get what she needed.

"Emory untie her hands." Slade pulled out of her but was kissing her legs as Emory worked with the knots.

As her arms came free Emory rubbed them a little before Slade pulled her up onto her knees. He slid underneath her and pulled her onto himself.

"Fuck you feel so good." She moaned as she moved with Slade.

"You still need more Angel?" Slade asked as Emory was behind her kissing her shoulders.

"Yes." She was not sure what he meant by this but when Emory pushed her flat against Slade, she tightened up on her hold inside of him.

She felt Emory's fingers brush over her back entrance and she tightened up again.

"Not there today love, but let's see if you can take two of us at one time in this sweet pussy of yours." Emory teased her with the tip of his dick. The pressure of him pushing into her alongside Slade was almost too much to handle.

"Breathe love, let me in." Emory kissed her shoulder as he pushed in farther. She gasped as he did, and he pushed all the way in.

"Fuck, it feels so good." She cried as they both began to move inside her and the pleasure pushing higher.

"So perfect Angel. You still need more?" Slade asked, holding her face as he kissed her.

"Please I need it all," she said just as Emory slammed into her hard with a slap on her ass as he did.

"Open up then Angel." Slade instructed and she followed

without question.

As she opened, she felt the smooth pre come tip on her lips and she licked it up before taking the tip into her mouth. She moved as Emory and Slade continued to push into her with their relentless pace. As she took the entire dick into her mouth, she figured out who she had in her mouth as he moaned her name.

"Gideon you taste so good." She pulled off quickly before taking him back into her mouth.

"Doll, you look so perfect like this. Taking three big dicks like a goddess. Shit your perfect for us." Gideon held her still with his hand in her hair.

The three of them matched pace for a while before Emory cried out and filled her up. She moaned around Gideon, and he slowed his pace. She was still so close but not quite done. Before she could say anything though she was being pushed into again alongside Slade and she knew Toby had enough watching and was joining them.

Now as she sucked on Gideon, Slade and Toby were rough with her body. She was closer to the edge now and she needed them to cum with her. She felt hands and a mouth on her chest as Slade pushed her up slightly. With Emory's attention she felt her body about to lose control.

"Give it to us Angel, give us everything your body can give." Slade said to her, and his words pushed her right to the edge.

"Doll, do as you're told." Gideon threatened and she felt herself get slick.

"Shit I am so close sweet girl cum with me. Choak my dick with Slade's and take us down with you." Toby's request did it to her and she felt herself crest that hill and fall hard down the side as all the pleasure hit her.

Gideon spilled into her mouth, and she swallowed quickly before pulling off him and crying out all of their names. She could not tell who came first inside her, but Slade and Toby cursed as they followed her and Gideon over the edge. The blindfold came off and she was being kissed by Gideon as Toby pulled out of her.

She shuttered as they were all still touching her, and she felt out of control of her body. She felt Gideon wipe the tears off her cheek that she did not realize she had let out.

"It's ok Lola, let it out while we take care of you ok. We are going to get you untied and into a quick shower." Gideon was taking over now. Usually Emory would take care of her, but she could see Gideon needed this control.

She let them untie her and she did not argue with Emory, who carried her into the shower. Gideon and Emory washed her and brought her back out after she was dry. Back inside the room, they set her on the bed, and she curled into the middle.

"You want to nap here for a while?" Gideon moved her hair from her face.

"Can you all stay?" She just wanted them all close; she felt their relationship was different now. She just felt more reliant on them, and it worried her now that she knew what it felt like.

"Of course. Slade and Toby will be right back and Emory too." Gideon moved under the blankets next to her and pulled her onto his chest.

The door opened and Emory and Toby came in. Toby was fresh out of a shower and Emory was holding snacks and water. He opened the water bottle and handed it to her.

"Take a drink and have a cookie then you can sleep ok." Emroy was always making sure she was taken care of like this.

She took the water and cookies, doing as she was told. As she was done Emory laid down on the other side of Gideon while Slade came out of the bathroom.

"We need a bigger bed if we are going to cuddle." Slade made them laugh as he slid into her other side kissing her shoulder.

She felt the bed shift as she expected Toby to join them.

"We definitely need one. I am going to fall off." Toby said and she tried to scoot closer to Gideon to give him more room.

"You're fine Sweet girl. Go to sleep ok." Toby said leaning over Slade to kiss her forehead.

"Thank you for showing up for me earlier." She whispered as her eyes got heavy. She thought she heard a choir of responses, but she was being pulled into sleep by Gideon's heartbeat in her ear. She would be fine if this was how she could end her days, she had fallen for all of them, and hard. It may have been a knee jerk reaction to start with, but it was more than that now, and she was terrified to lose them.

Chapter 18

Lola

Rolling over she realized she was alone in bed, but there was still warmth all around her, so they had not left to long ago. Looking at the clock on the best side table she realized they were probably still working on things for the day as it was only 5pm now.

She flipped the covers back and headed into the bathroom to go pee. As she did, she realized her clothes were missing and rolled her eyes. She headed to Slade's dresser when she was done and grabbed a pair of his boxers that were too big for her and a tee-shirt that covered most of her body.

Heading out of his room she could not hear them in the rest of the house, so she went into her room only to put on her own underwear and a pair of shorts. It may still be spring, but it was getting warm quick around here.

She looked around for her phone on instinct but then remembered what had happened earlier and groaned. How could shit have hit the fan so fast? This was going to make this season interesting with the guys there Greyson was going to lose his mind since it did not seem like he knew about them yet.

In the main area of the house no one was here but she could hear the music from the garage as she got closer to the door. She paused on the balcony to watch them work. They did not even need to talk to each other as they worked on one of the cars that had been under a cover. Anticipating what the others needed, it was like earlier they all worked in unison to claim her and remind her she was theirs.

Toby glanced up at the balcony, probably able to feel her watching them and smiled at her.

"How did you sleep Sweet girl?" He called up to her and she walked down the stairs but stopped at the bottom step.

"Great." She paused as Toby came over to kiss her, the others followed him over.

"What's up love?" Emory could see her anticipation.

"Will one of you take me to the phone store to get a new one? Did anyone save what was left of mine?" She felt embarrassed for her outburst with it earlier.

"Alaska and Noelle are on their way over with a new one for you. Your old one is in the kitchen." Emory kissed her forehead, and she felt a wave of relief washing over her.

"Thank you. Let me know how much it is, and I will pay you back for it." She did not want to put them out for her own actions.

"Duke paid for it, take it up with him. He also is getting the process started to make sure Greyson is a good distance away from you for the season." Gideon smiled at her, and it told her he was already in control of this issue.

"Thank you." She couldn't help but be thankful to them for this.

"Doll we are going to take care of you. Now are you hungry?" Gideon stepped closer to her and she backed up a step to be as tall as him.

"A little, I could really go for a huge salad with chicken on it though." She ran her fingers through his hair as she looked at him.

"Do we need to go get something for that or is there somewhere in town we can pick one up?" Gideon asked.

"Theres some salad but the toppings are missing here. There was an Italian place in town that has a good chicken Cesar salad if you would rather just pick one up." She did not want to be difficult.

"Perfect, we will order something for us as well and get your salad." Gidon kissed her now and she let him pull her into him, she had to wrap her legs around him as he pulled her off the stairs.

He began to carry her towards the car they were working on but when he tried to set her down, she held on tight and he laughed while looking confused a little.

"No shoes on." She would never come into a garage with no shoes and walk around.

"Then sit here and look pretty for us." Gideon set her on the hood of the car across from the one they were working on.

"Best hood ornament ever Angel." Slade came over and kissed her as Gideon left to work on the car.

She smiled at Slade as he turned to help the others. She tucked her feet up and watched them work. It seemed so simple, but she had never done thing sort of thing. She imagined their high school girlfriend did this and it made her a little upset to know she was not the first to be here like this with them.

"What is going on in there?" Emory stopped next to her.

"Just thinking how comfortable this feels. I never had this sort of friendship as a teen, and no one was comfortable with me in the shop except Tayler and Duke, so I never get to just hang out around cars. I used to live in the garage with my parents and I didn't realize how much I missed it till right now." She was honest even if she left out the part about their past.

"I could never imagine not getting to be in a working garage. I think there is oil and gas in my blood working with it to keep me alive at this point." Emory smiled at her, and she laughed.

"I definitely feel like that sometimes." She tried to hide the other question she had and looked back at the car.

"If you have a question love, just ask it ok." Emory was too good; he could see it on her face.

"Did your high school girl do this a lot?" They had never told her the girl's name and she was sort of thankful for that.

"She did for a while but then stopped. She got jealous of the cars and the time we were spending to make it in this world. She couldn't handle the long hours building a car or the time it took to get to the level we wanted to be." Emory moved in front of her now and she looked up at him.

"I am sorry, I hate that those questions come up. I guess I may be a bad ass on the track, but I can't escape the silly little girl worries." She hated how she felt when she thought about someone else with them.

"Lola, I love that you're a little jealous. Because when I feel like beating the crap out of Greyson, knowing your jealous of my past reminds me that it's normal." Emory pulled her face to his and kissed her.

He laughed when he pulled away and she realized his hands were covered in grease. Before she could say anything in protest, he wiped a finger across her cheek and on her nose.

"Hey!" She protested as he walked away from her leaving

her stranded.

Slade looked over and laughed before sneaking up on Emory and wiping his even dirtier hands on his face. The two of them chased each other around the garage and she burst out laughing.

"Look what you started Doll." Gideon came and grabbed her off the car, effectively getting her thighs covered in grease as well.

"Emory started it." She argued as Gideon carried her up to the loft.

"God you are gorgeous. Stand still for a minute." Gideon put her down and pulled out his phone. He snapped a picture of her, and she couldn't help but pose a little, it was the girl in her always trying and take a good picture.

"Alaska said they are almost here, and I guess the others want to come by if you're good with that." Toby called up to them as Emory and Slade stopped their chase.

"Of course. I should go change though if they are all coming over." She realized how short her shorts were at this moment.

"No, none of that crap. Change if you want but not out of worry of being inappropriate in front of them. We are secure enough in our relationship with you and them to not give a crap Lola." Gideon pulled her out of the thought quickly.

"Ok well I should at least put shoes on if we are going to be out here." She did not need to be carried around all night.

"We need to clean up anyways, it's too windy for a fire tonight so we will probably hang out in here anyways." Gideon opened the door to the house for her and she walked inside.

He took her back in his arms and she laughed as he carried her to his room. All their rooms were different and matched their styles perfectly. While Slade's room was dark and cozy Gideon's was brighter but very organized. Toby's room was very neutral, and Emory had purple walls and motorcycle memorabilia everywhere in there.

He set her down on the bathroom counter and then began to clean the grease off with a washcloth and the action made her body ache for him.

"How long till the others are here?" She asked as he wiped her thighs slowly.

"Maybe 10 minutes? Why, you still needy Doll?" His finger grazed her core, and she felt the heat rush to her there.

"I don't feel like I ever get enough of you guys." She ran her hands up his chest and into his hair.

"We definitely do not get enough of you Doll." He continued to tease her through her shorts.

She pulled him to her and kissed him hard. He moved his hand but grabbed the hem of the shirt and pulled it up and over her head, breaking their kiss.

"What I wouldn't do to see you covered in greasy handprints over your naked body." He said as he palmed her boob. She moaned and pulled his face back to hers, fuck she needed him more than she had thought.

"Please Gideon I need you." She broke away and ran her hands down his chest to the top of his jeans.

"Fuck, take it off Lola." He let her move to the ground as she began to take his pants off, she pulled his boxers down with them revealing how hard he already was.

In one motion she took him into her mouth, and she moaned as she felt her own body react to his taste.

"Shit Doll." He said before taking her hair in his hands and holding her head as he pushed into her mouth nicely as she sucked on him.

She pushed down on him to take him all the way into her mouth, and he quickly pulled her off him. He pulled her up to standing and turned her to face the counter before ripping her shorts down to her knees.

"So perfect Doll." He slapped her ass once before pushing himself into her hard, the motion taking her breath away as this angle was tight and filling.

"Oh shit." She cried out as he pushed in and pulled out faster, each time her need growing and her body tightening around him.

She looked at him in the mirror and as they made eye contact, they both cursed. He pulled her up, so her back was touching his chest, and he kissed her hard before pushing her back down to the counter.

Gideon's noises of desire were filling the bathroom and hers was mixed in with it. It made them both act like starved animals and the sounds that filled the space began to feed on her desires. The sound of him pounding into her mixed with their curses and moans was enough to get her right on the edge.

"Fuck, Doll cum with me. Let your body pull everything out of me like it owns me just as much as I own you." Gideon's words pushed her the little bit she needed, and she cried out his name.

"Fuck, fuck. Oh, shit Lola." He cried out as he filled her with his warm cum making her orgasm even harder. They both caught their breath before moving and then began to clean up.

"I have a question for you." Gideon was already dressed as he handed her Slade's shirt off the floor.

"Ok." She was not worried as she pulled the shirt on.

"The first time we were together when I asked you about birth control you said no worry about a baby. But you don't take the pill, you don't have an iud. Do you use the shot?" Gideon did not look mad or think she was lying to him she could see concern on his face.

"No," She couldn't find the words to tell him what happened.

"I am glad for that; I was worried you had. I heard bad thing about it from the other girls here and was worried. But what do you take then?" He was not going to drop the conversation, and she was worried it was going to end their relationship right here.

"I can't get pregnant Gideon. My internal injuries were so bad they had to remove my reproductive organs; they were severely damaged in the accident. I am sorry if that ruins ideas of a life with kids in it." She could feel the rejection coming and it hurt. She had let herself fall so hard already.

"Lola, look at me." Gideon pulled her face up to look at him.

"Have I thought about having kids? Yes. Does this change how badly I want you to always be in my life? No. If you want to have kids someday, we will figure something out ok. But know that this does not change anything between us, or the others and I am sure about that." He pulled her close to him and she let his comfort wash over her.

"Dinner's here." Toby's voice came into the bathroom making them pull away.

"Great." She tried to sound better but her voice betrayed her.

"What's up sweet girl?" Toby ran a finger up her arm as Gideon let her turn to face him.

"Lola was explaining something to me, and we will all have a talk about it when she is ready." Gideon looked at her for confirmation and she nodded.

"As long as it's not about you moving, you're fine, Lola." Toby smiled at her, and she couldn't help but smile at him as well.

"And not get to see you all everyday, hell no. Though I do need to go back and get my clothes for the season. Shit, I need to see if the PR team sent the outfits for press week too." She forgot about them sending her stuff.

"We can go by tomorrow, don't stress. Come hang out and eat ok." Toby pulled her to his side, and they walked out to join the others.

The night was great, they played cards with the others. Everyone was surprised by how good she was at poker, but she explained how they played a lot on the road. As the night wound down and the others left, she did not feel like waiting to talk to the others about earlier. She explained what she had discussed with Gideon and each of their reactions were calming for her. They echoed what Gideon had said, making the nerves fall away.

It had only been a short time with them, but their comfort and affection felt like it was healing a part of her soul she had forgotten about. That part of you that lets you rest and grow because everything around you is providing nourishment even in the simplest actions.

Chapter 19

Toby

Their travel day came faster than Toby had imagined, and the weight of their success was starting to weigh on him as they waited in the airport for their flight to leave. He, Gideon, and Lola were meeting Tayler in Colorado to head out to the east coast. Emory and Slade had left Thursday to drive the truck and car out there, though they both complained about leaving the whole time.

They were sitting at their gate now and Lola had run off to get another cup of coffee since it was early for them all. Tayler had landed about 20 minutes ago from his Washington flight.

"Are you ok?" Tayler nudged him as he looked out for Lola.

"Yeah, wishing I could have drove, but it should be fine." He did not hate flying but he preferred to be in a car.

"You and Lola are the exact same." Tayler laughed.

"What do you mean?" He had not heard her complain about flying.

"She hates to fly, its why Duke makes sure she's in first class. Sorry about the split in seats by the way. But she needs space when she flies, why do you think she is walking the airport waiting for the boarding?" Tayler explained and now he wanted to go find her.

"She said she was getting a drink." Gideon chimed in taking his headphones off, he loved to fly, sleeping most of the time.

"Yes, but I am willing to bet she went to the other end of the terminal to get that drink. It will also be decaf or a tea to not add to the anxiety." Tayler nodded up at the crowd coming towards them.

Sure, enough, their girl had a cup in her hand from a coffee shop way at the beginning of the terminal. She looked stunning in her green pants and tan tank top; she had a jacket for the flight but that was tied around her waist right now. Her hair was down, and she was in comfortable shoes, but he knew she packed slippers.

"Sorry, that took so long the line was long." She sat in the empty seat between him and Gideon. He looked over at Tayler as she spoke, and he just rolled his eyes at her.

"What did you get doll?" Gideon smiled at her, but he knew it was a trap.

"A chi tea latte." She took a sip not noticing Gideon's smile.

"And you just had to have the one from the shop all the way at the front of the terminal? The one a few gates down wouldn't do?" Gideon was not usually dominant outside of the bedroom, but Toby could see that her keeping her fear of flying from Gideon made him upset.

"Well that one was full so I thought a short walk would do some good since our flight is long. Sitting still for so long is hard for me, right Tayler?" She was catching on but did not know her best friend had ratted her out already.

"I already spilled the beans Bunny, own up to it." Tayler put his headphones in and sank into his seat more. Lola cursed under her breath but they both heard her.

"Why didn't you tell us you hated flying?" Gideon was

151

holding her thigh now.

"How stupid is it that I drive a car down a track close to 200 miles an hour, but I hate getting into a plane. I usually travel with the car but seeing as this time I was not ready when it left, this was the only option." She laid it out to them, and he felt for her.

"I hate flying too Sweet girl. But you should have told us, we could have worked in time for some stress relief this morning." Toby now realized why she was up so early this morning, trying to be sneaky with a run at 3am.

"I went for my run, that is usually enough. I just need to relax, once we get in the air, I am usually ok." She took a sip of her drink and took a breath.

"You have to tell us these things Lola, we want to help you all the time ok. Plus, we care about you." He took her free hand and held it. They sat like that for the rest of the time and when it came time to board, she and Tayler boarded first.

As Toby and Gideon boarded, they walked right past them, and she looked stressed out. It hurt him to know she was so worried. They got to their seats, but it was a little bit of a wait for the other people to get situated. Right before they took off Tayler came back to their seats.

"Alright, one of you has to go sit with her. I don't know if it's because her anxiety is higher because of the accident but I cannot get her to calm down for take-off." Tayler rushed to explain, and Toby was out of his isle seat before Gideon could try to take over. He would come to get Gideon if he could not help her, but he needed her too.

"Sweet girl, you're alright." He said slipping into the seat beside her and buckling his seat belt quickly.

"Toby this is insane, we can just drive." She was trying to get off the plan and he grabbed her hands.

"No there is not time. You have press week stuff to do when we land even. You are going to be fine. Look at me." He took one hand and put it on her face to turn her to him. Her eyes had tears in them and as the plane moved away from the gate, he could see the fear coming.

"Do you want a distraction sweet girl?" He asked her as they taxied.

She nodded as she took a deep breath again. He pulled her face to his and kissed her quickly. She smiled at him as he pulled away.

"See we should have helped you this morning instead of you running." He teased her and as he heard the engines getting louder pulled her to him again.

As they raced down the runway, he kissed her deeply. Not letting her come up for air as he demanded her attention be on his lips and tongue. He moved his hand to the back of her head and when she moaned into his mouth, he knew she was good. Just as they leveled out in the air, he released her.

"So much better than Tayler trying to distract me." She laughed.

"Is this the reason we had to get this early flight so that he could be with you?" He asked as she settled into her seat.

"Yeah, he always makes sure we fly together, or Duke flies with me but he hates being in an airplane and gets grumpy." She took a sip of her drink, and he could see her relaxing more now.

The flight attendant was coming around with meals for them now even though he knew the back cabin was not getting food on this flight. As she put the tray on his table, he looked at it, realizing this was a vegetarian meal.

"Is Tayler vegetarian?" He asked, almost disgusted.

"He gets the vegetarian meals for planes because he says they are better." She looked at him with a smile as she dug into her eggs that did not smell bad.

"Should I go give it to him?" Toby would be upset if he planned for a meal and did not get it.

"Eat it, serves him right for abandoning me." She laughed taking a bite of her food.

"What, you would rather have him here, I see how it is." He made himself sound offended and she slapped his arm.

"I would gladly take you over him but still, what kind of friend abandons his best friend. I am like the best thing in his life." She laughed then quickly stopped.

"The best thing in my life huh? I will take that, thanks." Tayler was standing there and took the food from in front of him. Before either of them could protest Tayler was gone again.

"Here have some of mine." Lola handed the rest of her eggs over to him while she took one of the pancakes out of the package before handing him the other.

"You have to eat too," he said, trying to hand it back to her.

"There will be food available when we land, there will be a lunch almost right after we land." She ate the fruit on her tray as he took a bite of the eggs.

They finished their food, then found a movie to watch but 10 minutes later she was laying on his shoulder sleeping. The rest of the flight was good, and he found himself falling asleep with her but when the attendants woke them for the landing, he could sense her anxiety coming back.

Toby kissed her while they landed, and she was calmer as soon as they got off the plane. Waiting for their bags and she was on the phone with Duke who was picking them all up. He pulled her bags off the belt since she was distracted.

"Thank you. Sorry travel is so complicated like this." She still seemed frustrated by having to fly.

"It's ok Sweet girl. Is Duke here?" They all had their bags and were heading out the doors.

"He is." She said but her phone rang again.

"Hi, yeah, we just landed. It was an ok flight, I guess. Oh, I am sure he did. I will call when we get to the room tonight, yes. Bye, drive safe." She was glaring at Gideon, and he couldn't help but laugh at her rage as she ended her conversation.

"How was your chat, Doll?" Gideon knew what he was doing, and it was hilarious to watch.

"You told Slade? Why would you do that? He's going to make you beat my ass when they get in tomorrow." Lola slapped Gideons arm as a black Dodge Durango pulled up to the curb.

"He may be on the right train of thought." Gideon dropped it as Duke got out of the car and grabbed the bags.

"You packed light." Duke said to them as he got the bags in the car.

"We packed some in the truck." Lola said giving Duke a hug before getting into the passenger seat of the car leaving the back to Tayler, Gideon, and himself.

"I will take the back." Tayler climbed in the car. Gideon walked to the other side and got in while Toby got in as well.

"Alright, do you need to change before lunch?" Duke asked Lola as they got on the road.

"Nope this is what they laid out for me to wear today. Where is the lunch?" Lola asked as they drove.

"At the hotel actually, most of the media and sponsors are staying at the same place you are so that made things easy," Duke explained, and they all listened to them run down their schedule for the next few days.

Toby was ready to be racing already, he couldn't understand how Lola delt with all of this. But as they pulled up to the hotel and got out, he could see the shift in her. She became Lola Bunny; she became the girl driver determined to beat the guys and show that girls could race. He saw her in a new light as she shook hands and gushed about her vacation that she did not actually take. Part of him worried how good she was at keeping the secret of where she had been.

"She hates this part too. She hates the press, and she became this person to protect her privacy." Tayler was beside him now as they watched her talk to sponsors and laugh like she did not just had an anxiety attack on a plane.

"But she is so good at it," he said watching Gideon join her with the group. Lola did not falter and played the part of the excited new teammate.

"She put up a lot of walls when that jerk was with her. He made her feel small in a room like this but look at Gideon. He is keeping the focus on her even though the people are asking him about her car. Greyson would have taken that shine for himself. Now go join them why don't you." Tayler patted him on the shoulder before walking off towards Duke.

Toby took a drink of his drink and headed towards them. Her laugh was her real laugh though as Gideon joked about coming for her record times and as he stepped in the group welcomed him.

Chapter 20

Lola

The lunch took close to three hours, and it was exhausting. She felt slightly bad about heading to her room alone, but she needed to decompress, she was out of practice. Gideon and Toby understood and went to their room after kissing her goodnight, looking equally exhausted.

She finished up her skin care and pulled on one of Slade's shirts she stole and Emory's sweatpants that she had to roll a few times to not fall off. Laying down in the bed she scrolled through her phone to see what was being said about today and most of the media things were good. The impact of her breakup was there but not by much. The comments about her chemistry with the new guys made her eyes roll, she wished they focused on the racing, but she knew better.

She snapped a picture of herself and sent it in the group chat saying how cozy she was but how lonely she was with a sad face.

I would gladly come to keep you company sweet girl if you want me. Toby replied almost instantly.

Well, you know where I am. She taunted him and could feel the excitement grow in her body.

The others reacted to the photo and messages with laughing faces or raised eyebrows and she laughed. There was a knock on her door quicker than she thought Toby could get to her with how far away his room was. She got up and looked out the peep hole and screamed.

"What are you doing here?!" She launched herself into Emory's arms before realizing Slade was there also.

"We could not stand another night away from you Angel. We may have not stopped last night like we told you." Slade took her in his arms as Emory set her down.

"I can't believe you two, did the others know?" She looked around for Toby thinking he didn't know about this.

"We keep no secrets between us guys." Slade walked her into the room and Emory shut the door.

"We do have one problem. We have no room for tonight." Emroy stalked over to her, his eyes hungry for her and she loved it.

"I think I can accommodate that." She smirked as Slade kissed her.

"I was looking for this shirt Angel, when did you steal it?" Slade pulled the hem of the shirt up and over her head.

"As soon as you took it off Monday, I hid it in my room." Smiling at him as he kissed her neck.

"Did you do the same with my pants?" Emory puling the pants down to reveal her green lace thong.

"Yes. I wanted to have you with me." She had not realized how much she had missed them till right now. She needed them as much as the others and she was not ashamed of it at this point.

"What are you going to do with us now that you have us in person?" Slade was holding her hips and she needed them to get naked with her.

"First I think you have to many clothes on for what I want." She reached for the hem of his shirt and pulled it over his head. Running her hands over his muscular chest and abs before getting his pants undone.

She turned to Emroy before getting distracted by Slade being naked and undressed him the same way. Before they could say anything more, she knelt on the floor and took Emory into her mouth and Slade into her hand. Switching to give them equal attention.

"Shit Angel, I have missed your mouth." Slade held her hair in his hands as she took him all the way into her mouth.

She moaned around him feeling herself getting slick as she sucked on him. Emroy knelt behind her and snaked his hand around her front to find her sensitive core. He rubbed her in circles with just enough pressure and she was moaning around Slade ever harder as he took control of thrusting into her mouth.

"God you are soaked." Emory kissed her shoulder as Slade continued his relentless pace in her mouth.

"Ride his hand Angel, take what you need." Slade told her and Emory pushed two fingers inside her making her body tighten around him.

As Emory matched Slade's rhythm, she rolled her hips into him. He was pushing her closer to coming and she needed it after the day she had. She let out a muffled scream as Emroy hit the spot inside her that craved their attention. She came all over his hand and Slade pulled out of her mouth quickly.

"Bed now." Slade pulled her up and Emory followed them to the bed.

Emory pulled her onto him facing him as he pushed inside her quickly. She was going to lose it again so soon with how full she felt.

"God, I missed your ass." Slade slapped her ass as Emory

160

pounded into her from underneath her.

"Fuck please." She cried out not even knowing what she needed but knowing she needed more of them.

"You have some lubrication, Angel?" Slade dragged his finger down her spin and settled on her ass.

"Small bag inside my suitcase, its pink." She said as Emory slowed down a little. Her body was anticipating what was coming next. They had not done anal, but they had played enough that she was ready. The though of both inside her made her shiver.

"You like the idea of us both inside you love?" Emory pulled her face to his kissing her deeply as she felt Slade's weight back on the bed.

"Yes, please." She felt the cool lube on her ass, and she tried to not tighten up as Slade pushed one finger inside her.

"Just breath love." Emory pushed into her slowly keeping her attention on him and not what Slade was doing.

Emory's hand found her clit just as Slade pushed a second finger into her and she cried out his name.

"You are perfect." Slade kissed her shoulder before taking his fingers out of her. Before she could react, he pushed the tip of his dick into her.

"Breath love." Emory had stopped moving to give her a moment and as she took a deep breath Slade slid into her farther, the stretch was painful but only slightly.

"Oh, fuck you are so tight." Slade pushed in all the way, and she moaned around Emory's neck as she laid all the way on him.

She took a few breaths before pushing back onto Slade hoping he would move now.

"You ready for more Angel?" Slade pulled her up and the change in angle made her feel so full.

"Please I need more, move please." She begged and they both began to move in sync with each other.

"You are so tight love. I am not going to last." Emory said to her as she moaned and got closer to another release.

"Wait for me please, I want you both to come with me please." She was so close, and she wanted to feel them both reach that release with her.

Slade started pounding into her harder now and she could barely catch her breath, as she crests the peak of her pleasure she cried out. Slade bit her shoulder and Emory swore as he spilled into her. Slade was right behind them filling her full, well almost she would love to have one of the others in her mouth.

"So worth not sleeping the other night." Slade said as he pulled out of her, it was tender, and she hissed a little as he did.

"You ok love?" Emory already went into aftercare mode and his kisses were soothing as he pulled out of her as well pulling her into his hold as he rolled to the side.

"Yeah, more than ok it's just tender. But fuck it was so good." She was blissed out and did not realize Slade had left to get a washcloth.

"Let me clean you up Angel." Slade tapped her legs, and she opened them for him. The warm cloth felt good.

She was already cozy and when Slade joined them in bed Emory slipped out quick to clean up. She snuggled into Slade who kissed her head and told her how perfect she was. As she was nodding off, she was so at peace.

"Good night, I love you guys." She whispered as sleep pulled her into its warmth with two of her guys around her, no worry about claiming them. She couldn't hear their response to her before she was out cold.

Chapter 21

Gideon

They had just wrapped up with interviews and Gideon had forgotten how brutal it could be to be interviewed. Of course, they asked them about their connection to Lola, to which the agreed response was that they all cared for her very much. The team and her major sponsors did not care about their relationship, Duke told them that last night. But they did not want negative press before the season, so they agreed that it was early to say they were all together.

The harder questions were about how he felt being back after the years of being gone. He had not thought about his accident in years so to be asked about it brought it right to the forefront of his mind. But with it came thoughts about Lola and her accident, which now terrified him to think would happen again.

"Hey, get out of your head." Emory nudged him as they walked through the hallway towards the photo shoot area.

"I am sorry, I forgot how interviews dug into you is all. It makes me worry about Lola doing hers in a little while." He was eager to get to their girl since he did not see her after the events yesterday.

"She seemed ok this morning before we left." Slade still had a shit eating grin on his face from getting to be with her all night. Heck had he heard that girl say she loved him he would look like that too.

"Being ok and actually doing an interview is different." He said as they reached the room for photos. The door was shut, which meant someone was taking their photos, so they all stood against the wall.

"You are worried they are going to press the issues with Greyson?" Emory looked worried as well.

"That and pulling her back into the wreck. The mindset of having to talk about it makes you relive it." He knew all too well the truth.

"They are not allowed to talk to her about it." Tayler came around the corner having heard their conversation.

"What do you mean?" Toby asked, pushing off the wall.

"We have a list of things they cannot ask her about, which is a first for her but given the circumstances necessary." Tayler stopped right at the door.

"Well, that is a relief." Emory said as Tayler opened the door.

"You guys coming in? Lola should be done soon." Taylor held the door open, and the noises of the room came into the hallway, there was country music playing and he was curious.

"She is still not done?" Toby walked forward into the room.

"While you guys have maybe two outfits, she is on her last one." Tayler told them as they all came into the room.

"Oh fuck." Slade whispered as Lola came into view and he felt the sentiment.

Lola was in a short set of overalls, and by short you could almost see her ass in them. It was paired with a teal leather top that her boobs were about to spill out of. She had checkered shoes and was holding her helmet. Her long hair was curled, and she had more make up on than he had ever seen on her.

Gideon wanted her in his bed in this outfit so he could rip it off her and he felt the energy from the others wanting to do the same. She then gave them a smile that told him she was just as needy as them and it took all his willpower to not go over to her.

"How were the interviews?" Duke was in a chair on the edge of the photo area as they walked up.

"Good, asked about Lola and of course Gideon's wreck." Toby took a seat, not taking his eyes off Lola as she moved and changed her poses. She looked very comfortable out there.

"You good?" Duke asked him, knowing how that wreck messed with him.

"I am, I think spending time with Lola helped me get over my own issues a little more." He was sure about this. He never would have been able to re-watch his wreck and not get angry.

"That's good. You guys should go around the side there and get changed." Duke pointed to the side of the room where there were clothes lined up.

They went where he said as Lola also came off the photo area. She had that sexy smirk on her face that made him want to spank her red.

"Hi Doll, how has your morning been?" He asked keeping his distance since there were a ton of people here.

"Long, this is my last of five outfit changes and I get to do it all again later with the car." She sounded exhausted but still smiled the whole time.

"You look incredible." He said as the stylist handed them all clothes.

"Do you get to keep these clothes?" Slade asked getting close enough to her to trace the bottom of her ass in the shorts.

"She does." The stylist said, handing Lola another outfit. They all let out a satisfied growl that made Lola bite her lip a little.

Gideon moved over to where they had a blocked off changing area and began to change into the team shirt and jeans that were handed to him. The others came in as well and they headed over to where Tayler was pointing to while Lola went into the same blocked off area.

"Better not let anyone else here see you naked Doll, you are ours and we don't share with others." He whispered to her as they passed by so close their shoulders brushed each other.

"I wouldn't dream of it." She smirked at him as she pulled the makeshift curtain to hide her completely.

The photographer positioned them around with Toby in the center to start. They all followed their instructions but when Lola came out, they all lost focus. She was now in a team shirt, hers being teal and grey, her Dodge jacket again the same colors, and a black leather skirt. Her black combat boots giving her a little more height.

"Lola, will you step in for one more photo. We need a team photo and it's easier to photoshop only one group in rather than two." Tayler had a grin across his face knowing they all were about to fuck her here and now.

"Sure." She smiled but then shot Tayler a glare as she put her purse down.

"Great your team is on their way also but let's get some with just you and Toby first." Tayler was trying to get Lola to beat him up.

Emory, Slade, and he stepped off so Lola and Toby could be photographed. They had the typical pose like they were just teammates but when the photographer made them get closer, he could see Lola's desire get thicker.

Toby put his arm over her shoulder, and he knew the photos would look amazing. The image would look like friends with how comfortable they were together. Before they got any more comfortable the rest of her crew came in with their crew shirts on.

The stylist handed them their crew shirts as well and instead of going behind the curtain to change Gideon pulled his shirt off right there. Lola lost focus and he smiled loving his effect of her. They were positioned again with Toby and Lola in front with the team around their back.

"Your team colors work so well together. It's going to be a shame to add the red of Greyson's team to these." The photographer said and they all started laughing. Apparently, this was good for photos because he took more as they moved out of their positions.

"Alright Lola, you head to interviews. Kip, Marv, Wile, Sam you are with us for the interviews also." Tayler called them and Lola let her hand float over each of their arms as she walked away.

After they left, Toby got in his fire suit and then they were done. As they were wrapping up, Greyson and his crew were walking in, and he could not help feeling the rage that came to him.

Gideon looked at Slade and shook his head at him with a glare, his best friend wanted to destroy Greyson for what he did to Lola. He knew it was more after she told them all about the full extent of her damage from the wreck.

Greyson's crew paid them no attention but before they left Greyson was talking loudly with the photographer.

"When are we doing the whole team photo?" Greyson asked.

"We are photoshopping your team into the ones we just

took." The photographer said.

"That's stupid, just go get Lola and the new guys and have them come take them." Greyson was finding any excuse to have her in the same room as him.

"We are not doing that. Lola has other things on her list right now." Duke shut it down, but Greyson glared at Duke.

"Let's go." Emory pushed Gideon's shoulder, and they headed out to go to the conference room where they were having lunch and an all-hands meeting.

They were the first ones to the room, and they grabbed food and took the table with their team's name on it. It was not a long time before Lola walked in with her whole team smiling and laughing with them.

"You really going to do the tire challenge?" Kip was asking her as they came in.

"I mean I am sure they are going to ask me this year about it so I might as well do it." Lola laughed and winked at them as they grabbed a plate for food.

"They are going to lose their mind when they realize you can actually work on your car." Kip shook his head as they all filled their plates.

"I think it's a good thing we show her working on the car this year. She always has in the past, but some have not let it be photographed." Marv rolled his eyes, and Gideon already knew who was responsible for that.

"Yeah, this is Lola's year to show she is not just some pretty girl in a fast car." Sam made them all laugh as they got to their table.

Lola put her plate and water down but came over to them.

She quickly kissed each of them before going to her table.

"So, you all are really all together?" Wile asked with a curious look.

"Yes, you saw us together not that long ago." Lola did not sound upset at his question.

"As long as you're happy and they don't hurt you we don't care Lola. But you all better not hurt her." Kip spoke for the team, and he was intimidating for sure. Being her tire changer, he was large and all muscle.

"I would not dream of hurting her and if we do somehow you can crush us because we do not deserve to be here anymore." Slade was serious as he began to eat.

Before anyone else could say anything Greyson and his team came in with Duke and Tayler close behind. This would be the first time they were all in the same room together. He could see Lola tense up a little. Kip leaned close to her and whatever he said made her relax but not completely as she looked over to him.

"Guess your worry was wrong dude, she looks completely on the market from where I am sitting," Greyson's friend Logan said taking a seat at their table. He was tall and muscular as well, nothing compared to Kip but close. His hair was dark brown but short on his head.

"It's just for show." Greyson muttered as he sat down glaring at Lola as he did.

Taylor took a spot at the front of the room, "Alright, so as we get into this week, I need to let you all know some events that are new to the schedule. We all have track photos this afternoon and tonight with cars since they are finished being wrapped. Tomorrow night is the big official dinner with sponsors and the 'signing' for HPS, what you do during the day does not matter but if you leave the hotel, please wear something team related. Wednesday, Lola you were invited to a track day to switch cars with drifters. You're meeting there at noon, bring whoever you want. Thursday is nothing for everyone but Lola again, we already talked about what you have. Friday, we have a track night at the local dirt track, all hands in team gear."

"Why is it only Lola for Wednesday? Last year we were both part of events like that." Greyson looked pissed.

"Because she was the only one invited." Tayler was cold in his response, and he could tell her best friend was sick of Greyson already.

"This is bullshit; I am losing out on opportunities now." Greyson was directing his comment at Lola as if it was her fault, but she did not look up from her food.

"You were only invited last year because of her, Greyson, we had to get them to agree to include you while you were dating. Seeing as you are not this year, she is free to do these things by herself or with whoever she invites. If you have an issue with it take it up with your manager who couldn't be bothered to show up this week." Tayler was savage and Gideon loved the fighting he did for Lola.

"You see what you are messing up for me. Your lies about us not being together are messing with my opportunities." Greyson stood up and headed towards Lola, but he did not make it. Her entire team stood up at once and made a wall blocking him from her.

"If you want to be able to drive this year, I suggest you go sit the fuck back down." Kip was in his face, and he could see Greyson back off a little.

"Greyson if you are going to act like this I will have to go to Jason and re discuss how this partnership is going to work." Duke's words made Greyson back all the way off now.

After Greyson sat back down, Duke did the run through of how track days would work, and he told them the schedule. They would be driving to all the races, each were about two weeks apart, but they would spend the week leading up to them at the locations working on the cars or whatever needed to be done. It was going to be a packed next few months.

When they were done, they all headed to their rooms, and Gideon was not surprised when Lola came to theirs before they left for the track. She was not as worried now that she realized Greyson would lose his chance to race if he messed with her, but she still was worried about being around him.

They promised they would try to always be around, and he knew they would. Even if they weren't able to, her team would always be there. They were not going to leave her alone around him at all.

Chapter 22

Lola

The next few days went well but Lola was worried about tonight's dinner. She was finishing getting ready in her room and she loved the dress they found for her. It was a darker teal color which paired nicely with her gold jewelry, it had a thigh slit but was just barely to her knees. The body con fit of it made her feel incredible and so happy she had been able to work out so much. The nude heels gave her some height, but she would still be shorter than her guys.

They had been so present this week, and while they were not being affectionate in public, they definitely stole private moments. Between them being protective of her and sexy as hell in their publicity outfits, she was already excited thinking about seeing them in suits tonight. As long as she could keep her little secret to herself tonight, she would be fine.

There was a knock on her door, and she smiled knowing it was them. They agreed to walk down together and since they were all paired up for the past week Tayler agree it would be ok.

As she opened the door her breath was lost as they stood there in their dark grey, black, and brown suits. Slade was in all black with his hair pulled back in a low ponytail which made his clean-shaven face look sharper. Gideon and Emory were in grey and if you did not know who was who you would get them mixed but. But Gideon's hair was styled a little and Emory had just had his cut. Toby was in brown, and it suited him so well with his darker hair and skin.

"Damn I hope this dinner does not take too long," she said letting them step into her room.

"Why's that Angel?" Slade smirked at her, and she knew they felt the same way she did.

"Because I want you all to myself." She stepped into him and kissed him hard. His hands falling to her ass pulling her closer.

"I think we are all on the same page Doll." Gideon stepped into her side and pulled her from Slade in a playful way. He kissed her hard and she could feel his affection digging into her side.

"It will probably be a 3-hour thing at least though." She hated it but she knew these things took time.

"That's fine we can have you all night. Your day tomorrow doesn't start till noon." Emory smirked at her next to Gideon.

"That makes me very happy." She smiled and leaned toward him for a kiss.

"Are we ready to go then?" Toby sounded nervous and she got the feeling he was worried about tonight.

"We are, are you ready?" She moved away from the others and walked over to him.

"Yes." He was nervous she could see it now.

"Toby, it's going to be fine tonight. You are an amazing driver and Duke would not have chosen to bring you all on if he did not feel you were." She got the sense that this was about the press and sponsors.

"Sweet girl." Toby pulled her into him, and she could just

feel the worry wash away a little. He held her for a moment then took a kiss.

"You smell amazing Lola." He said to her as he let her go.

"Thanks, I got a new perfume from a press box and thought it would be nice." She couldn't deny that the perks of the job were good.

"Tell me the name later and I will make sure you always have it ok." Emery smiled at her as they headed to the door.

She just shook her head and took Toby's arm as they all headed out. Tayler and her crew met them at the elevators, and they all headed down together. She loved the idea of one day being able to be open with her relationship, but she knew right now would not work. But holding onto Toby's arm as they walked through the lobby was enough to draw attention.

She kept hold of it all the way to the event room. If someone asked, she could say her new team mate was just being a gentleman and escorting her to the dinner. She could hear some comments being made as they all walked in and took their seats. The teams were separated again so as she sat down Tayler gave her a shit eating grin like he always does.

"Not a word, Taz." She glared at Tayler as they settled into their seats.

She looked around and could see there was a girl sitting with Greyson and she suspected he had called his manager to be here. It was a surprise to her that he had one since he always made it sound like he handled all his own things. She was more surprised that it was a girl, not that she was jealous if they were together but more so that she didn't think he would think a woman could be competent to handle the job.

175

"That's Stephanie, she is his manager." Tayler leaned in and told her. She turned her attention to the stage where Duke and Jason were taking to the podium.

"Thank you all for coming out for the official start to the season." Jason was not as old as Duke, but he was starting to get some salt in his dark hair, his face was always clean shaven, and his green eyes sparkled when he met hers. He was like an older brother and, like the rest of the guys she was surrounded by, protective as hell of her.

Duke and Jason addressed the group welcoming Greyson up to again congratulate him on his win last season. They showcased his team and car build for the year. The room clapped as they gave him a new patch for his team jacket.

"Now we are glad to have our very own Lola Bunny back with us this season." Jason motioned for her to join them, and the room whistled and clapped as she walked up.

"We all know how her season ended but even with the wreck, she was able to pull second for the entire season. You have a patch as well and we are excited to see what you do in your car this year. The build is nothing anyone has seen and Duke, Tayler and the team have outdone themselves this year." Jason handed her the patch with silver writing and her name on it, he pulled her into a hug before letting her go back to her seat.

"Now for our exciting announcement. I am sure you all have taken note of the new members of our group in the past few days. Some of you are aware that we have decided to take on a grass roots team. HPS Motorsports placed first in the prequalifying events for the season and after their work with Lola and her team on her car we officially offered them a position on our team. So please give a big welcome to the team. Co-owned by Gideon and Emory Henderson, car driven by Tobias Smith, worked on by Slade Presley." Jason called the guys up and the room clapped, and her table cheered for them as they went up.

"You are one lucky girl, Bunny." Tayler nudged her as they all got up there to accept their team patch and jackets from Jason and Duke. They were like hers but were orange and black and she was ready to see them in them.

"No complaints here Taz." She smiled at him as the guys went back to their seats.

The room filled with talking as the food came out. They all ate their fill and when the sponsors began going around congratulating everyone before heading out, she was glad the event seemed to be ending early. She did not like the way Tayler was acting tonight and something told her he was up to something. As she was about to sneak away to the bathroom Duke got the room's attention.

"Before everyone heads out for the night, we would like you all to join us as we wish our girl a very Happy Birthday, Magnolia Rae get up here." Duke was on the stage and the room started clapping.

She cursed under her breath and glared at Tayler who was standing with the guys. Every one of them looked like they wanted to punish her for not telling them, including her sweet Emory. As she got on stage Duke and Jason pulled her into a hug and there was a cake being brought to the center of the stage.

The room burst into a chorus of Happy Birthday, and she just turned on her people pleasing smile to the crowd. As she blew out the 24 candles, she met Gideon's eyes, and they told her she was in so much trouble.

"We know you don't like to celebrate but we could not pass up the chance when Tayler suggested it." Jason smiled at her as he handed her a piece of cake.

"I will be sure to thank him for this specifically." She took a bite of cake as everyone came up to get a piece and tell her happy birthday on their own. Some had cards and she knew Tayler had been planning this for a while.

"Magnolia, you give that boy a break, he cares about you like we all do. He wanted to show you that you can celebrate today." Duke pulled her close and kissed her forehead.

"I know Duke." She had a sadness to her that she hated today but it never went away.

As the room emptied, she grabbed another slice of cake and headed towards Tayler who was sitting at their table still.

"Taz, you didn't get any cake." She smiled as she stood next to him holding the plate out to him.

"Awe, Bunny you didn't have to." Tayler reached for the plate, and she smashed it in his face before he could move his head.

"Oh shit, Lola you better run." Kip yelled at her as she could see the look Tayler was giving her.

She was able to slip out of his reach and was heading towards the door, but Slade was standing beside it with a look that dared her to try and run past him. Instead, she turned to where Kip was and raced behind him as Tayler ran after her.

"He's not going to save you Lola." Tayler got closer and Kip just laughed before she headed towards the other side of the room with Marvin and Sam.

"Help." She yelped reaching them. They did form a small wall but before she could take a breath a set of hands was on her waist pulling her through the back door of the room.

"Wait, help Sam." She cried out but Sam just laughed when he turned around and saw her. She twisted to look but she already knew it was Gideon.

"We will see you up at the club." Gideon shut the door and the room they were in lost all the light. She shivered in his hold against her choice.

"Gideon." She whispered as she realized his hands were gone now. The room was quiet, far too quiet for the three men she knew had to be in here.

"You are lucky we told the others we would meet them at the club on the roof tonight, Doll." Gideon's voice was close but not where she felt she could touch him. There had been a bit of convincing on her part to go party with them, she really did not want to go party. Her team had begged her, and Duke even told her it would be ok to have a night of fun before the season.

"I will apologize to Tayler; he should have known better." She was trying to move towards the door, but she hit a hard body and froze.

"Angel, you are in more trouble than that." Slade grabbed her and threw her over his shoulder. Before she could protest a hard slap landed on her ass and she cried out.

"Shit sorry." She did not think this through, she should have just told them. A light kicked on and she could see they were in a small media closet. The others were standing to the side and after slapping her ass again Slade put her back down on her own feet.

"Why did you not tell us it was your birthday today, Lola?"

Emory looked hurt while the others looked angry.

"I just don't celebrate ok. It has always been a busy day because of when it falls, and it slips my mind sometimes." She was not lying but she did not feel like breaking out the emotions today held for her right now.

"Try again." Gideon was staring her right in the eye and the pressure was too much and she quickly dropped her gaze to the floor. Before she could say anything though she heard Gideon's phone go off.

"Hello. Yes. Absolutely. I understand." Gideon put his phone back in his pocket and his expression changed quickly to one she knew well. The look of pity and remorse in his eyes was something she would never escape. Once a person knew the story of today their attitude always shifted.

"Who was on the phone?" She asked backing up a little before he could grab her.

"Duke." Gideon always held onto the not keeping things from her, but she did not want to be this girl right now.

"Ok, good so you know. Now move past it. Let's go party ok. I want to party." She looked over at Emory to try and get him to reign in Gideon. She usually wouldn't drink during the season, but it looked like the only way out of this situation. If Duke spilled her secret, she was going to need a drink for this conversation anyways.

Emory gave her a consideration look before putting his hand on his brothers' shoulder. Slade snaked his hands around her waist again and pulled her to him, he put kisses on her neck, and she was willing to melt into him right here.

"Let's go dance with our girl." Toby grabbed her hand and

twirled her away from Slade who followed them out the other door in the room.

They broke apart just enough to get to the elevator but as soon as they hit the darkness of the club knowing no one here could see them well enough to realize she was dancing with all of them the mood changed. Each of them pressed into her as the songs changed and she got lost in the feeling of being with them. It probably helped that Tayler had brought her shots to make up for spilling her secret before getting the DJ to play a birthday song remix with all her favorites and she laughed as they danced.

Chapter 23

Emory

Emory watched as Lola danced with Tayler knowing they had to get her back to her room soon. She had a driving event in the afternoon, and she would need sleep. He nudged Gideon as he walked up to where he was watching her.

"We should get her to bed." He took a drink of his water; he had switched after Tayler made them do a fourth round of shots.

"After the birthday songs." Gideon was already tracking it and it just made him realize how wrapped up in this girl they all were.

"What did Duke have to say that changed your tune?" He wouldn't usually ask but he did not know his twin to change tune so fast.

"Let's just say I am pretty sure she will spill her beans if Tayler gives her one more shot, and I don't think it will be a good thing." The look Gideon had said it all. Whatever was going on with Lola today was not simple, especially to not acknowledge her birthday.

Emory nodded over to the edge of the dance floor where Tayler was handing her another shot. Gideon whistled to Slade who looked up and followed their gaze, Gideon gave him the cut it out look and Slade moved towards Lola. He did not get there fast enough and she threw the shot back and Tayler handed her the other one.

Slade took it from her hand, and she gave a pout that made Emory feel like shit for cutting her off. Slade threw back the shot before talking to her, he was telling her it was time to go to bed and Emory could tell Lola was not happy with that idea. Slade turned her toward Tayler and whispered into her ear, she moved to Tayler, giving him a hug. Before she moved back to Slade though Tayler poured his shot into her mouth and they both laughed.

"She is trouble when drinking." He said to Gideon who was watching the interaction. There was something so innocent about her right now that made him excited to get her to the room. The only issue was she was hiding something big from them.

"I have a feeling that if she is not the Lola Bunny all those people portray her as. She is a firecracker, and that will always have her in trouble, brother." Gideon smirked at him and shook his head.

Slade now had Lola over his shoulder again, Toby behind them making sure her dress was not showing off anything and they were heading towards them.

"If you don't put me down, I will puke." She was slurring and talking slowly as they got closer.

"Shouldn't have taking that shot then, Angel." Slade walked right past them towards the club doors. They had found a back elevator and realized it was one no one used.

"But it's my birthday, and the birthday girl gets whatever she wants." She was giggling now reaching for Toby as they walked. This was going to be interesting.

"Angel, you can have whatever you want always, nothing about the day changes that. But you did not eat much dinner and one piece of cake is not enough for over five shots, and whatever Tayler

183

gave you." Slade pushed the elevator button and they waited.

"Oh, come on, I'm fine. Seriously put me down though." She wiggled so much Slade had to put her down to not drop her. She stumbled into Slade and her hands roamed over his chest and arms.

The elevator opened and they all filed in just as Tayler was coming out of the club.

"Make sure she drinks some water and takes medicine." Tayler yelled at them as the doors shut on the elevator.

"Mmm. Happy birthday to me." Lola was touching all of them as they rode the elevator up.

She reached for him, and he pulled her to his body. She may be wasted, but she was cute as hell, no walls up, just going for what she wanted. She reached down to cup him in his pants, and Emory could not help thrusting himself into her hand.

"Love, let us get to a room ok." Emory said into her mouth before kissing her. He was just tipsy enough to still not really care about where they were.

"Oh, mine has a big bed lets go there. You can all stay with me, all night so I don't have to be alone." She was cheerful as she talked but he looked over at Gideon who had his worried look again.

"We will be wherever you want us, Doll." Gideon's words made her face change like she just remembered he was here.

"I am so happy you guys are here." She tucked herself into Gideon and the door opened to her floor.

They led her to her room, pulling the key out of her small bag. Inside they headed right toward the bed, and Emory made her sit down so he could take her shoes off. She lay all the way down and would not quite moving her legs.

"Love, you have to stop moving so I can get these shoes off."
He grabbed her leg harder and held on which just made her laugh.

"Sit up Angel." Slade and Gideon came over with water and a
bottle. Toby was pulling a shirt out of the dresser, because of course
she was someone who unpacked in a hotel room.

She sat up and took the water but looked very upset that it as
water. Gideon gave her a look that scared even him, and she took the
medicine without argument.

"Stand up sweet girl." Toby came to his side and helped her up.

They both helped her out of her dress, ignoring her lace bra
and matching underwear was hard, but she was in no position to be
with them right now. She needed sleep and they all knew this was not
the time. Toby slid the shirt over her bare body but before they could
get her back into bed she walked towards the bathroom.

"I have to pee, be right back." She was fine now that she was
not in the heels.

"Ok drunk Lola is hot but what the heck is going on?" Toby
kicked off his shoes and they all did the same.

"It's the anniversary of her parents' death. Duke warned me
she would try and numb it, I guess Tayler always takes care of her
today." Gideon's words hit Emory in the chest like a knife, the pain
hurting more than just for their girl. If one comment could sober him
up that was the one.

They were quiet as they got undressed, in only their boxers
they turned to the bathroom when the toilet flushed but Lola did not
come out.

"Maybe she needs a minuet." Emory said as the others
stiffened up, but then he heard the soft sound of her crying, and his

heart broke into a million pieces.

But none of them moved into her space, if she needed alone time, they would not interfere in that. Toby moved to the bed and sat on the edge and Slade followed him, they both grabbed water and just staired at the bathroom entrance. Gideon took a chair by the bed, and he just paced back and forth waiting for her.

This was the hardest part of being how he was, he wanted to fix all her issues. Emory did not want her to ever be sad or upset. He wanted her to be happy and smiling all the time. So, when she came out of the bathroom tears still streaming down her face and fighting for air, he moved quickly to her. He pulled her close to his chest and held her as her body shook from the sobs.

"It's ok Love, we got you." He whispered into her hair as he kissed her.

He could feel her body growing weak, so he lifted her into his arms and carried her to the bed. With Lola on his lap, he sat on the edge next to Toby. Toby kissed her shoulder and began to rub her back. Slade came over to the other side of him and ran his fingers threw her hair, Gideon looked so worried from the chair. He could see the confliction in his brother at the distance Gideon was keeping between them.

"What do you need Love? Can we do anything or get you anything?" He needed to have something to do for her.

"Nothing, just go enjoy your night." She tried to climb off him, but he held onto her tighter.

"No, we are going to stay. Now if you want to be in bed alone, we will understand, but none of us are going to leave. We love you Lola, and being here for you is more important than anything." He held her face in his hands now and her tears just kept flowing.

"Let's lay down ok. We can see what movies are on the tv and order food if you want." Toby suggested it and she gave a small smile.

"Ok." She let them take control of the night.

She let Slade pull her into him with they all got the room moved around so the tv was closer. Gideon ordered some food and Toby went and grabbed more water. Emory climbed next to her on the bed and just held her hand. It felt like home to be like this with her, even though she was hurting and sad.

Everyone was on the bed when the food got there but Gideon went to get it with no concern about being in her room. When he came back with a large pizza Lola just laughed and took a piece. After eating she made them move around to where Gideon and Toby were closest to her as they watched a movie. She was laying on Gideon's chest and Emory thought she was asleep before she started to talk.

"They were going out to get a new cake. The one mom had tried to make burnt in the oven and she was so upset dad said they would just go get one before I got home. He texted me when they left but I was at school late. I got home to find the cops at the door. Someone was not paying attention on the road and ran into them on the bike. They died on impact, so thankfully they did not suffer. Duke and Tayler were there the whole time, and after, I went to live with Duke. Most days it doesn't hurt so bad but, on my birthday, when anyone goes out of their way for me it hurts. If they did not feel like I needed a damn cake they would be here to see me now." She was quiet from all the crying but as she talked, he could feel the pain, it was still so fresh to her even after the years.

"Lola, I doubt your parents would believe that. They loved

you; they wanted their only daughter to have a good birthday. I don't believe they would regret their choice to go out that day." Gideon smoothed her hair as he talked.

"I know, Tayler reminds me of that every year. But we usually just ignore it, we don't do cake today. We do it tomorrow, we celebrate the day after. I have let this day just be a blank day for so many years. I could keep it in till he gave me shots. I am sorry for ruining the night, you guys should be celebrating the accomplishment you have made." She took a shaky breath in.

"We can celebrate tomorrow, Doll. Just go to sleep now ok, you need to rest and let the day be blank for the rest of it ok." Gideon kissed her head.

"I don't know what I did to deserve you all, but this might be the best present I could get." Her words hit home as Emory realized she was on the same page as him.

"Lola you are the brightest star in the dark sky for me. I love you." He leaned over Toby and kissed her.

"We got the best Angel from heaven that's for sure." Slade did the same and Emory could see a smile on Lola's face.

"I am thankful for getting to spend the day with you, I cannot wait to see you in a car tomorrow though. Because you are sexy as hell behind the driver's seat." Toby pulled her face to his for a kiss before letting her go back to her spot-on Gideon's chest.

"I am pretty sure we are the luckiest men on the planet to get to have you warm our beds." Gideon kissed her head, and she snuggled closer to him.

It was not five minutes before her breath evened out and she was asleep. Slade had crashed out as well and Emory could tell Toby was almost asleep. He looked over at Gideon and could just tell he was going to hold her like that as long as he could.

"We have to find a way to make her birthday not a blank day." He looked at Gideon and knew he was thinking it too.

"Next year, right now we just need to be what she needs. Tomorrow we will get her cake and celebrate her birthday. Tonight, we just need to protect her from her sadness." Gideon kissed her again and she made a noise as he did.

Gideon stayed just like that all night, when they woke up the next morning Lola was not hungover at all and asked not to talk about it. She said that was yesterday's talk and today was going to be fun. So, none of them brought it up and headed out separately to their rooms to get ready for the day.

Chapter 24

Lola

After her birthday meltdown the guys were even more clingy, and Lola couldn't say she hated it. She loved having them close to her and as she got ready for the night, she was excited to hang out with them. There was a knock on the door but as she looked at her phone realized it was early for one of them to be here.

She looked in the peep hole to make sure it was ok to open it up and saw Duke standing there.

"What are you doing here?" She was happy to see him, but it was a surprise as she opened the door.

"I had to bring you your car keys for the night." Duke held out a set of keys to her and she tilted her head in question.

"I figured Tayler would have gotten a driver." She was sure that had been the plan.

"Well, he did but when Dodge offered to send you over the newest track hawk after how well your YouTube episode went, I figured we could change the plan." She smiled so hard her face hurt as she took the keys from him.

"Are you serious?" She was shocked.

"Yes, they want you to drive it for the season and then keep it. We have room already made in the trailer for it." Duke smiled at her as she hugged him.

"I was meaning to ask you about the truck situation." She needed some clarifications and had an idea.

"Greyson has his own truck this year, as do the guys." Duke had his serious tone of voice on again.

"While I am glad about the first, the second shouldn't be needed though. If my trailer can fit four cars then it can surlily fit the two racecars, the track hawk and Emroy's bike. The sleeper area will easily sleep all of us." She had thought about it after waking up this morning, she did not want to sleep separately from the guys. Being able to sneak around the track was going to be impossible so this idea came to her.

"It very well can work, but are you willing to deal with the argument that is going to come of it?" Duke moved to the chair and took a seat. She moved over to the mirror to finish putting on her jewelry. She had a team shirt in dark grey on with her short jean shorts, she would bring her team jacket and wear her teal boots.

"I am willing to explain that I agreed to have them ride with us to save the team money. Because logically we would have to run two trucks either way, this way I don't have to be with Greyson, and I can be with those who make me happy. My entire team and them get along great. We know it will come out eventually and I know we'll deal with it, but I think it makes perfect sense to have us in one truck." She turned around and saw the proud look Duke had on his face.

"You better slow down girl, you're sounding like a team owner already. I will get things ready tonight and tomorrow. With the first race here, we should be good to get it moved over. I will let you tell the guys though." Duke got up and pulled her into another hug.

"Thanks for listening to me." She couldn't help being thankful for him.

"Lola, if a man doesn't listen to an idea from you, he is not worth your time. Heck, Jason already has your next five years with us planned out." Duke headed to the door and as he opened it Gideon was standing there with the others getting ready to knock.

"Everything good here?" Gideon looked past Duke to her to ask that question.

"Yes, just giving Lola a present and discussing a great idea of hers. You all have a good night ok." Duke patted Gideon's shoulder as he walked past him.

"You having some ideas in here love?" Emory walked right to her giving her a kiss before she could answer him.

"I was thinking that it would be better to only run two trucks for the season and seeing as my truck and trailer has plenty of room for you guys that we should just join camps. Because honestly, it's going to happen anyways." She smiled at them as they looked like they wanted to eat her.

"You are trouble, you know." Slade said, giving her a hug that turned into him spinning her around.

"How is that trouble? I am clearly trying to save the team money." She smirked at them as Slade put her down.

"So that explains part of Duke's comment. What was your present?" Toby came over and gave her a quick kiss on the cheek and it made her feel all warm and fuzzy inside.

"A new toy." She dangled the keys in the air.

"Oh, tonight is going to be fun." Gideon laughed as she grabbed her team jacket.

"It will be, but you guys are not all going to fit with me. Tayler needs a place to ride also." She was almost tempted to make Tayler ride with the other guys but that might draw to much suspicion.

"That's ok we have the truck, and I was going to ride the bike anyways. It is such a nice night here for a ride." Emory winked at her, and she wished she could get on the back of his bike with him.

"I mean one of you could come take the passenger seat if you wanted to piss Tayler off." She smirked at them as she put her phone in her jacket pocket and the keys.

"Shotgun." Toby called out before Slade or Gideon could and she laughed at the look they gave him.

"What it will just look like she is giving the new driver a ride to the event. It's good to be close to your team mates right." Toby pulled her into him and just touching her she was wet and wanted him.

"Fine but I call dibs on the way back here." Slade was right by them now.

"Before we go, we have something for you." Gideon was holding a blue box in his hands now.

"Oh?" She raised her eyebrow as he walked over to her.

"We went and found you something for your birthday. We wanted you to have something with you all the time that would make you think of us." Gideon opened the box as he explained and revealed a gold necklace with a piston pendant, a helmet, a wrench, and a gear with a heart in the center.

"Guys this is so perfect." She ran her fingers over the pendants.

"Turn around." Gideon pulled the necklace out and she turned and moved her hair. As he secured it around her neck, he kissed her before pulling her hair back.

"How did you get it so fast?" She was sure they had not found these things in town.

"You will be surprised by what you can get delivered in a short amount of time. Now let's go have some fun." Toby took her arm and led her out of the room with the others to follow them. She was ready for a fun track night with the grassroots teams.

Chapter 25

Slade

Waking up at the track for their first race day was definitely a different experience. Slade could see why Lola had insisted they stay here. It made you wake up ready to go, even if it was 6am and no one was around. The track was quiet outside of the truck and it had been so nice last night they just left the windows open. Slade climbed out of the bunk he had claimed and tried to be quiet as he moved along the cabin. There were three stacked bunks on either side of the truck leading to the back bigger bedroom. Then the two couches laid out to be beds.

They were all comfortable with sharing a bed with Lola to leave more space but Gideon and Emory had climbed in with her late last night. This left a bunk for Tayler under him and Toby. Everyone else was still asleep so he slipped on his boots and headed out the door. When he got outside, he realized his assumption was wrong and his Angel was jogging in the return lane of the track.

She had her hair braided already and she was in a pair of workout shorts and a sports bra. With her headphones on, he could see she was in the zone of her run. When she turned to head back, he almost had a heart attack to see her climb up onto the wall. She balanced the wall, every few steps he could see her taking deep breaths as she stood on the wall.

He walked over to watch her, taking a seat on the bleachers behind her as she walked. When she reached the end of the track she hopped back down from the wall and ran back towards him. When she saw him, she pulled her headphones off and the smile on her face was the sweetest thing ever.

"You are up early," she said climbing over the fence to come to him.

"So are you." He met her as she dropped down and kissed her while cupping her amazing ass.

"I couldn't sleep so I came out for a run." She just smiled kissing him back.

"You taking up a new skill of balancing?" He raised his eyebrow at her, and she rolled her eyes making him grab her ass harder.

"Think of it as getting closer to the wall, I respect its place and, if I trust myself around it, today should be good." They all knew there was a chance she ran next to the wall today and it worried them all, to include Duke.

"You will be perfect Angel. This wall is not going to do anything to you, or I will have it torn down. You hear me?" He was serious but her laugh lightened his heart.

"I hear you. Want to get some food? The driver's tent should have food out by now." She had an excited bounce to her as they walked.

"Food and coffee sound good." He had become a different morning person as long as she was around, the mornings when Emory woke him up were the worst.

They headed towards the large white tent and the smell of food filled the air. There were a few other people from various teams there, but they were still the only ones from their camps up. Lola grabbed a protein shake and fruit while he made some coffee. After getting what they wanted they headed back to their set up.

There were chairs out still and he sat in one pulling Lola onto his lap. They had pretty much exposed themselves at the track night and it was nice to be able to touch her like this. The team had been really cool about it and other than some social media comments there were no big issues with it. This girl made Slade want to touch her all day every day and he did not care what anyone thought.

It seemed like right now that no one in their world cared if she was with all of them. The only person making things difficult was Greyson who was still making comments around the team. Thankfully, there were no cameras at the track for the qualifying days and practice before today, that is when Greyson is the worst. It's the reason they all feel he is just trying to do it to get under Lola's skin.

They drank their drinks in silence as the track woke up. It would be a few hours before cars got running since the opening ceremony started at noon. But there were crews setting things up and getting the track prepped.

"There you are." Gideon broke their silence as he came out of the truck. He was fully dressed for the day and Lola shifted on his lap as she saw him.

"Dang, he found us hiding out in the open, I told you Slade it was too easy." She laughed as Gideon came over.

"Brat." Gideon held the back of her head as he kissed her hard. Lola just smiled as Gideon broke their kiss.

"If you want coffee or food, the driver's tent is up and running." Lola settled against him again as Gideon looked around.

"I think I will go grab something." Gideon smiled at them as he headed towards the tent. This was the way everyone came out of the truck. Eventually they were all around the pits with coffee and some form of food. As they talked about the day more and more people showed up at the track Slade expected Lola to get up at some point, but she didn't.

"Good morning, everyone." Jason's voice was cheerful as he and Duke came around the side of the truck.

"Good morning." Lola chimed with a big smile on her face.

"How are you all feeling? Sleep well?" Jason gave Lola a knowing look and just smiled at her as she nodded and took a sip of her coffee. While Duke was more like her dad, Jason was the cool uncle or older brother who just liked seeing her happy, with a side of hurt-her-and-die to him also.

"Good to hear. Gates open in an hour. All drivers get one test run down the track this morning so get ready and head to the lanes." Duke's words made Lola feel tense in his lap and he rubbed her back.

"You got this Angel. Go change and we will get the cars ready." He tapped her ass a little and she met Toby at the door of the truck.

The crew got to work. They had the cars already out since they were here last night, and he joined Gideon and Emory to get theirs ready. Firing up the cars to warm up made the adrenaline hit him hard. This was their shot, and he was excited about what this meant for them as a team. But when Lola came out of the truck with her grey and teal fire suite with Toby in his orange and black behind her, a new wave of excitement came over him.

They were both smiling, and she looked excited, no more of the girl trying to hide her fear of the wall. She looked ready and he hoped she was not faking this look.

"You look incredible, Angel. Feel ready?" Slade pulled her into him, she wouldn't be able to lie to him if he was touching her.

"I feel beyond ready." She was telling the truth, and he kissed her quickly before anyone came over. The cars drew attention, and he knew after her wreck all eyes would be on her first few runs.

"Good, cars are ready, lets go racing." He was ready and she skipped to her car and team.

They all gave her hugs and high fives as she got into her car. Toby was getting into the seat with Emory there to do final checks. He could see Gideon unable to help checking Lola's harness straps, since the first track day he always double checked them for her.

Slade went behind their car and pulled the pins for the parachutes and saw Kip do the same, they walked over to each other and tapped them together before putting them in their pockets.

"Glad someone has superstitions like me." Kip smiled at him as the cars began to back out.

"Always." He looked into Lola's car as she backed out and she gave him a salute and he just shook his head. She was ready, the confidence she had was radiating off her at this point. The girl who only a few months ago was shaking so hard just sitting in the car was gone.

They all headed to the staging lanes and Lola and Toby were first in line. She chose the lane away from the wall. Tayler and Gideon were in the staging area as they warmed up their tires. They pulled both cars forward and Slade was having a hard time standing still.

The lights dropped and both the cars launched perfectly. Lola overtook Toby easily but that was not the point. The time flashed a 6.5

for Lola and an 8.8 for Toby and they all made excited sounds. If they could pull those out all day, they would be in perfect range to win the event. With the bracket style racing they would have to make sure to stay in their levels.

Lola qualified 3rd last week for her bracket and while they expected her to be mad, she had been happy with that spot. Toby had gotten 2nd place in their bracket, and they were good with the adjustments they made since then. Both had faster times now than their qualifying times.

They made their way back to the pits before the cars came down the return lane, but he knew when Lola went past. The people that were in the stands cheered so loud they could hear them in the pits.

"They love her you know." Duke stood beside him as he watched the cars coming towards them.

"It's hard not to." He turned to Duke and saw the admiration for Lola in his eyes. He may not be her dad, but he loved her like his own.

"You boys hurt her, and I swear I will make it look like an accident." The seriousness in his voice made him nod.

"I hope you do." He walked toward Toby and their car as he pulled into their pit.

"Fuck that is amazing." Toby pulled his helmet off and hugged them all before going over to Lola's pit.

She was getting a round of hugs as well and Toby went right in and grabbed her and spun her around.

"Best feeling ever chasing you down sweet girl, god I don't ever want to not do that." Toby kissed her as he set her back down.

The mood was amazing right here, it felt right and perfect. They celebrated and decided they did not need another run before the event. The gates opened and the pit area was flooded with people, it was only open at the beginning of the event and at the end thankfully. Lola looked incredible, she had pulled the top of her suit off and was just in the sports bra under.

She was signing autographs and taking pictures with as many people as she could. When a group of little girls came up, she pulled them under the ropes of the pits and had them get in her car. Her team went and grabbed some extra shirts, and she signed them for the girls. In a brief moment she looked up at him and smiled the best smile in the world. She lived for these moments, and Slade could see her world light up with those little girls. That was it, he thought he was hooked on this girl before. but now, he was sure.

Chapter 26

Lola

Qualifying 3rd meant Lola was in a good starting spot for the races when they started. With a 16-car roster she would be in the second half of the races and the second to last to go. She knew the guys were surprised when she was ok with this starting spot. But this gave her a chance to watch the others from the pits. Had she been 1st she could have been nervous as hell. Was she happy Greyson was first, no but she couldn't change that.

After gathering for the opening, they all came back to the pits. Toby was on the other side of the bracket for his races as well, so they were all in her pits watching the live stream of the races on the tv on the side of the truck. Duke and Jason were with them as they watched Greyson head down the track, he beat his opponent, but he only hit a 6.7 and it made her laugh.

"I am going to have a heart attack if it is you two in the finals Magnolia." Duke looked worried and she felt it now.

"Want me to peddle it in the semis if he gets that far?" She as joking and knew he would never ask her to do that but the concern on his face looked like he was about to say yes.

"Never. I just won't watch." Duke pulled her in for a hug as the next racers got ready for their run.

The next races were close to the same as the drivers' qualification times. She was in the zone now though, but she could not sit still. She got up and went to the covered area of their pits and grabbed her headphones. The first half of Toby's bracket still had to go but she needed to do her warmups and find that centered part of herself. Stretching, she began her routine, a light jog for the length of the truck and trailer back and forth about 20 times. Each time on the turnaround she did a few squats or jumping jacks. Just before she was done, she saw Emory watching her and it took all she had not to stop early.

"She's getting in the zone; don't worry she's fine always has done this. Usually, she runs the pits so be happy she stayed here." She could hear Tayler explain to Emory when her music changed songs.

Tayler was right, she would usually run the pits, but she didn't want to run into anyone else right now. 'Champion' by Carry Underwood came on and it was her power song, she walked over to the car as it came on. She sat in her seat listening to the song with her eyes closed, her playlist was perfectly timed and when Tayler handed her helmet into the car, she knew it was time.

"Thanks." She said, handing her headphones to him and getting ready to go. The only change was after Tayler checked her harnesses Gideon was right there and it made her smile.

"You're good Doll, kick ass, go fast, and enjoy the ride." Gideon tapped the harnesses and gave her the thumbs up.

"Lola, you ready?" Duke's voice came into her helmet, and she just shook her head, he would of course not be able to step back on this part.

"Yes, let's go," she said Tayler's voice came to her now, they must both have a head unit today.

Tayler backed her out of the pits, and she headed to the staging lanes. She knew the driver in the 14th spot, and he was a few seconds slower than her. It would not be a chase, and she was ready. She was not on the wall, and it made her feel even better.

They moved into the burnout box, and she got ready to go. Tayler moved her up to the lines and she waited for the other driver.

"You got this." Tayler said to her as he tapped her window walking back to the middle watching area.

She staged and watched the light. On the green she let the car fly, she felt fast as she shifted through the gears. Before she knew it, she was at the end and pulling the parashoot out of habit. It felt just like it had before, she felt like she never had an accident, and nothing was different.

But it was different because now all she wanted to do was make it back to the pits in time to watch Toby's run.

"Bunny, you killed it. Fuck you are back baby!" Tayler screamed through her helmet, and she just smiled.

At the end of the track, the attendants helped with the parachute, and she was on the return lane past the stands.

"Take your helmet off Lola." Tayler said and she did. The sound from the crowd overwhelmed the sound of the car as she slowly drove by them. Tears formed in her eyes, and she puts her hand out the window to wave at them all.

She loosened her harness as she got back to the pits. Duke is right there pulling her out of the car spinning her around as he does.

"Your amazing." He put her down and the team comes over and celebrates as well.

"What was the time?" That's all she cared about right now.

"6.5 just like practice." Tayler handed her the time slip and she smiled, her times were perfect.

She jumped for joy and Emory was by her side with Slade now. They hugged and then turned their attention to the screen. Toby's race was up, and everyone was focused on the screen. Gideon was lining Toby up after the burnout.

"Breath." Slade whispered to her, and she didn't realize she was holding her breath. His hands on her sides grounded her now.

She took a breath just as Toby left the line and pulled on his opponent. She watched him keep the car straight and the time flashed an 8.8 when he crossed the line. They all cheered as the winning light came on for his lane. This was a high she would never be able to come down from and she was ok with that.

Slade turned her around to face him and kissed her deeply. His hat tipping and she grabbed it from his head, turned it around and put it back on.

"Trouble." Slade said as Gideon came back into the pits followed by the car.

Gideon pulled her into his arms before anything else and hugged her tight.

"You were perfect, Doll. Everything I knew you would be today." Gideon dropped a kiss on her forehead and then went to Toby who was out of his car now.

She rushed over to him and launched herself into his arms, she didn't care that everyone could see her being affectionate with all of them. She loved them and she did not care if it had been such a short time.

"That was amazing." She kissed Toby's cheek as he put her down.

"Best feeling ever." Toby laughed as Emory came behind her and kissed her head before going to wrap up his parachute.

The teams all got ready for the next runs, and she was riding the high. She did not even think about it when she stepped in to help Marvin and Wyatt with the car. It was at this moment she realized there were a few cameras in the pits on her while she worked to get the car ready with the guys. Tayler came in and they talked about how the run felt and they decided not to change anything with the car.

Lining up for her second race she felt even better than the first run. She went through the same steps and when she won the race as well, the high she was feeling even better. By the time the semifinals came around she was filled to the brim with adrenalin. She felt like the car was faster than the other two runs, but she still had a 6.5 run, this won her the race and put her into the finals.

"He didn't make it! Lola you're not against Greyson in the final he was too slow." Kip scooped her up out of the car when she got back to the pits. They were all worried that she might have to run against him today but now she wouldn't have to.

She turned her attention to the screen to watch Toby's semifinal run and was excited to see him win his race as well. She could not help the celebration she let out when he got back to the pits. But now she was beginning to worry about her race. She would be on the wall side for the finals, which she had not been for any of the other races. She slipped into the truck to use the bathroom but while in there she grabbed her headphones again. She needed to fall into her mind a little and clear her thinking. This was the last part of healing for her.

To be able to run next to the wall and not freak out. But she wouldn't let that wall worry her, it was there to protect her not hurt her. Her car would go straight, and she would be done before she had time to think about it. She was seconds faster than the other car and she would win, winning her first race back would prove to everyone that she was back.

She came out of the truck and saw everyone waiting for her, but she waved them off and went over the final checks of the car with her headphones on still. She saw Tayler talking to Gideon and could see the others back off a little. She wasn't shutting them out because she didn't want their help, she just needed to be able to do it herself.

Kip tapped her and nodded towards the car, and she knew it was time to go get staged. She pulled her fire suit up, zipping it closed and climbed into the car. She pulled her headphones off and handed them to Tayler, who did not say a word to her, and she got strapped into the car. But as she went to take her helmet from him Gideon took it from him.

"I know you want to pull into yourself at this moment Doll but hear me ok. We all love you so much and are so proud of you for what you have done today. No matter what happens out there on this run that is not going to change, ok. You are safe in this car, you are strapped in correctly, the car is sound, and nothing is going to go wrong. Now go win so I can celebrate with you tonight." Gideon kissed her hard before handing her helmet over.

He did not give her time to respond as he shut her into the car, she pulled the helmet on and secured the neck brace. Taking deep breaths, she headed to the staging area. She could see the fans going

207

crazy in the stands and it helped her anxiety as she pulled into the burnout box by the wall. When she looked up and saw Duke and not Tayler pulling her forward, she calmed down even more.

"I got you Magnolia, you got the car, but I got you ok." Duke's voice came to her ears, and she focused on the lights as she staged.

"You do exactly what you have been doing all day and give these people a good race. You're faster than he is, and this will be an easy win." Duke gave her the thumbs up and double tapped the car as he passed.

The only thing she heard now was her car as she watched the lights drop. She let herself feel the car and be in the moment with it. She looked straight forward as she shifted through gears and then shut the car down at the end of the track. She knew she had won but the track attendants' excitement as they put her parachute on the car confirmed it. She left her helmet on as she drove back to the pits to hide the tears she felt flowing from her eyes.

At the pits she did not unlatch the door or shut the car off after pulling in. No one moved to make her get out and she pulled the helmet off and just cried in the car. She had beaten the wall, she controlled her car, she won, and no one was ever going to take this feeling away from her ever again.

Chapter 27

Toby

They had made it to the track late last night for their 6th race out of the 21 for the season. Toby was second in his bracket for lead while Lola and Greyson were tied up currently. The energy in the truck on the drive here was a little tense with Lola being frustrated but not talking to them about whatever was bothering her.

Duke and Jason were regular fixtures at the races, but they were not with them on travel days, and he wondered if not having Duke around was upsetting her. He found Tayler up before anyone else drinking his coffee out front of the truck set up.

"Morning." Toby said to him after shutting the door.

"Morning, though I still feel like I should be asleep." Tayler looked a little worse for wear today.

"I feel that, but this is the best time for testing the cars." He hated that it was true. Their testing and track times were important to get an accurate read on the cars.

"True, doesn't mean I like it anymore." He laughed while taking a chair next to Tayler.

"I have a question for you." Toby was nervous.

"Why do I feel like this is going to be a Lola question that puts me in a difficult situation?" Tayler was on to him already.

"It's not bad, it's just something I noticed. It seems like she is frustrated with us. I know with the points where they are it can be frustrating and that last race taking second to Greyson made her very mad. But she seems to be more on edge when Duke is not around. Do you think she is mad at him for not being on the road with her?" He hated the thought, but it was the only thing he could think of.

"It's could be, I don't really know. You should just ask her." Tayler closed up with his answer and it was more telling than the answer given.

"Is she mad at something we did?" Toby needed to know now for sure.

"Listen ok, she is my best friend before she is my driver. There is no way I am going to tell you what is up with her without her telling me I can. That girl is scary when you make her mad ok. So, talk to her ok." Tayler got up and headed back into the trailer without another word on the issue.

But Tayler's comment made him think. There was nothing that happened this last week that Toby could think would have made Lola mad at them all. Hell before the last race they all had a moment alone with her to alleviate some of the sexual tension they were struggling with due to sharing a trailer with the whole team.

He was going to have to talk to the others about it, but they were still asleep. So, he headed to the driver's tent to grab food and get the day started. By the time he was back the others were up, but everyone was getting ready for the day and time got away from him. After lunch and before the first race of the day he was able to get Gideon alone for a moment.

"Have you noticed Lola being frustrated with us today?" Toby asked as he pulled his fire suit on.

"Yes, but I cannot think of why she would be like this. I asked the others and they said they couldn't think of anything else either." Gideon looked worried.

"I asked Tayler this morning and he said to ask her myself, he wouldn't break friend code basically." He saw the realization on Gideon's face.

"Shit, we fucked up somewhere. We need to talk to her." Gideon headed out of the trailer but when he got out there, he couldn't see Lola anywhere.

"She is on her run; she'll be back." Tayler told them seeing their surprise to Lola being gone.

They must have really done something if she was running the pits. She had been doing her warmups in their pit this whole time. But now it just felt like she was putting distance between them, and it was not sitting right with him.

The pits became a mad house as they got ready to go for their first runs of the day and they were unable to talk with Lola before their runs.

Waiting in the lanes behind her Toby just felt terrible about how she was feeling. They might not have been together for long, but this felt so unlike her. She didn't keep things from them like this, there was a level of trust they had achieved so quickly.

He watched as she did her first run but when the time read 6.8, he realized something was off. She was consistently at a 6.5 or higher at this point.

"What's up with Lola's run?" He asked Gideon over the radio.

"Tayler is saying she felt the transmission slipping at the end.

211

She still won her race." Gideon's answer calmed him a little. It sucked that her car was not running right but he was glad she was ok.

On his turn up he killed his run getting an 8.5 putting him as the fastest for the day in his bracket. As he pulled into the pits there was chaos all around.

Lola's car was up on jack stands and her entire team was working around it. There were cameras on the other side of the roped off area and as he walked over, he could see what the commotion was about.

"Kip I need a longer extension." Lola yelled from under the car. All you could see were her checkered Vans sticking out from under the car. She was out of her fire suit and her long bare legs were mostly hidden by the car.

"Here." Kip came over and handed her an extension and waited for her next instruction.

"Alright all my bolts are out. Get me the creeper so I can move it out from under the car." Lola was commanding as she worked, and it made him hard as fuck.

Wyatt moved the creeper under the car, and he could see Lola moving around to get what he assumed was the transmission onto the tool to get it out from under the car. As she wiggled out from under the car covered in grease, he had to stop himself from grabbing her.

"Fuck Sweet girl look at you." He smiled at her, but she gave him a look that said she was not happy with his presence there.

"Got a problem with a girl doing the dirty work Toby?" She snarked at him as the rest of her team swapped the old transmission for the new one, they kept in the trailer.

"No problem at all, I was just saying how incredibly hot you look covered in grease." He was very confused by her frustration.

"Well, that's what happens when you have the smallest hands to get the bolts out, I guess." She turned to look back at the team who were now taking their positions to get the new transmission in place.

"We will get it installed and you can put that last bolt back in for us ok." Wyatt told her as he slid under the car.

"Thanks Wile E, let me know when you need me." She was nice to them, so her frustration was solely towards him.

"Angel, are we ok?" Slade was there now after getting his car set up to cool down before his next run.

"Yeah, just fine." Lola snapped.

"Doesn't sound like it. Are you frustrated about the run or is there something else?" Slade asked, reaching out to her.

"Of course, it would be the run. So sorry to disappoint you on my time, sorry to lose your bet." Lola lashed out to him and quickly disappearing to the back of the pits where the cameras were unable to see her.

"What the fuck." Slade said before following her. Toby nodded to Gideon and Emory to follow them as he walked over towards Lola.

"What are you talking about Lola? What bet?" Slade was mad but he could see his friend pulling back because he was talking to Lola.

"Don't act like I am some dumb blonde Slade. I know your betting against me." Her words hurt him deeply.

"The fuck we are." Slade was losing his control.

"Hey, hold on, start from the beginning Lola." Gideon put a hand on Slade's shoulder to get him to calm down.

"Greyson told me how he overheard you all talking with some other teams about betting on my times and chances of keeping the same consistency over the season. He said he heard you all bet that I would keep them up and that you would win big time for it." Toby had never seen her this angry and the fact that Greyson was behind it made him see red.

"Magnolia, I swear to you that is not how that conversation went." Gideon stepped towards her, and she stood her ground.

"Why should I care Gideon? Am I just a way to win some more money? Are you using me, is that what this is?" She waved between them all.

"Enough, no you know that is not what this is. God damn it I am going to kill Greyson." Gideon was losing it now and he was not sure how this was going to go.

"Lola, first we will always bet on you winning because you are our girl. Second, we do have a bet with the team on when we think you will get a new personal best, but there is no money riding on it." Emory, of course, stepped in to explain to her, he could see her start to soften towards them.

"Why?" She was still mad, but he could see her trying to understand them.

"Because we are guys and betting on things is part of how we function." He answered before the others could. All he got from her was a glare.

"Lola we were betting on the losers having to pay for your tattoo at the end of the season ok. We are all so sure you are getting a new one that when we were talking about it, we came up with the bet. I am sure that is what Greyson overheard the other day." Emory moved closer to her holding his hand out to her trying to get her to come to him.

"Seriously?" She dropped the anger now.

"Yes, Angel. Even Duke and Jason are in on it. The only one who doesn't know about it is Tayler." Slade's explanation made her laugh.

"Of course, that would explain his preaching about how no guy is good enough. Fuck I am sorry." Lola took Emory's hand letting him pull her into a hug.

"Lola, we need you." Sam's voice called breaking them up.

"Ok Yosemite be there in a second." She called back.

"Hold on, before you go, I have to say this to you. Magnolia Rae, I swear there is never going to be something that we keep from you like this ok. I also need you to understand how hurt I am because of your lack of trusting us with this. I love you so much, I would do anything is the world for you. But you cannot hold on to something like this again." Gideon took her face in his hands as he talked to her. His use of her full name made even Toby feel intimidated by Gideon.

"I am sorry, I was just so frustrated when he told me. I was stuck in my head about it." Lola had tears in her eyes, she understood how much she had hurt them.

"I understand that, but we don't work if you keep these sorts of things from us. Beyond that why would you believe that jack ass over us?" Gideon pulled her into him now holding her tight.

"I don't know why I believed him. I have known him for years and I think I just slipped and forgot what he did to me for all those years. He was talking about how he still cares for me and how he is worried about me with you all. I know logically that all those things are false, but this dark part of my brain latched onto it." Lola looked so upset with herself.

215

"Sweet girl, there are going to be changes in every relationship. You are learning that you can trust us in a way that is different from what you thought was trust before. We have seen how Greyson is with you. The way he talks to you makes my skin crawl thinking about how long he was trying to control you like that. But like Gideon said, you have to come to us about these things so we can talk about them." He hated that she felt she needed to keep these things to herself.

"I am sorry." Lola sniffled and it broke his heart. All of them went over and gave her a group hug, knowing they were running out of time.

"Lola, we really need you." Wyatt's call for her broke them all away.

"Alright go out there and fix your car so you can get back out there." Gideon kissed her forehead as he let go of her.

"I love you guys too." She smiled at them as she walked back towards the car.

"That sucked." Emory looked defeated.

"It did, I don't think any of us realized how much Greyson got into her head while they dated." He hated the thought, but it was evident that it still troubled her.

"We need some time with her alone soon. Our halfway break is not close enough." Gideon was right.

"Let me talk with the others. Maybe we can take the car and go to a hotel tonight and drive to meet up with them tomorrow. I think one night away might help." Emory was on top of it already and he loved that his friend could jump to take care of their girl without needing to much help from them.

"You get on that while we go see if they need any of our help also." Slade headed towards Lola's team and Toby and Gideon followed him out leaving Emory to plan. They were going to make it up to their girl no matter what the situation was. But they needed to finish the day out strong first.

Chapter 28

Lola

Somehow even after a blown-up transmission Lola was in the finals, and unfortunately it was the first time she would be up against Greyson. Trying to focus on the last race was starting to rattle her brain and she was not sure she was going to be able to get in the car. Everyone else was working on last minuet things for the last run while she was in the trailer trying to calm her mind.

Even with her music she was having issues focusing on calming her nerves. Today had been long and exhausting so far with the car breaking down and then the thing with the guys. It all felt like to much to deal with right now. The door to the trailer opened but she didn't turn to see who it was.

The tattooed arms of Gideon pulled her back close to his chest as her headphones were taken off.

"Doll they are ready for you." Gideon said kissing her cheek.

"I can't do it Gideon; I am going to drop the race and take the DNF for today." She was convinced this was the only option.

"You can do it. There is nothing out there that is going to hurt you." His words calmed her a little, but it was not working the way she wished they would.

"No, we are tied in points, and he is not going to be ok with me winning plus he is wanting a perfect weekend. After his comments I am sure he is already feeling the pressure to push in front of me in points." She hated thinking like this, but it was how her brain was working right now.

"Lola, you can do this. You have never had a DNF in your entire career and you are not going to start today after all the work you have done." He was right but it didn't matter to her.

"I can't Gideon. Look, I can't stop shaking." She held up her hand showing him how bad her hands were shaking now.

"Listen to me." He turned her around to face him.

"You have beaten him before; you are in a position to win this season if you keep going how you are right now. He is not going to try what he did before, it's possible someone will question it. As much as I hate him, he is not stupid to try that. So, you are going to go out there, get into that car and win this race. Because after you do that, Emory has a surprise planned for you and if he doesn't get to take care of you, he is going to lose his mind." Gideon looked at her with his blue eyes boring into her soul. These men were meant for her, and she was beginning to see it more and more each day.

"Ok. But can you be on the radio with Taz?" She needed extra support.

"I might have to fight Duke for it, but I will be there." Gideon made her laugh because she knew Duke was probably freaking out right now.

They headed out of the trailer to join the others. No one talked about what was about to happen, as if they all felt the same way she did right now. She got into her car and started to strap herself in, waiting for Tayler to hand her helmet in.

"Listen, I am not going to tell you to lose this race but so help me god if it looks like that idiot is coming into your lane shut it down Magnolia. I don't care about the damage to the car, you make sure you are in a safe position to avoid getting hurt." Duke was there with her helmet.

"I will do what I can." She couldn't think of anything else to say. She knew the car would keep her safe but Duke being worried made her worry even more.

"I will be on track with Tayler ok." Duke handed her helmet in and patted her leg.

Gideon came to the door next and checked her harness straps but did not say anything to her. He shut her into the car, and she could see Kip behind the car with Slade as they tapped the parashoot pins and giving her the thumbs up. Everyone else was in front of the car waiting for her to head out to the staging lanes. Taking a shaky breath, she gave them her salute and began to back up the car.

"You are not on the wall Bunny, so crush the burnout and do what you do best." Tayler let her know her placement and she had to wonder if Duke had intervened with her position.

"Before you ask, yes I had it changed do not argue with me." Duke made her laugh because he was always going to know how she was thinking because he was her person for so long.

"I love you guys." She couldn't help the shakiness in her voice as she pulled into the burnout box. The red car of Greyson lining up next to her, but she looked straight forward ignoring everything around her.

"For the first time this season we have teammate against teammate on the track for the win. In the left lane in the red dodge we have Greyson, with the top qualifying spot for the weekend he is going for those extra perfect weekend points. In the right lane Lola Bunny with the 2nd place qualifying spot is going to try to upheaval Greyson's attempt at that perfect weekend that we have yet to see this season." The announcement was loud enough for her to hear, and it made the shaking in her hands get worse.

"Don't think about it Doll, it's just a regular race nothing special about it." Gideon's voice made her smile as she got staged with Tayler lining her up.

She did not respond, just taking deep breaths focusing on the lights. As they dropped, she launched the car like she would usually. Shifting and keeping her focus on the end of the track. As she passed the end, she pulled the parashoots and glanced back to see that she had won.

"You did it! You beat him!" Tayler was yelling on the radio.

"Great job Magnolia, now get back to the pits so we can celebrate." Duke was all business to her best friend's excitement.

Back in the pits everyone was going crazy, there were camera crews all around to catch the moment between the teams. She got out of her car and was swept up by Tayler who basically passed her along the team. Each spinning her around and telling her they knew she could do it. She was looking over the time slip to see that she had a 6.2 run which was the best they had run the car so far.

"Fastest run so far!" Tayler was still celebrating. But she had turned her focus to the tv to see Toby's run. He was a second slower than the other car but would take second for the weekend.

"Lola, how does it feel to get a win today?" One of the reporters asked her and she walked over to the fence.

"It feels great. The team behind me is the best and I couldn't ask for a better one." She gushed about them.

"This is your fastest run of the season so far, do you think you are close to the max for the car?" the reporter asked.

"I think the car can do more, crazy I know. But I know Sam is working his hardest with all the data and stuff to make this the fastest car of the year." She really was so happy to break out of the same pace they were in so far.

"Do you think your driving is better this year compared to previous years?" The question caught her off guard a little.

"I think I grew as a driver last year. A wreck like mine would make most step away, but I saw it as a growth opportunity. I had to learn to trust my car again, and trust that my team has my back when building that car. I think that trust allows me to get in a different head space yes." She really did feel more connected to her car this year.

"How about your relationship change? Does that have any effect on your driving?" She laughed because right then Toby was pulling back into the pits.

"If being happy in a relationship makes me drive better than I guess it does." Everyone laughed and they got some more photos before there was shouting behind her.

"You are not turning my car up the same way you are hers." Greyson was yelling at Sam still in his fire suit.

"Your car is at the point that you can handle it. You know that even though they are the same platform each car will perform differently. Lola's car handles more power put into it. You spin the entire way down the track if we turn it up." Sam was not yelling, but the conversation was drawing attention.

"So, what are you saying I can't drive a car turned up as high as hers? That's bull shit and you know it. I am the best driver on this team, and I deserve the best car as possible." Logan and Ripley were here now behind Greyson as he continued to yell at Sam.

"I am not saying that." Sam was standing firm, but Kip and Marvin were there now behind him.

"That's exactly what you are saying. You think she can handle her car better than me." Greyson pushed Sam now and she moved towards the altercation.

"Hey, stop, go cool off. Quit being a sore loser. We all win some and lose some." She pushed in between Sam and Greyson.

"A sore loser? That's bull shit and you know it. I am a better driver than you, any day, in any car. You are their little Lola Bunny, wrapped around their fingers. You get the better car and I get shit. God it's all your fault with your bull from last season." Greyson grabbed her arm, and all hell broke loose.

Sam punched Greyson then Logan and Ripley swung at Sam, only to meet Kip and Marvin blocking them. Lola was pulled out of the way and realized Wyatt had pulled her out of the middle of it. While they beat the crap out of each other she kept screaming at them to stop. Finally, Duke and Tayler came over and got everyone pulled apart, but the damage was done. The media was going to have a field day with this.

"What the hell do you think you are doing. We are a team; we do not fight within this team." Duke was yelling at them all after he finally got everyone to the back part of the pit away from the media, even though they could still hear them.

"That's a joke. A team wouldn't be treating one member

223

better than the other." Greyson shouted and stood up before Duke pushed him back into his seat.

"Enough, you know we are working with your car to get more power out of it. You also know that your driving style is different to Lola's, and we have to work with that. I know you were hoping for a perfect weekend, but this is not how you are expected to act after a loss." Duke was absolutely terrifying right now, and when Slade ran his hand along her arm, she shivered hard.

"This is crap, ever since last season I have been getting shit on here." Greyson was on a roll.

"Keep it up and you are going to be on probation with the team." Jason finally spoke up from where he was sitting. Greyson did not argue with him after that, taking his seat with his team.

"Good, now you all need to get to the podium. Teams stay here and start cleaning up and stay the hell away from each other." Duke instructed them.

They all headed out of the tent. Gideon came with them, but Toby held her hand the whole way keeping their distance from Greyson. Of course, when they got to the podium the media was going crazy and she did her best to just smile and not make comments to them.

"You know what I said was true. You are getting special treatment and it's not fair that I have been shunned because of your choices Lola." Greyson said to her as she watched Toby get his 2nd place trophy.

"You did it all on your own Greyson." She walked away from him before he could respond because she was done with his thoughts on this.

She met up with Gideon and Toby before heading back to the pits." She was exhausted and ready to crash into her bed and sleep for hours.

"I am going to go change. You guys let me know if I can help with clean up," she said to them as they got back to the pit.

"No help needed. But you need to pack an overnight bag love." Emory said to her as she heading past him.

"Why? We don't have a break for a few weeks." She definitely needed one but halfway was not here yet.

"Don't worry about it. Just pack and come back out." Emory kissed her and pushed her into the trailer.

Inside the trailer she hurried to get changed and packed. She threw some of her nicer clothes into a bag not knowing what they were going to be doing. It was still late afternoon so they could be going to do anything at this point. Usually, she would shower after a race, but she was too curious to see what was going on to bother with that right now.

Running her brush through her hair after pulling out the braid and throwing it into her bag, she had everything. Slipping on her Vans and grabbing her phone, she headed out of the trailer. She saw the track hawk unloaded and raised her eyebrow to Gideon who was watching the team load up the cars.

"You guys packed up quick," she said joining them to see that Toby's car was already loaded as were their tools and gear.

"We have somewhere to be tonight. Say goodbye to the guys you will see them tomorrow." Gideon said to her as the team looked up from what they were working on.

"Bye guys." She waved to them getting a laugh from them all.

Gideon was guiding her over to the car as they all told her to have a good night.

Gideon took her bag and opened the passenger door for her to get in. Emory was already in the driver's seat with Toby in the far back third row and Slade in one of the captain's chairs.

"I can sit in the back, so you guys have more room." She offered but Emory pulled her into a kiss.

"We are fine Angel." Slade said as Gideon got into the back with them taking the other captain's chair.

"So where are we running off to?" She was going to at least try and figure out what was going on.

"It's a surprise. You have time to take your after-race nap so just get comfortable." Emory started to drive out of the track, with her music going already. It was not long before she was asleep between the music and being comfortable in the car.

Chapter 29

Lola

"Hey, love wake up we are here." Emory's voice was soft to wake her up nicely and she appreciated it.

"Where are we?" She sat up in the seat of the car and rubbed her eyes to wake up all the way.

"We found an Airbnb to stay at tonight. It's about halfway to the next stop. Duke gave us the day off tomorrow. Sam is going to run the tests on the cars for us when they get there." Emory was pulling up to a small cottage nestled in the woods. The east coast was a gorgeous place to be able to explore but with their tight schedules they did not have time to do that.

"Emory, this place is amazing." She was in awe over how simple the cottage looked.

"It was easy to find a little one-bedroom place and since that's all we really need I booked it, then got clearance with Duke. We figured even if we only had the night to ourselves that it would be enough." Emory pulled the car into the driveway and turned it off.

"This is perfect. Seriously this is amazing." The whole thing brought a tear to her eye.

"What's wrong love?" Emory of course noticed.

"It's just I feel so bad about earlier and then this. I just feel so lucky. Like how are you guys real?" She laughed as she wiped the tear away.

"Oh, we are real Angel. Wait till we get you all to ourselves after sharing space with people for the last six weeks." Slade laughed as he got out of the car.

"Gideon is going to go grab some food from the little town while you take a shower or bath ok. Just wait till you see the bathroom." Emory was excited as he got out of the car.

"There are a few choices in town anything you are specifically wanting?" Gideon asked as he got out of the car letting Toby climb out as well.

"Not really, nothing to greasy the track food has been so greasy this year." She usually did not care about it, but it had been making her feel off recently.

"Something fresh and on the healthy side got it. Enjoy your cleaning up time sweet girl." Toby kissed her as he helped her out of the passenger's seat and took it from her as Gideon got into the driver's side. Slade had their bags and was waiting for Emory to lead them into the house.

She followed them inside and was shocked to see that the back of the cottage was all glass overlooking the forest. It was a simple design inside with a living room and small kitchen. Emory walked them right to the bedroom and the large bed almost took up the entire room with a large bay window looking out at the back as well.

"Come check the bathroom out love." Emory called her over and she looked into the attached bathroom. While the rest of the house was simple and what you would expect out of the location the bathroom looked like it was out of a resort.

"This is amazing." She walked to the shower that was the length of the wall with the bathtub inside.

"I figured you would like it." Emory kissed her neck when he came behind her.

"Shower and we will get everything unpacked." Slade said to her as he dropped their bags on the bed.

"Unpack?" She looked at Emory. Slade left the room with a smirk on his face, they were up to something.

"We grabbed some snack foods and stuff to make breakfast in the morning. Just relax and we will come get you when the others are back with food." Emory kissed her and left her as well. She heard the bedroom door shut and went to find her bag.

As she pulled out her shower things, she decided to just take a bath. Gathering her things, she went back into the bathroom and began to get the water warm in the tub. She was scrolling on her social media and the clear news was the fight from today. She decided to post a photo of Toby and her on the podium with their trophies with the caption 'So grateful for all the hard work of the team for today's win even after the issues with the car.' Setting the phone down with some music playing before she climbed into the warm tub.

The water was getting cold, so she pulled the plug on the tub and started up the shower to actually wash off. As she was washing her hair, she heard the door to the bedroom shut and assumed dinner was ready.

"Look at you, perfection." Slade was sitting on the edge of the sink watching her when she opened her eyes.

"Why don't you join me to see if it can get better?" She was definitely in the mood to have them all and was missing having them at her disposal.

"There is not time for that, I was sent to get you for dinner." He smirked at her, and she knew she could tempt him.

"Seems like a terrible choice to send you." She turned the water off and grabbed the towel on the hook, wrapping it around her body.

"Oh, and why is that, Angel?" Slade just watched her with a hooded gaze as she walked towards him.

"Well, it seems like you don't care about eating dinner right now, maybe you want to start with desert." She took the towel off and dried her hair off a little before stepping in front of him.

"Oh, I would love nothing more than to start with desert, but Gideon would punish me for that, and I am not the one on the list for that tonight." Slade's words made her shiver as he reached out and palmed one of her boobs.

"He is mad about today?" She knew it was going to happen.

"He is upset still yes, and you know him well enough to feel that a punishment is justified." Slade kissed her quickly and got off the counter.

"Save me." She begged.

"Oh no, not going to work. You can't get out of it by begging me or the others we don't work like that you know it. Now get dressed and out to dinner before you're in more trouble." He left the bathroom, and she was equally excited and terrified of what awaited her tonight.

Lola finished towel drying her hair and put on all her skincare before grabbing a t-shirt and a pair of shorts. In the living room the guys had laid out dinner on the coffee table and her stomach growled loudly as she smelt the food.

"Someone is hungry." Toby laughed from the kitchen; he was in just sweatpants as he brought drinks into the living room.

"I guess I didn't eat enough at lunch." She thought about it more and realized she missed lunch.

"You didn't eat lunch." Gideon grumbled at her as she took a seat on a pillow on the floor. There were two small chairs where Emory and Gideon were already sitting both in sweats as well. Slade was on the couch but there was not a lot of space there.

"I guess I forgot." She reached for one of the bottles of water.

"We grabbed Italian, there are a few different types of pasta and then a big salad also if you just want that." Gideon reached for the containers, beginning to open them.

"Sounds good, maybe a little pasta and then the salad after you guys get some if you want." She did not want to eat all of it if they wanted some too.

"We got you your own Doll." Gideon handed her the larger take-out container, and she could smell the chicken on the salad.

"Thanks." She opened the container and added the dressing from the small container inside. They all ate and just talked about their runs and possible changes they wanted to make to their cars.

"How was your bath?" Emory asked her as she finished her salad.

"It was great. This place is amazing." She was seriously impressed with this house.

"I figured you would like the bathroom. I was thinking about trying to get the one at the house redone so it could have a shower like the one here." Emory just looked at her with a raised eyebrow.

"That seems pretty nice for a guest bathroom." She was not

going to read into this more than she should, she couldn't let her mind go there.

"It wouldn't be a guest room anymore; you need your own space." Emory was doubling down; they were going to have this conversation right now.

"Are you asking me to move into your house permanently?" She looked at them all now. Slade was watching her with a look that said she was going to be in trouble in a moment. Toby was just smirking at her, and Gideon looked like he was daring her to say no.

"We want you to be with us all the time. We understand that before the season there were different circumstances for why you joined us. Now that we are officially together, we would all like you to live with us at the house permanently." Gideon took over the conversation and she just sipped her water.

"I don't want to sell my house." She was attached to it and what would happen if they decided they didn't want to be with her anymore.

"Fine, we can rent it out if you want." Gideon had a challenge in his eyes, and she was not sure she wanted to push him anymore.

"Ok that sounds like a plan. Should we pick up? I think bedtime is coming up fast my nap was not that restful." She was lying through her teeth, but she was so horny that she was not going to be able to focus on anything else.

"We can go to bed, but we are not going to sleep. You have a punishment waiting for you Doll." Gideon stood up from the chair and walked over to where she was sitting.

"But I said sorry." She did not take his hand that was now outstretched to her.

"Oh, but sorry only gets you so far. You questioned our dedication to you Doll. That needs to be rectified." Gideon reached down for her hand, and she let him take it.

Lola let him pull her up from the floor and walk into the bedroom. She was sure the others were following but she did not dare look at them. Gideon was upset with her still and he needed this as much as her aching body did. There was something unlocked inside her by his control, something she never realized she needed.

"Take your clothes off and get on the bed. Hands and knees Doll." Gideon was pulling his shirt over his head, and she was distracted by his body for a moment.

Pulling her shirt over her head before her shorts, the moment Gideon realized she was not in underwear a sharp slap came on her ass.

"Fuck." She cried out of surprise.

"You are a brat aren't you, Doll. No underwear at dinner? Were you expecting your punishment?" Gideon got behind her and pulled her into him with an arm around her chest holding her still.

"I was." She was not going to lie; she wanted this punishment, maybe even needed it.

"How did you come to that conclusion?" Gideon pushed her onto the bed, forcing her into the position he wanted her in.

"Slade warned me that you were in a punishment type of mood after this afternoon." A slap on her ass made her core grow warm, she arched into the sting.

"Oh, he should have kept his mouth shut. Maybe he needs to be punished also?" Gideon ran his hand over her ass soothing the sting.

233

"He told me I couldn't avoid it." She had no clue how to respond to the question, to lost in the desire to have them all around.

"Toby what do you think? Should Slade have to sit out while we play with our girl?" She looked up to see Toby sitting on the window seat watching them.

"I think it would be a punishment for them both. She looks so needy right now. Slade's form of punishment might give her to much pleasure." Toby smirked at her, and she stuck her tongue out at him. A quick two slaps on her ass came from that move.

"Brat. Fine, Slade you can sit right there and watch till Toby thinks you have suffered enough to join us." Gideon slapped her again and she heard Slade groan as she moaned.

"Oh, make more noises like that and he is not going to make it love." Emory was in front of her and the thought of both the twins controlling her made her shiver. While Emory was usually soft and loving she had a feeling he was willing to do whatever his brother told him to do right now.

"Doll, do you think you deserve to suck Emory's dick?" She could feel Gideon's hand roaming her ass waiting for her answer.

"If that is what you would like. I want to show how sorry I am." She arched into Gideon's touch as he trailed his finger over her entrance.

"Good answer. Go ahead, show Emory how sorry you are." With Gideon's words Emory pushed his pants down. His hard length popping out already with a bead of pre cum on the tip.

She opened her mouth not daring to move from where Gideon had placed her. Emory pushed into her mouth, and she licked and sucked on him. The tastes and feeling of him in her mouth making her moan. It was not till being with them that she realized how much she enjoyed giving them head.

"Fuck Lola. You are perfect." Emory held her head and pushed into her mouth harder now.

"Harder, make her choak on it." Slade's voice called to them, but Gideon slapped her ass in response making her moan around Emory.

"Keep talking and your Angel is going to take the punishment for you." Gideon said as he pushed two fingers into her entrance causing her to arch into him begging for more. She knew this was a punishment, but she was desperate for them.

"Fuck." Slade groaned and she knew he could see Gideon punishing her with his slow pace. They both needed him to fuck her faster, but they were not going to get that.

She sucked on Emory harder and took him all the way back till she gagged a little. Gideon pulled his fingers out and spanked her twice and Emory pulled her off him.

"Shit." She cried out as Gideon landed two more spankings on her ass, the sting growing with each one.

"You know better." Gideon rubbed her ass now and she was about to lose it, she needed more.

"Please I am sorry, I should have talked to you. Please just fuck me. Please." She was beyond need as Gideon continued his slow pace with his fingers.

"I am not sure you understand yet, what do you think Toby?" Gideon pulled her hair a little to make her look right at Toby.

"I think she is sorry, but I don't think she is to the point you want her at." Toby's words made her shiver, and she felt her

235

release right there.

"Agreed." Gideon pushed a third finger into her but spanked her at the same time. The split between pain and pleasure blurring. She was lost to the desire of this man, she needed to show him she was sorry.

"Gideon, please. I won't do it again, I promise. Please I want to be a good girl for you." She was almost crying as he pulled out quickly.

Before she could catch her breath Gideon pushed into her with his dick hard and Emory was back in front of her. Taking Emory into her mouth the twins set a steady pace, giving her close to what she needed but not quite what she wanted. They picked up the pace and Emory began shoving her farther down his dick as Gideon slammed into her.

"Fuck Lola." Emory cried out as he spilled down her throat.

"Right there Doll, right there." Gideon slammed into her harder as Emory pulled out of her mouth and she swallowed his release down.

"Gideon!" She screamed when Gideon found his release with her at the same time. Her entire body felt on fire with sensation. She was theirs and did not ever want this to change.

Chapter 30

Toby

Watching Gideon and Emory punish their girl was almost too much for Toby tonight. She was already almost spent, and Slade was struggling to stay where he was sitting. Emory had a towel to clean Lola up knowing he was going to want to taste her.

"You ready for more love?" Emory kissed her before cleaning her up. She was still on her hands and knees; probably worried Gideon was not done.

"Yes please." She moaned and he went over to her.

"You think Slade can take watching me get another orgasm out of you sweet girl?" He trailed his finger down her back, she moved into his touch.

"I don't know is my punishment over?" She looked over to Gideon who was laying at the top of the bed now.

"Your punishment from me is done, but I think Slade should have to wait." Gideon was being mean tonight, and it made him laugh.

"Lay down Lola. Let me get a good taste of you sweet girl." Toby let her move before pulling her to the edge of the bed, displaying her right in front of Slade.

"Fuck you guys." Slade was not going to last much longer; it was surprising he was listening to Gideon at all.

"Just me after they say so babe." Lola answered but was quickly silenced with a kiss from Emory.

Gideon held her legs open for him, and he began to lick her. Each pass of his tongue Toby could tell how sensitive she was. This would not take long to get her to the breaking point again. He sucked on her sensitive nub causing her to arch into him, glancing up he could see Gideon pinching her nipples as Emory continued to make out with her.

"Oh, fuck Toby!" Lola pulled away from Emory as he sucked on her harder and pushed two fingers inside her warm center.

"Give me one good one and I will let Slade have his way with you." He said to her as he curled his fingers insider her finding the right spot.

"Fuck, Angel. Give it to him I need that sweet pussy to be mine." Slade was on the edge now he could hear it in his voice.

"Toby, fuck." Lola arched into him again and Gideon and Emory took her nipples into their mouth now. This took her over the edge and her release soaked his tongue as he pulled it out of her.

He moved away from her quickly knowing Slade was on the verge of taking her from them all already. As soon as he was out of the way Slade was there licking her and biting her center as he kissed and bit his way up her body. It was desire driven and animalistic, Toby could not remember the last time he had seen his friend in this state.

"God damn Angel you are intoxicating." Slade consumed her moans as he slammed into her. His friend had their girl tucked into him so close that you almost couldn't see her in his arms.

"Fuck, Slade please!" She cried out and Slade moved them quickly. Pulling Lola off the bed and turning her around fast and hard.

Slade pulled her ass up to him hard and began to slam into her with so much force Toby could tell Lola was struggling to catch her breath. They both were lost to their desire and watching it was making him need her at the same level.

"You up for sharing?" He caught Slade's eye, and he could see the answer.

"I am not going to be nice. Angel, do you want Toby at the same time as me?" Slade asked Lola slowing down.

"Yes, please I need it all." She answered. Gideon passed Slade the lube as he pulled out of Lola.

"Get on Toby, Angel." Slade was in charge now and he moved onto the bed so Lola could climb up.

Toby took her face in his hands as she lowered herself onto him. The moan that came from her making him jump a little inside her. He could tell when Slade began to work her up to take him in her ass. Her body tensed up a little before giving over to the pleasure she was feeling also.

"Oh fuck. Slade." Lola pulled away from their kiss sitting up a little as Slade entered her. Toby could feel her getting tighter as Slade pushed in, hell he could feel him a little as they shared her.

"Look at you taking him so well love, so full of dick." Emory was beside them kissing her as Slade let her adjust a little.

"You are so fucking tight." Slade pulled out and pushed in a little and then gave him the look that she was ready.

They set an unforgiving pace as they pound into their girl. She was moaning and crying out their names as they pushed her into another release. As she fell into him Slade did not quit chasing his own release and as he felt him finish Lola cried out again. She was in a state of floating with pleasure and every little touch was making her pussy tighten around him trying to take what it wants. With a few more thrusts into her he found his release as well.

"Fuck I love you sweet girl." Toby said into her neck as she lay on top of him completely spent.

"I love you too, all of you." She mumbled and he could tell she was out of it.

"Go wash up and we can go to bed." Emory was there helping Lola get situated. Lola looked at him as if she was going to ask why he didn't want her.

"I will get you in the morning love, no pouting I am completely happy with how this night went." Emory kissed her and helped her into the bathroom.

Gideon was coming back in with water, and they all took a drink. When Lola came back, they had her get in the bed before they all went to clean up as well. By the time they came back out she was passed out in the middle of the bed.

"If you don't think it's big enough the couch does pull out." Emory let them know as they got situated in bed with Lola. It was usually only two of them in bed with her but tonight just felt different.

"We will make it work," he said turning the light off and turning his back to Slade who was curled up next to Lola. Emory was on her other side with Gideon on the other side of him.

He was not sure how they managed to stay in the bed all night but when he got up in the morning before them all he laughed at how Lola was practically on top of Emory with Slade trying to pull her off.

Chapter 31

Slade

They were all on fire today, Lola and Toby were both in the top bracket for the event and they were getting ready to line up for their last races. After a streak of crappy qualifying and finishes for Toby it was great to be having a good weekend. Lola was on fire these past few weeks. She had won the last three of the 5 since running against Greyson and she had a great lead on him with 81 points to his 69.

Slade pulled the pins on Toby's parashoots, and Kip did the same with Lola's. They tapped them together and put them in their pockets. Tayler and Gideon backed them both up and they headed towards the staging lanes.

The rest of the teams headed up to watch the races, they were both set to have perfect weekends. They also had the next week off and they had gotten another house for them all for the week a day away from the next track, but on the beach this time, so they could relax. He was ready to have his girl to himself not in a truck for a while. Their night away a few weeks ago had shifted their relationship even more.

Being around her so much made him realize how head over heels he was for this girl, and he could see his friend felt the same. She had agreed to move in completely when the season was over, and they were all ready to have her in their home to make it hers.

The fans were going crazy as Lola pulled into the burn out box. They had been this way at every track they had been on the entire season. Her fans were some of the best and most respectful, though Slade was not sure if that was just how they always were or because she was surrounded by strong men the whole time.

They had been photographed kissing her and holding her and her fans were not upset about it for the most part. They had worried when the first photos of her kissing them all had come out, but no one seemed to care except Greyson, who was making comments about how she had to go get four guys to replace him. This along with his continued accusations about Lola getting special treatment was starting to get on Slade's last nerve.

"I think this is going to be her fastest lap, Sam and Tayler were talking about how they turned it up a bit for this since she is so close to that 6.0 mark." Emory said into his ear careful not to let others around hear them.

"I think so too, she is in the zone this week. Her reaction times are unbeatable, but that is always the case here with the track conditions." Lola had a different fire in her this week. Even her practice laps were faster than when she started this season.

Tayler lined her up and they watched as the lights dropped. Lola took off right as the last light came on it seemed and flew down the track. At the end the board flashed 6.00 and the crowd went wild, but Slade could not pull his attention off her car, her parashoots were not coming out. The other car was already almost stopped, and Lola's shoots were not out.

"Pull the shoots Angel," he said and realized he and Emory were moving down the return lane already.

When her shoots did not come out and then a cloud of dust came from the end of the track they moved into a run. The crowd was screaming but he did not stop with Emory at his side. Tayler and Gideon were on the golf cart on the track racing past them. Time meant nothing right now, she didn't pull her shoots. That means she went into the net at the end of the track close to 200 miles per hour.

As Slade got to the car Gideon and Tayler were pulling the door open and accessing her before the medics could get to her.

"Magnolia, are you ok? Fuck!" Gideon was yelling and Slade realized Lola was not responding to him. He rushed over to Gideon's side looking in to see her slumped in her harness.

"No! Angel, wake up right now!" He screamed lifting her visor on her helmet. Lola's eyes fluttered and he knew she was coming back to them.

"Fuck, that fucking hurt." Her voice was quiet, but she was there.

"What the hell, why didn't you pull your shoots?" He was yelling at her and only realized it when Gideon put a hand on his shoulder and a look that said calm down.

"I tried but it wouldn't come out." She said it and Slade moved to the back of the car.

"What the fuck. Tayler." He called him overlooking down at the pin in her parashoot.

"I took that out, its right here." Kip pulled the pins out of his pants pocket and looked at him; Slade hadn't realize the whole team was around them now.

243

"Somone put a pin back in her shoots," he said to Emory and Gideon who had backed away from the door to let the medics get Lola out.

"It's a team pin though look at the tag." Tayler pulled it out and sure enough it was a team tag but the red on the stitching meant it belonged to only one person. Each of their teams had special tags distinguished only by the stitching colors. Lola's was teal, Toby's was orange and Greyson's was red.

Slade grabbed the pin and heading away from the others. Gideon and Emory were screaming at him, but he was filled with rage. That ass hole had put his girl in danger and there was no denying it at this point. Tayler came up next to him in the golf cart.

"Get in." Tayler looked just as murderous as he felt, and he got into the cart.

They drove to Greyson's pit where when he saw them both he took off running. His team disappeared as well, and they knew they had been caught.

"Get back here you waist of air!" He screamed as he came around the corner and found Greyson trying to get into their truck.

Slade grabbed him by the back of his race suit and threw him on the ground. He kicked Greyson in the side and then began to sit on him. Hitting him once in the face before Greyson was able to roll them both. But Tayler was there to pull Greyson off him and land a few punches to his gut before Duke came around the corner.

"What the ever-loving fuck is happening here?" Duke yelled at them all.

"Tell him ass hole." He grabbed Greyson by the hair and turned his head to Duke.

"I didn't do anything; you can't prove it." Greyson tried to say

244

but Tayler hit him in the gut again.

"Fuck, fine. Logan put one of my parashoot pins back in Lola's shoot so it wouldn't pull when she tried." Tayler threw him on the ground at this point and Duke looked like he was going to kill him.

"Stay right here, you two make sure he doesn't move." Slade realized right now that Duke did not know about what had just happened on the track.

"She's ok, lost consciousness but she is ok." He called out to Duke who took their cart and took off.

As Duke took off Kip, Marvin, Wyatt, and Sam came around the corner with Logan and Ripley in their grips.

"Sit down now." Kip shoved Logan to the ground next to Greyson.

"She is not even that good." Logan said which got him a kick in the side from Marvin.

"She's only winning because they put more into her car than mine anyways." Greyson looked at Sam who just shoved Ripley down.

"She's winning because she can handle a turned-up car whereas you can't and threaten to blow it up any time we turn it up more than it is now." Sam said before leaning up against the truck.

"It was a 6.0 run by the way," he said to Sam who nodded, they couldn't even be happy about it now.

"Looks like you took away happiness from her again as far as a race goes." Tayler was holding himself back from kicking Greyson which was good considering Jason came around the corner at that moment.

"Good you got them all that makes my job easier. You three are fired immediately, your contracts and sponsorships disbanded at

245

this moment. The cops are also on their way to take you and press charges for attempted murder." Jason's words made them all try to get off the ground, but the team just pushed them back down.

"Attempted murder, fuck that. She wouldn't have died just been too scared to finish the season." Logan argued.

"That may be true but with how fast she was going there is no way to prove that it was only the parashoot you tampered with. If you had cut her brake lines, she would have hit the sand and net at 240 and possibly rolled. Even with safety equipment she could have died, just like last year." Jason looked at Greyson who was glaring at him now.

"That was a car failure." Greyson tried to argue again.

"Actually, we tore her car apart, there was no issue other than your paint on her right side of the car." Jason's words hit Greyson and the fear in his eyes was enough for Slade.

"You guys got this; I need to go make sure Lola is ok." Slade looked at Jason who just nodded to him to leave.

Heading towards the medical center in the middle of the pit area, Slade pulled out his phone. There were people everywhere and he was trying to get to them as fast as possible.

"We are still in the medical tent at the track. She is refusing to go to the hospital." Emory's voice was worried when he picked up the call.

"I am on my way back over. Jason fired the whole team." Slade jogged to the tent now and people moved out of his way when they saw him.

There were cameras all around the tent and the curtains had been shut all around to give Lola privacy and there was a guard at the entrance.

"No one is allowed to enter." The guy said to him blocking his way.

"I swear to every god known to man if you keep me from my girl, I will kill you." He threatened but the guard did not move.

"Let him in please." Lola's voice called and the guard looked at him questioningly still. Inside Lola was on a bed being looked over by the medical staff with Emory and Duke by her side.

"Let them take you to the hospital Angel. Please?" Slade rushed to her side and could see the bruises on her chest from her harness holding her in the car.

"I am fine just some bruises. Plus, I want to do the podium, it was a 6.0 and I won the event it was a perfect weekend." She was stubborn and he loved that she still had the fire in her right now.

"How about after the podium we go and get you checked out." Slade was bargaining with her now because he really needed to get her checked out, if not for him for Emory who looked like he was going to lose it.

"Deal." Lola stuck her hand out to him, and they shook on it before he took her face in his hands, and he kissed her.

"What happened anyways, why did the parashoot not deploy?" She had not been told, and he looked at Duke for guidance now.

"We will talk about that later Magnolia, rest now. I will come get you for the podium." Duke kissed her head and headed out of the tent. Just then he heard a car stop outside.

"I swear I will beat the shit out of you if you do not let me in there." Toby's voice was yelling at the guard and Lola rolled her eyes.

"Let them in please but other than Tayler no one else." She called out. Toby and Gideon rushed into the tent and over to her.

"Why are you still here? You need to go to the hospital." Gideon was fussing over her now. Slade could see the exhaustion on Lola's face at all of the fuss happening.

"Slade said I could stay for the podium and go after." She did not hesitate to throw him under the bus on that one.

"Did he now? And what would you do if I forced you to go now?" Gideon was not playing games with her right now as his eyes landed on her shoulder.

"I will kick and scream the entire time. I had a perfect weekend with a 6.0 Gideon, please do not let the celebration be taken away from me. I will go after I promise, you can drive me yourself and stay the whole time if you want." She did not soften her fight even a little in Gideon's glare.

"Fine, but only because Toby just put down a killer winning run also and we all need something good from today other than the fact that your alive." Gideon's words made her smile and reach for Toby.

"Winners podium here we come." She kissed Toby and Slade could see her wince a little as she moved to much.

"You are going to be the death of us Angel." He grabbed her hand and held on to her but could not help looking over her exposed skin, she was covered in bruises now. He wanted to go back and beat the crap out of Greyson some more.

"I think the car is trying to be the death of me Slade, thank God we have a week off." She looked exhausted as they waited for the podium ceremony to start.

"It was not your car, Greyson had Logan put a pin back in your parashoot that's why it did not deploy." He hated telling her, but she needed to know, with Greyson being fired she was going to ask why.

"That's it I am killing him." She was trying to get out of bed now, but Gideon glared at her, and she stopped.

"Jason fired them all Angel. Plus, I am pretty sure the cops are coming to take them to jail for attempted murder." Slade kissed her hand as he watched her process the situation.

"Good, but I wish I could have hit him once." She was fisty and it made him chuckle.

"I got him good, and Tayler landed some good hits for you." He just smiled at her as Tayler and Duke came back into the tent.

"Jason and Duke hit them all also but don't tell anyone." Tayler announced and got a head slap from Duke as they came over.

"Good." Lola just looked at them all taking some shaky breaths now.

"Podium is starting now if you still want to go." Duke looked at her with worry.

"Yeah, let's go, I need to cover my shoulders though." She tried to pull her fire suite back up but stopped with a groan.

"I swear you make noises like that, and we are going to the hospital right now." Gideon was helping her get her arms into the suit.

"It's just sore Gideon, 200 miles per hour into a net is not easy." She got her other arm into the suit, and Slade could tell she was keeping the pain off her face as she did.

"Alright lets go." Tayler walked towards the door as Toby looped his arm in Lola's.

This was their night, both with perfect weekends. Both with

faster times than the whole season. Slade climbed into the second golf cart and followed Tayler and Duke to the podium. The crowd was wild when Lola pulled up and he was happy they were still here for her.

Lola did not show a sign of being in pain as she climbed up to the top step of the podium with help from the other two drivers. She was the queen of this domain, and he wanted to live in the glow that was coming from her even when he knew she was in pain. When it was Toby's turn to get up there the crowd went wild for him as well and he could see Lola off to the side clapping for him as well.

After photos of all the groups they regrouped at the truck and got individual pictures of Lola and Toby together, but Slade could see the adrenaline was wearing off for Lola.

"Time to go Angel." He took the trophy from her and took her into the living part of the truck.

"That's fine." She let him take her suit off and he caught his breath when it was all the way off. The entire outline of the harness was bruised into her skin, her legs had bruises from her seats and by the way she was breathing he figured she had a broken rib.

"Want to go in this or change?" He did not know if a sports bra and shorts were ok right now but he couldn't bare to hurt her more by trying to take it off.

"Maybe a shirt, I don't want to try and take this off right now." He grabbed one of Gideon's large team shirts and pulled it over her.

"Alright shoes and lets go." He pulled her Vans onto her feet and headed out the door with her.

Gideon and the others were already in the car waiting for them and the team was packing everything away. Slade could see the race officials with Jason and Duke and when Tayler waved them off, he knew they had it covered. He helped Lola into the car, and they headed off to the hospital. She was almost asleep when they got there, and he hated waking her up. It was going to be a long night as they took her back to an exam room with Gideon by her side.

Chapter 32

Lola

Lola groaned as she rolled over in the soft bed, she hated that she had to pee so badly. Maneuvering herself out of the bed to head to the bathroom was probably the worst part of waking up at this point. But with a cracked rib and bruises all over her chest that was to be understood. She did not have any brain injuries, which was a relief to everyone. Her legs were sore as well but as she shuffled to the bathroom she couldn't help laughing at the guys.

They refused to sleep with her for fear of hurting her, so their solution was the pullout couch and chairs in her room. Gideon and Emory were on the couch bed while Slade and Toby took the chairs. They were all asleep and she glanced at the clock on the table to see it was only 4am.

"You should be sleeping Angel." Slade's deep voice scared her as she came out of the bathroom.

"Shit, I had to pee, and I am pretty sure I need some more of the meds they told me to take. But I can't remember when I took them last either." She slowly made her way back to the bed as Slade got up from the chair.

"Emory wrote it down and yes you need more. Let me get you a water." Slade held the blankets for her to slide back into the bed before going to the mini fridge and coming back with a bottle of water and a package of crackers.

"Thank you." She took both from him as he took out the pill for her to take.

"You need anything else?" Slade smoothed her hair back as she took her medication.

"I do actually." She was not ok with being this far away from them.

"Anything Angel." Slade took the water from her and put it on the table.

"I need cuddles and kisses." She almost pouted as she told him because she really needed him to just lay down with her.

"I don't want to hurt you, Angel." He looked torn between not hurting her, but knowing telling her no was hurting her.

"You won't, plus in 15 minutes I will be passed out and you can sneak off again." She knew this was what Emory did when they first got back last night.

"Fine, but only because I need to hold you too. Scoot over to the middle." Slade waved her over and climbed in under the blankets with her.

"You are so warm." She snuggled into him, and his warmth soothed her body.

"Feel good?" He kissed her head as she kissed his chest.

"Perfect." He played with her hair as she drifted off to sleep.

When she woke up again the bed was empty as was the other bed in the room and the sun was coming in bright now. The clock was now at 9am and her body was screaming for more medication, but she didn't want to take more quite yet.

She grabbed her phone off the table and dialed Gideon to figure out where they all ran off to.

"Doll, are you ok?" Gideon sounded worried as he answered.

"Great other than I am alone and feel like I got run over by a truck. Where are you guys?" She slowly got out of bed and headed to the bathroom.

"We went out to get you something better for breakfast than what the hotel had and coffee. We will be right back." Gideon sounded rushed and she could hear the others rushing with whatever they were doing also.

"No rush just wondering, I am going to take a shower." She was sure she could handle that.

"A bath please Doll? Unless you wait for one of us to shower with you." Gideon asked.

"Fine, a bath sounds better anyways. See you all soon." She turned the water on to get it warm.

"Love you, Doll." Gideon's words made her choak up a little.

"Love you too." She hung up the phone and pulled the clothes off slowly.

The amount of bruising was worse today and it looked like she really had been run over by a truck. She sank into the warm water and her body felt instantly better as she did. Before her mind could over run her, she dialed Tayler and put the phone on speaker on the small table next to the tub.

"Bunny, are you ok?" Tayler's voice was worried too.

"I think I will make it Taz." She smiled knowing he was just worried.

"Good, how are you actually feeling." He called her out on

254

her bullshit.

"Like I relied on my car to keep me alive again but not as bad as last time. Where are you?" She turned the water off as it hit her shoulders.

"In my room in the same hotel you are in. Are you alone?" He sounded worried again.

"I am but not for long the guys went to get food. I am taking a bath. What happened after we left." She needed to know.

"They pulled Greyson's racing license, and the cops have pressed charges. His records for times are being taken away from him and almost every team on the circuit had black balled him." Tayler's explained. Something like this would spread fast in their community, it would be hard for Greyson to do anything involving a car.

"Good. Now how is the car? Is it going to be ready in a week?" She was worried this would set them back.

"It will be ready to go don't worry. If nothing else Duke said we would just wrap the other car. You'll race that one. The work is getting all the sand out of it, you had to go make a mess." Tayler laughed making her smile for a second.

"But what about you will you be ready?" The tone shifting to concern so easily for her best friend.

"I will be fine, this is minimal." She took a deep breath.

"What's going on in your brain Lola?" He could tell she had more in there than that.

"I am in love with them all Tayler, how the hell did this happen? They were all gone this morning and I panicked that they had left me." She let the emotions in now thinking about it all. She was committed to living with them, but the back ground pain of them leaving one day lingered.

"They all love you Lola, so let them ok. They were so worried about you yesterday, hell Slade almost killed Greyson ok." Tayler's voice made her feel a little better.

"But what if they change their mind. I can't deal with the heartbreak that will come Tayler; it hurts to think that they might leave me." She started to cry at the thought.

"Lola, you listen to me. They are not going to leave you by choice. I know this because what they did yesterday was different than last year. That loser did not even come to the hospital to see how you were. Those men did not leave your side ever. One of them with you the whole time, hell they ran the track to get to you. If that is not true love, I don't know what is." His words only made her cry a little harder and the silence of the room just filled the space.

"You need me to come over?" Tayler broke the silence after a few minutes.

"No, I will be fine. I just wish my mom was here you know." She missed them right now so much.

"I will call mine for you, she has been blowing up my phone asking if you're ok." She laughed as he told her.

"Tell her to come to the next race, I am sure Duke will get her tickets." Tayler laughed at her now.

"Oh, those two will never admit their feelings for each other you know that." Tayler said.

"I bet we could get them too." She heard the door to the room close.

"Sounds like your guys are back. Let them love you Lola, see you soon ok." Tayler hung up the phone just as Emory came

256

into the bathroom.

"You alright love?" He was in a t shirt that showed off his tattoos this morning and his hair looked a little unruly as well.

"Yeah, just needed a best friend call." She stretched out in the tub a little, letting the water sooth her body.

"You want food in here or out there?" Emory walked over to her and bent down to kiss her in the tub.

"Out there is fine I will get out." She leaned up and he straightened up to wait for her with a towel.

"I grabbed some Epson salt from the store for you for your next bath." Emory wrapped her in the towel as she got out. She made sure not to wince at the touch because they would never touch her if she did.

"Thank you." They headed into the room after grabbing her phone.

In the room the others had spread out all her favorite snacks on the bed and were lounging out as well.

"God I am a lucky girl," she said taking a seat before getting dressed.

"I think we are the lucky one's love." Emroy handed her a bottle of water before sitting at the bottom of the bed.

"I really am lucky though. You guys are here taking care of me. Anticipating things that I need before I think about it. You know Greyson left me at the hospital and never came to visit the whole time I was there. Granit I would not have been ok with him being there but still." She took a drink of the water as they watched her.

"Well, I think the difference is love Doll. We love you for you and not for what you can do for us." Gideon said kissing her cheek.

"I am thankful for it. I wouldn't change a single thing right now."

She got back up and went to her bag to grab a shirt and underwear.

"I would change how much pain you are in." Toby looked at her like the wind would break her.

"I am not in too much pain right now, the bath helped. Oh, and all the sleep." She knew that the pills were knocking her out and she needed the rest.

"You should take some more medicine. The doc said you should be religious with it right now to stay ahead of the pain." Emory grabbed the pill bottle off the nightstand where Slade left it last night.

"Ok but only half because I do not want to sleep the whole day away." She grabbed a muffin from the pile of food they brought her.

"Fine. But if you are in too much pain you take the rest." Gideon was worried and she could see the concern on his face.

"Promise, I will let you all take care of me. But please tell me we are still going to the house?" She was so excited about the house they found on the beach for the week that she didn't want to miss it.

"Yes, we were planning on heading out tonight depending on how you felt. Duke insisted on us staying here last night so if you had to go back to the hospital he was here." Emory handed her the one pill, and she took it grabbing the water as well.

"He wants to come talk about the car though, when you feel up to it." Toby looked concerned and that worried her.

"I thought it was not to bad that's what Taz said this morning." She was going to kill Tayler for lying if it was not ok for the next race.

"It's not but I think he just wants to prepare you for the possibility of the next race being in Greyson's car. Though I know they are already planning on making that a backup car for you at this point in the season." Gideon would know more about this since Duke talked with him about team things.

"I am fine with that if it needs to be done for a race. But I really don't want to finish the season in his car. Call me crazy but when Sam says my car is faster, I believe him." She laughed but it hurt too much with the cracked rib.

"Ok enough of that. Eat and we will find something to watch." Emory shooed her further into the bed to get comfortable.

They stayed like that for most of the day even when Duke came by. It was a simple conversation, and she was surprised by how well the team was going to be able to come back without Greyson. Apparently, most of his sponsors wanted to jump over to her and Toby, which was great so the team would not lose any funding. That night they headed out to the house. She didn't argue about taking the whole amount of pain medication for the drive. She was uncomfortable in the car despite laying across the back seat.

Chapter 33

Lola

Going into the last race of the season had Lola's nerves on end. The last eight races had been right on the money, and she was well in the lead for winning the season, though the second-place spot was catching up to her now that Greyson was out of the season. The pressure was still there, she had been able to pull out two perfect weekends after setting a new top speed at the 18th race. But she was stuck in the 6.0 range, and she knew there was more in the car.

The first race back after her wreck had been in Greyson's car unfortunately. Lola had been frustrated with the 3rd place finish there. But now she was back in her car and felt on fire. Toby was on a role as well putting down his top speed last weekend with an 8.0. They both had qualified 1st for the race today and after practicing this morning she felt another joint perfect weekend coming their way.

The teams were out getting the cars set up for the first runs and she was debating her jog. She felt like she needed the entire pit area today but did not want to go on her own. Grabbing her headphones, she headed out to find Toby waiting for her.

"You want company on your run sweet girl?" He held up his headphones with a smile.

"Yes please." She laughed, putting her playlist on and heading out. They ran the entire pit area before heading back. She was less nervous but still on edge, seeing the entire team ready to go helped her out though.

They all got her ready to get into the staging lanes, with her 1st place qualifying position she would be the first run of the day. She was used to this, but this track was still something she had to tackle. She would be on the wall side for the race, the same wall that took her out a year ago. In practice and qualifying she had stayed in the right lane away from the wall, but she was going to face the left lane now. Duke had offered to get it changed but she told him no because she needed to do this.

"All right race fans who is ready to kick off a great day of racing?" The announcer came over the loudspeakers and the crowd went wild. They had told them the event was sold out and they even let people come in for standing only this morning.

"That's great to hear. First up, this afternoon we have our points leader, our very own Lola Bunny. She is going to try to clench the championship today with some solid runs. Her competitor is our grassroots team with a solid season Brendon. This team has done so well for itself in this first season at the level. Let's get those cars in the burn out box and down the track." The announcement got them moving as Tayler waved her into the box.

"Let's go Bunny, you got this." Tayer made her smile as she did her burnout before getting lined up.

She got staged and gave Tayler the thumbs up as he tapped the car walking behind her. Watching the lights she launched the car at green and sored down the track. Pulling her parashoots at the end and seeing the winning light pop up she gave a small fist bump. The adrenaline was rushing through her and as she pulled back into her pit the team was on fire.

"What was the time?" She felt fast.

"6.0" Sam told her as he handed her the slip.

"Damn it. Can we turn it up anymore?" She wanted that 5.9 run so bad.

"I think it has just a little more. Let me take a look at it." Sam grabbed his computer and went to work on the car while the others began the cool down process.

As she watched Toby's run, the driver she just ran against came up to her pit.

"Hey, Lola." Brendon called out, still in his fire suit, his dark hair a mess from his helmet.

"Hey great race, and great season. You guys have done so well this season." Lola went over to him giving him a hug. She had gotten pretty close with the teams this year and all the drivers. Their small community helping them all feel like family.

"Thanks, I just wanted to come say it was an honor to race against you today. I was here as a spectator last year and your wreck almost made me quit racing. But seeing you come back and literally crush the season is amazing." His words made her choak up a little.

"Thanks. Racing is in my soul nothing would have kept me away. I am just glad I had such a great competitor; you all made me work for it. I couldn't slack off at all." She laughed.

"Your slacking off right now." Marvin yelled at her from under the hood of the car.

"Whatever Martian. I got to go, but I hope you have a great off season." She patted Brendon's shoulder before heading over to the car.

"You know I was messing with you." Marvin joked with her as she grabbed another bag of ice to cool off the car.

"Yeah, I know." She laughed as Toby was pulling into his side of the pits.

"Great run Doll." Gideon came and hugged her as Toby got out of the car and Slade started their cool down.

"Thanks, it was still a 6.0 though, Sam's going to make it faster, right?" She raised her voice at the end so Sam could hear her inside the car.

"Slave driver." Sam called to her making them all laugh.

They worked on the cars. She and Toby were running great for the next two runs. She was still stuck in the 6.0 but her reaction time was a little off on the last run.

She was sitting in the staging lanes behind Toby. They switched up the running order on the last run so that her run would be last, and she was happy to be in the lane behind him for once.

"Alright everyone here it is. The last two runs of the season and let me just say what a fire season it has been. Up first we have the rookie to beat Tobias Smith in the HPS Dodge. He is up against the top seat for the season Beckett More who may have qualified second for today, but he is having a winning day." The announcer queued them into the burnout box.

She watched as Toby did his burn out and then Gideon lined him up. As Toby launched the car she was in awe as it was a blur of white and orange as he pulled on Beckett. At the end the light for his lane lit up, he did it. Toby clenched the perfect weekend again.

"The winner of the race is Tobias with an impressive 8.0 run. He may have won the race but with a second palace finish Beckett still has more season points than him. The top three for the season will go to Beckett More in 1st, 2nd will be Tobias Smith in his rookie season, and 3rd will go to Luke Holmes. What a great season." The announcement made the crowd get louder as she pulled into the burnout box.

"Now we have the finish for the pro season. Lola Bunny is going to try to follow her teammate and boyfriend. Going for an unprecedented 3rd perfect weekend in a row. We also know from her team that she is chasing that top speed record for this track, going for a 5.9 or faster. In the right lane Axel is going to try and upstage her. He has had a great weekend with his 3rd place qualification pulling him into 3rd in points as well. Looks like their tires are all warmed up let's get some rubber laid down for the last time." She was finishing as the announcer wrapped up.

"You are a badass no matter what happens. You already have the season trophy Bunny, so no pressure just fly." Tayler tapped the car, and she gave him a thumbs up.

Taking a deep breath, she watched the lights and as soon as the green light lit up, she let the car fly. She felt it as she was going, each shift perfect. As she crossed the line pulling the shoots, she saw the winning light on her line. She won, she did it, her comeback was complete.

Chapter 34

Gideon

"How is she almost falling asleep?" Slade asked him as they watched their girl getting her tattoo. She had gotten a 5.9 on her final run last week and so here they all were getting a new tattoo.

"She always falls asleep." Tayler told them as he was finishing up with his tattoo. The team had decided to get the team logo this year because of how special of a season it was. Each of them also had their nicknames under it in Lola's handwriting for something extra.

"I am not asleep just relaxed." Lola made them laugh as Gideon looked at Toby who was getting finished with his 8.0 tattoo on his arm. None of them would let her convince them to get it on their ribs like her. They all knew that was crazy.

"Enjoy it love." Emory kissed her forehead. He was the first of them to be done and was just sitting with their girl.

They were back home finally; Lola had refused to fly home. Her reason being that she faced more fears in the last months than anyone else and so she shouldn't have to fly. None of them felt like arguing with her. Leaving the car with the team to take to the team shop. There are plans to go back in a month to get ready for next year. With a few smaller races they wanted to do in the off season. Even Lola was going to drop back into their bracket to run with them.

The team had flown in last night and were staying at Lola's house since she officially moved in with them when they got home. Duke and Jason were coming today for a party they were having. The big team and sponsor party is in a few weeks, but they all wanted to celebrate with their friends at home.

Once everyone was done, they went back home to get ready, and Lola was enjoying her time with everyone when Duke came up to him.

"I have a favor to ask of you." Duke took a drink off the table.

"Why do I feel like this is going to result in me having to work." Gideon joked as he watched Toby pull their girl into his lap by the bonfire.

"I need you to convince Lola to race in the international season. I know she said she wanted to take it off, but the sponsors really want her to go and with this sort of momentum. It could take her career far. I know you understand and know that we would fly you all out with her as support team with the others." He gave Duke a raised eyebrow as he talked. Duke was right though; she should continue with momentum this year.

"I will talk to her but know she may still say no." Gideon was sure he could reason with her, but he knew she wouldn't do something she didn't want to do no matter who talked to her.

"Well, the season is not as demanding as the one here, so there would be a week off after each race. Jason and I are willing to put you all up in some destination places if you get her to go. With Greyson gone we have a little more funding to push her way." Duke just laughed as he looked over at Lola. She was in a heated conversation with Cody and Granger with Brighton on the side shaking his head.

"I will let her know." Gideon walked towards the group and all the girls were laughing.

"Angel, you're going to give them a heart attack." Slade was kissing her head giving her another bottle of water.

"What they want to talk smack. They can put their cars where their mouth is." Lola shot at his friends.

"You couldn't beat us in a basic track car, no matter how good the reaction time was." Cody was digging a hole he couldn't get out of.

"Gideon, can we go to the track? It's the only way to show them I am right." She turned to look at him and he could see his entire world in her eyes.

"Whatever you want Doll. What car do you need?" Gideon was pretty sure he knew already.

"I think it's time the Supra went down the track. Then when I beat them it's in a girl car too." The other girls laughed.

"Oh god you got her on that crap too. You guys really don't know what you got yourself into." Tayler laughed as everyone got up.

"Let's go." Gideon pulled her up off Toby. Everyone laughed and joked as they got in their own cars. Though Emory grabbed his bike, he knew his brother was dying to get back to racing the bike again.

At the track Lola did in fact beat each of the others and Gideon even ran a race against her. It was a great night and back at the house they were all snuggled around the bonfire talking and drinking.

"Doll, I have a question for you." He was hoping she was willing to be understanding.

"Yeah babe." She turned around in his lap to face him.

"Why don't you want to do the international races?" Gideon watched her reaction.

"I don't want to be away from you guys that long. You have the shop here so I figured you couldn't leave to go with me for another four months." She tipped her head to the side as she talked.

"What if we could come with you? With time off in between each race to sight see also. Would you want to go then?" He asked.

"Duke got to you didn't he." She was on to him already.

"He did. He also said the sponsors really want you to go and how good this could be for your long-term career." He loved that this was an opportunity for her.

"Duke you better get everyone first class tickets if I am going on that long of a flight." She yelled to him after thinking about it for a minute.

"They are already booked Bunny." Tayler responded from next to Duke with a laugh from them both.

"They knew you could convince me huh." She smirked at him before he pulled her into a kiss.

"They knew you would see reason. You boys ready to run the shop some more so we can watch Lola win on a global scale?" Gideon asked Brighton.

"Hell yes, you know we got your back." Brighton raised his beer to the sky while they all cheered. This was the life, and it would not be his if the girl on his lap had chosen a different town to heal in. Pulling her close, Gideon kissed her as the rest of the night dissolved around them.

"I love you Lola, you are the best thing to happen to me and my family." He told her.

"I love you too Gideon, even if that means Duke now knows how to get me to do what he wants more." She laughed and snuggled into his lap more.

6-months later

Lola

"God it's good to be home," she said as she jumps into the now extra-large bed in her room. The pillows engulfing her as she lands.

"No sleeping, jet lag love." Emory calls to her as he drops her bag in the room.

"Just a quick nap." She snuggled into the pillow but was pulled down the bed.

"No, we have to go to the shop." Slade had pulled her all the way out of the bed.

"Fine." Lola huffed grabbing her phone from her backpack on the floor. They had just gotten back from Europe and though she slept on the plane she was exhausted.

It had been a whirlwind season abroad and now they finally got some time off actually. She took 2nd place in the season there, her times were consistent. But they had a break at the halfway mark that took them till the next race to figure out. She heard from Duke that the sponsors were so impressed that they were building their contracts larger for this year. There was now room to bring Brendon in for the other pro spot.

The guys had played around with Toby moving up but decided to stay where they were and improve there first. But Lola could not help wanting to race with Toby, so she has Duke working on a car for her to run both circuits this upcoming season. Jason had almost cried when she told them she wanted to run two cars. The response was great, and she was excited to tell the guys over dinner.

"Hold on. Lola can stay here and nap. Just us at the shop." Gideon called down the hall and she looked at Slade with a raised eyebrow.

"Oh, heck no. I am going now." She rushed out of the room and past Gideon who was calling out to her.

Emory was already in the garage getting the bike ready to go and she grabbed Slade's helmet off his bike.

"Go, go, go." She pushed Emory as she climbed on the back of the bike. He took off not asking her about it till they got away from the house.

"You are trying to put that new bed to the test tonight aren't you love." Emory laughed as they went around the corner for the shop. The others were right behind them in the track hawk she kept after last season.

"I will take it to see why Gideon wants to keep me from the shop." She laughed as they pulled into the parking spot at the front of the building.

"You are not allowed in there!" Gideon shouted from the car as he jumped out, but she was already at the door pulling it open.

As she did, she heard Alaska yelling watch out as four puppies came around the corner towards her.

"Puppies!" She reached out for the little baby pit bull puppies, stopping them from going outside. She let them take over her balance and she was now sitting on the floor being mauled with kisses from them.

"Damn it." Gideon said shutting the door behind him as they all came inside.

"Your home." Alaska came around the corner and laughed when she saw her.

"I told you not to have them where she could see them Alaska." Gideon was so mad now.

"Oh, look at the babies. Who's are they?" She asked Alaska as Noelle came around to see them all now.

"They are our foster puppies. Granger is keeping one already, Brighton is taking one so is Cody." Noelle told her.

"What's going to happen to the last one?" She looked at them all. Three boys and a little girl fighting for her attention.

"She will go back to the shelter when she is big enough to try and find a home." Noelle watched her and Gideon groaned.

"I want her." She snuggled the little brown pup who was licking her face.

"Doll what are you going to do with her when you are out racing?" Gideon was trying to logic his way out.

"Plenty of people bring their dogs with them to the track. She will be fine." She was going to keep her, and he could argue all he wanted but a puppy was exactly what she wanted right now.

"I don't think you're going to get out of this one man." Granger came in now wiping his hands on a rag.

"She can be our baby." She looked at them all, knowing this would get them to her side. Never would she pull the 'I can't have a

271

human baby' card, but man she wanted this puppy.

"Fuck." Gideon threw his hands up and bent over to kiss her.

"Yay! Now to find a name for you." She looked over the baby now thinking of how she would fit into the team. Seeing the little white dot on her belly she figured it out.

"I got it. Dot like the little sister from the Animaniacs." She pulled out her phone and snapped a picture of her for the group chat.

Gideon, let you get a puppy? Kip asked.

Let is a strong word. She was ambushed by them, and I couldn't argue with her begging. Gideon responded.

Hello baby Dot, your uncle Taz loves you. Tayler send a million hearts with his message.

"Never mind give her back." Gideon said but she just laughed. Toby came to snuggle the puppies, followed by the others.

They spent the afternoon at the shop with the guys going over some things there while she hung out with the puppies and caught up with the girls. Granger had proposed to Aurora before they left so they were planning their wedding. She was asked to be a bride's maid and she was excited to see them get married.

It had brought up the conversation with the guys but right now they were all happy with how their relationship was going. But she would love to have some sort of commitment ceremony with them, or something that says they are hers. But that could be a conversation for later, she was truly happy with where they were in their lives right now, nothing was going to pop the bubble they were in right now.

2 years later

Slade

"With that impressive 5.8 run Lola has clenched her third consecutive season win, the second with a perfect weekend. Congratulations what a way to end an impressive racing career." The announcer says over the speakers as Slade watched Lola fly across the finish line from the tv in the pits.

She had announced this week that she was moving away from racing at this level. She felt like she had gotten to where she could and was not interested in going to a full drag car. Duke had been so upset when she told them, but Jason was excited. Lola was going to move into a team manager for the new girl she brought in this year to the team.

Page is only 17 and remined the entire racing community of Lola when she got started. They had all gotten to know her parents back home and Lola took the girl under her wing the last two years before getting Duke to get her a spot in the secondary class for the season.

"What an exciting race to see teammates battle, but I would not want to be a fly on the wall of their trailer when Toby realizes how close their points are." The announcers talk back and forth, and Slade laughs.

"Yeah, she's going to gloat the whole drive home." Toby's voice came over the radio.

"Winner, winner baby. You owe me dinner and a new tattoo. Yeah!" Lola was so happy and in the return lane she waved to the crowd cheering for her.

"Get back to the pits so we can get ready for the ceremony. Great job you two." Gideon and Tayler were already back at the pits waiting for them.

"Your mommy won Dot, what are we going to do with her now." Slade looked at the dog laying under the table. Dot was a good dog though lazy unless Lola was making her run with her. Little did they realize how easy she was going to be compared to her brothers. The other three made a mess of the shop as their self-designated shop dogs now.

Toby and Lola made it back to the pits and the team all give them hugs while the media came over to get the celebration. They asked her questions, and Slade just watched as she soaked in the high of this. She worked so hard to be where she was, 2 seasons a year and countless track days to make sure the car was perfect.

Slade walked up behind her and kissed her neck as she stepped back to let Toby answer some questions with Duke and Gideon.

"You ok babe?" She asked.

"Perfect, just thinking about how amazing you are. I can't believe that four years ago you almost died at this track. To come back and be on your third season win. While bringing in the next generation of bad ass female racers." Slade was sappy right now, but he loved this girl so much.

"It is pretty amazing isn't it." She chuckled a little.

"What's funny?" He turned her to look at him.

"I heard someone say Greyson was here with another team as a crew chief, but the team is on the bottom end of the brackets. I guess he has been keeping a low profile. But I can't help but laugh at how I have what he wanted. He tried to use me to get it and is all the way at the bottom now while I am at the top of the top." She just smiled and he kissed her forehead.

"It's because you are the best Angel." He pulled her into a hug.

"Let's go celebrate!" Tayler came hyped up to get to the podium.

They all took the golf carts to the podium, and it was in fact a huge party up there by now. The fans were going crazy for everyone and the high of it was like nothing else. Of course, Lola had Dot on stage with her now, she brought Dot everywhere and the fans loved her just as much as they loved Lola.

"You guys still doing that thing tonight?" Tayler nudged him as Slade watched Toby spray champagne on Lola.

"Yeah, is the team all ready?" He was nervous as hell about tonight.

"Yeah, all ready. I am going to go with the plan and get her to the hotel you guys just handle the rest." Tayler smiled at him, and Slade was grateful for the friendship he had with him.

"Taz I can't walk in these heals blindfolded anymore." Lola's voice made them turn to see her coming towards them. It was dark at the track now, but they had gotten the track owners to let them use the end of it for something special.

"Just a little farther Bunny. Stop being a baby." Tayler shook his head as he walked their girl towards them.

He was with Gideon, Emory, and Toby in front of the finish line at the track, the very spot where she wrecked her car four years ago. All their friends and family were here because they were surprising her with a commitment ceremony tonight. They had Tayler get her into the off-white dress she looked like a wet dream in and get her back here while they got everything set up.

As Tayler stopped her and pulled the blindfold off everyone said surprise and Lola got tears in her eyes as she looked around. Duke was by her side in the spot her dad would be to give her away.

"Guys what is this?" She looked at Gideon first expecting an answer.

"We wanted to have our commitment ceremony right here Doll. This is the spot that ultimately got you to us and we thought it would be perfect to do tonight." Gideon's words made her drop a tear on her perfect face.

"I hope you will let me give you away Magnolia?" Duke asked and she took his arm.

"You already gave me to them once for safe keeping you might as well do it again." Lola laughed a little as Duke began to walk her towards them. Duke placed her hand in Gideon's while they waited for Tayler to get started.

"Alright let's get this show on the road." Tayler walked up to be in the middle of them all as he was going to lead the ceremony.

"Thank you all for coming to this less than traditional ceremony. While we all wish a big wedding would happen, we know Magnolia would not go for that. So, to start the guys have all written something for her and we are hoping she will have something to say back after to each of them." Tayler made them all laugh because it was true.

"Gideon, your first." Tayler said.

"Magnolia, you are the best thing to have ever shown up in my life. You came in with a fire so bright I was worried we would all get burned by you. But we all came to realize that you were exactly what we needed. Loving, caring, understanding, and a little bit of trouble." Everyone laughed as Gideon paused.

"I have cherished every day I get to wake up with you in my life and I want the world to know your mine and I only share with the others here with us. I love you." Gideon was done and he handed her hand to Toby.

"Lola, I never thought I would find someone who challenges me as much as you do. On and off the track. It has been an amazing journey this year to race against you and it made me realize how much I love you. I go to bed each night not knowing how I could possibly love you more than I do that day. But every day you make that love grow. Everything I have is for you and I can't wait to love you more tomorrow." Toby handed her hand to Emory next.

"Sweet girl, you are everything to me. I love the life that we have created. I love the dreams we have built our life to be, and I can't wait to do it forever. Being alongside you has shown me how much can be accomplished when you push and fight for what you want. You push me to be a better man for you every day and I can't wait to see where we end up. Because I know it is right where we are meant to be." Emory held her hand out to him, taking it letting her warmth take over the small shake in his hands.

"Angel, I don't know what else I can say that they others have not. You are my world; you are my dream come true and I don't want to do anything without you. You make the world bearable when everything around us feels like it's going downhill. Watching you be yourself and push the boundaries of this sport for other girls and women makes me so proud to call you mine. I love you so much and I can't wait to see what you do in the coming years, and I want to be by your side while you achieve it all." Slade kissed her hand but did not let go.

"How am I going to top that, geese. Slade you are my partner in crime in this relationship and though it may get us both in hot water I wouldn't change it. Having you in my corner means so much to me. Emory you are always there for me, anticipating things I need before I even realize it. You may drive me crazy when I try and hide things. Toby, you push me to be better every day, not only on the track but in our lives. Your passion for life makes me so happy to be by your side in whatever crazy adventure we are going on. Gideon, god I would not be standing right here without you. The ability you had from day one to see me for me and not what everyone else thinks I am made me feel safe. That safety net let me fall and know I had the support to climb my way back to where I am now. Making that climb with you all behind me just made my love for you all grow so fast, it was incredible. I love you all so much." Lola was fully crying now, and Tayler passed her a tissue.

"Gideon do you take Magnolia to be your partner for life, no matter what she does to make you crazy?" Tayler asked.

"I do." Gideon smiled and slid a thin gold band onto her left ring finger.

"Lola, do you accept that Gideon will always keep you safe and be your partner for life?" Tayler asked her before handing her the silver ring Gideon had picked out.

"I do." Lola smiled and pushed the ring on.

"Toby, do you take Lola to be the push in your life to be the best you can be as her partner in life?" Tayler continued.

"I do." Toby pushed another thin gold band on her finger.

"Do you take Toby to be your partner in adventure for life?"

"I do." Lola pushed the similar silver ring onto Toby's finger.

"Emory, do you take responsibility for the rest of her life to take care of Lola despite how annoying she is about it?" Everyone laughed as Emory lined up his gold band.

"I do." Emroy smirked, pushing the ring on.

"Do you promise to let Emory care for you and try not to be a pain in his ass about it?" Tayler was laughing at himself now handing Lola Emory's ring.

"I do promise to try." She smirked as she pushed the ring on his finger.

"Slade do you take this fallen Angel as yours to keep from the rest of the world and protect from those who would hurt her." Tayler's choice of words made him laugh thinking about his history of beating up Greyson.

"I do." Slade put his ring on her finger finishing the stack of rings that matched her other jewelry.

"Do you take Slade to be your partner in crime to make the others crazy for life?" Slade could almost hear Gideon's eyes roll.

"I do." She pushed the gold ring on his finger, and he felt the weight of it on his hand and soul.

"I now pronounce you all life partners and if you hurt my best friend, I will still kill you all. Kiss your girl." Tayler announced and everyone cheered as they pulled Lola into them all.

Kisses were put all over her forehead, lips, cheeks, and neck before they turned to celebrate with their friends. There was a tent set up so they could party for a while before they took their girl away for a weekend away. But she was theirs forever, no matter what happened now she was never going to leave them, and Slade was perfectly ok with that.

Acknowledgements

First to my husband Jager, thank you for always believing in my dreams sometimes more than I do. This book would not be here without you and your encouragement. Thank you for sticking with all my questions, and for being the first beta reader of this. For forever and always babe.

To my kids, who I hope won't read this till they are much older, you three are amazing! You all support me with such passion and it means the world to me. I love you all and I am honored to be the author you dress up as for spirit weeks.

To my dad, who I hope only reads this page, thank you for being in my corner and being so invested in me. You might not read a lot but you have always supported not only my reading habits but encouraged me to get this far. I did it, I became invincible, and I hope I made you proud.

To my mother-in-law, thank you for taking this book and editing it with your heart. I grew to be a better writer because of your input. Your enthusiasm when I called to give you updates on my process warmed my heart. Now its time for your next book, we are all ready to hear the story you have in your heart.

Last but definitely not least, to my grandparents, you two have been in my corner for longer than I can remember, and I am a better person because of it. From short stories in high school that you would listen to me talk about all the way to this point. You both stuck with me and encouraged me to just keep writing and not give up. I love you two so much, thank you for being my cheering section always.

About the Author

Elise is a mood reader turned mood writer. Creating the stories her mind begs to be written. Spending her days being a mom and wife while trying to consume as many stories as possible.